Neil Bailey lives in Greenwr
and Dexter the poodle. *Whe*

Manay,
Thanks for
all the
support!
love
nb

When
She
Was
Bad

Neil Bailey

Copyright © 2016 Neil Martin Bailey

All characters and events in this publication, other than those clearly in the public domain, are fictitious and any resemblance to real persons, living or dead, is purely coincidental.

The moral right of the author has been asserted.

All rights reserved. No part of this publication may be reproduced, stored in a retrieval system, or transmitted, in any form or by any means, without the prior permission in writing of the author or publisher.

ISBN-13: 978-1535084024
ISBN-10: 1535084022

Published by Neil M Bailey

Printed by CreateSpace, an Amazon.com company

For more information about the author and his work, please visit www.neilmbailey.blogspot.co.uk

Cover design by Jenny Bailey
Set in Baskerville 11pt

There was a little girl,

Who had a little curl,

Right in the middle of her forehead.

When she was good,

She was very good indeed,

But when she was bad ...

Henry Wadsworth Longfellow 1807–1882

For Jen

Later...

I had aimed at his shoulder but it was the side of his head that exploded. So much for shooting to wound rather than kill. Shit. Barclay would be furious.

So I ran. Ran like I'd never run before in my life. Drop the gun? Keep the gun? My fingers felt welded to its grip. I couldn't let go, the warmth of the metal strangely seductive.

Run.

Was she chasing me or seeing to what was left of her fallen lover? I wasn't waiting to find out, didn't even turn to see. I just ran. Arms pumping, cheeks puffing, breath already shortening. Run, girl, run.

I turned left, down the dark alleyway that led round the side of the abandoned warehouse. There were no lights, no paving and I stumbled on the uneven surface but I couldn't stop, I ran as fast as I could, my legs, sides, lungs all protesting at this sudden call to action.

There was wire fencing a few yards ahead. Could I take it in my stride like in the movies? From behind I could hear a shout for me to stop. At least she'd stopped screaming. I slipped the gun into my coat pocket and jumped at the fencing, surprising myself by getting a firm grip with both hands and hauling myself up like I was on an assault course.

'Stop, bitch!'

Well that's nice, I thought as I dropped over the other side, my ankle turning slightly on landing but just a tweak. I could understand she was upset, but there was no need to make it personal. I brushed myself down then started to run again, though every muscle was howling for me to slow down. Just too out of condition for this running lark. If it hadn't been for the adrenaline rush I'd have been finished already.

I could hear the blood hammering in my ears, felt my lungs close to bursting. Any further and I was sure I would collapse. I turned left around another building and then suddenly there was a pool of light ahead, a single streetlamp picking out the familiar Fiat parked at the roadside.

Had he heard the gun shot? Or was Barclay oblivious to the drama I'd suddenly ignited?

'Barclay!' I attempted to shout as I neared the car, so short of breath I thought I would die.

He saw me and wound the window down.

'All go to plan?' he asked.

'No it…no it fucking didn't.' I fell against the passenger side and wrenched the door open, clambering in.

'Where's the money?'

'What?' Barely able to speak.

'The money. Where's the money?'

'He's dead. I shot him. He's dead. Drive!'

'Fuck.'

He turned the key and the engine coughed into life. Slamming it into first and flooring the accelerator, we shot off, as fast as the little rust trap could manage.

Chapter 1

Before I found the man who would change my life, I found his bag.

It was a December Thursday and the morning commuters had long since shuffled from the platforms when I arrived to catch the train for yet another boring job for my pompous paymaster at Marshalls Design. 'Got a mission for you, Claire. Go pick up a package from Thompsons,' he had commanded, not even looking up from his laptop and critical game of Candy Crush, sending me, his always-obliging Intern, away with a careless wave of his hand. Git.

I didn't know what would be in the package – I didn't care, to be honest, I wasn't paid to think, just do – so off I went, entirely at his beck and call, picking up or dropping off, whatever he deemed was essential to keep the planet spinning and the gods happy.

The bag was a lonely black Prada rucksack, resting against the glass wall of the Waterloo sickly-sweet doughnut place. Did I mention it was a Prada rucksack? Not any old bag, not even an expensive rucksack but a *ridiculously* expensive one. It was certainly not something you would expect to see left and forgotten at Waterloo station on a cold winter's morning. I quickly glanced around. No obvious owner in sight. I couldn't believe my luck.

I should have reported it to a member of the police, but I was, for once, walking on the wild side that morning. Besides, terrorists don't buy Prada, surely – that just draws attention and they don't want attention. At least, not until things go bang.

I walked over to it and knelt down, admiring this neglected example of decadent luxury that had been so sadly abandoned by one careless owner. I'd never owned anything so glorious and instantly wanted one of my own.

It was such a very nice bag even though it was about to become second-hand – pristine condition, not leather but synthetic, Prada synthetic, probably even better than leather. It was in perfect nick, spotless, scuff-less, not a mark on it, and even the buckles looked freshly polished, the chrome sparkling in the unseasonal December sunshine. It looked so new I was surprised it didn't have a price tag still attached. I didn't know my luxury goods back then but I knew expensive when I saw it, felt it, smelt it (and it smelled divine). This was top of the line.

And I'd been thinking of getting myself a new bag.

So, a few more quick furtive glances left and right, just to be sure, and I took it, hoisting it over my shoulder and walking quickly, purposefully, for platform 8 and my waiting train.

It was heavier than I'd expected but not excessively so. I decided I'd throw the contents when I got to Reading. I had never stolen anything before in my life, but I was enjoying this adrenaline kick and the danger of my sudden impulse. A guard's whistle blew and I jumped, my anxiety getting the better of me. I skipped through the closing doors and the 11.07 lurched into life, departing platform 8 a few minutes' late but not that anyone really noticed or cared. I didn't realise it at the time but looking back that was the beginning. It wasn't just Waterloo station I was leaving, but also my tedious life of the 9-to-5, of Claire MacDonald being a good girl and doing as she was told. Blame a moment's unbidden impulse for me turning to the Dark Side.

I had the carriage pretty much to myself. There was a spotty kid in a dishevelled school uniform sitting a few rows down, ears plugged into her music, staring out the window at the factories and warehouses as the train pulled out and started to pick up speed. She should have been at school – I had no idea why she was on a train at this time of day. Maybe she was bunking off. I'd never had the courage to do that when I was that age. Good for her.

I hoisted the rucksack onto the small table. It was quite beautiful (as rucksacks go) but not so beautiful as to probably justify the ludicrous price its (former) owner had likely paid for it – a small shiny brand label the tasteful reminder of its quality and price tag. There was another even smaller label that just had a printed mobile number on it, presumably the owner's, useful if my guilty conscience finally got the better of me. There was no lock and the zip easily yielded to my impatient pressure.

The first thing I took out was a laptop. A gossamer thin, featherlite top of the range slice of Apple, designed in California, forged in China, a computer so elegant I wanted to stroke it and purr at its delicate sleek brushed aluminium finish. Beautiful.

Sadly I realised that this would be useless to me. It would be secured and encrypted with passwords, possibly even booby trapped to delete everything or explode if my clumsy fingerprints should glance over its state-of-the-art keyboard. The bag may not have been secured but I'd put money on the laptop being locked from prying eyes and fingers. Bugger. This would have to go back; just too good to throw away, too hot to sell, too password-protected for a simpleton like me to use. Besides, said my guilty conscience suddenly finding its voice; the laptop may have critical stuff on it for someone. I would need to call that mobile number and return it – I may just fifteen minutes earlier have become an opportunist thief, but the rucksack alone would need to be enough.

Putting the laptop to one side I dug a little deeper into the bag. There was a bright red cashmere scarf and a copy of *Catcher in the Rye*. A well-worn, well-thumbed vintage seventies edition that looked much loved as though it might be a much-travelled constant companion. I was starting to feel bad about digging through someone's most personal possessions. It was not a good feeling. I was invading a stranger's privacy. But still I dug deeper. It's what us Bad Girls do.

Rootling a little further I found a boxed Epipen, one of those hypodermic things for people with serious allergic reactions, anaphylactic shock and all that scary stuff.

No messing now. I really should get that at least back to the owner if it was for medical emergencies. My angelic conscience was no longer whispering and was getting the upper hand over my newfound criminal intent. The Epipen's box was unopened and although its Use By date had long since expired I needed to return it or I'd never sleep at nights ever again. Thief? Maybe. Killer? Definitely not.

The other contents were less interesting: a packet of travel tissues, Rennies, a broken Chunky KitKat, a packet of three ('ribbed for heightened pleasure'), a Tom Ford glasses case (empty), some keys (including an impressive looking one for an Aston Martin), leather gloves (presumably Prada too) and a handful of USB thumb drives, unlabelled.

There was something bulky in a compartment at the back of the bag that was zipped shut. Whatever it was would be what was making the bag feel heavy. I unzipped it and, before I realised what I was doing I placed a gun on the table.

'Fuck me!' I whispered to the almost empty carriage (fortunately the girl was still lost in the music). A gun. I'd never seen a real gun before, let alone touched one. Keeping an eye on the girl lost in her daydreams I picked it up and tried the grip for size. I was surprised just how heavy it was. I didn't know anything about weapons back then, but it looked the real deal, a serious handgun for serious crime. Unlike the bag it was old and dirty, slightly oily, and looked like it had been used a number of times.

(It was probably my imagination, but I'd swear it felt slightly warm, as if it had been recently used.)

Mild panic took hold. I couldn't put the stuff back into the rucksack fast enough. I scratched the laptop's pristine surface ramming it all back in (sorry, my beauty) but I didn't care. Any thought of keeping this deluxe treasure trove immediately left. I should leave the bag on the train, dump it, throw it away, run a mile.

I suddenly went cold. I'd have been caught on the CCTV with it, the cameras at the station and would be seen dumping it in a bin at the other end. They even had CCTV on the train ('We are watching you for your protection' proudly boasted the sign on the carriage wall). Hell, they may even have me on CCTV getting the gun out. I quickly looked around the carriage. I couldn't see any obvious cameras. I tried to convince myself that they wouldn't be looking that closely for my 'protection', would they?

I'd call the rucksack's owner. I got my ageing Nokia phone out but saw there was no signal. Damn. The call would have to wait.

I decided my bad girl days were already over. Barely half an hour all told, off the straight and narrow. I was reverting to well-behaved type – this was not a world I was comfortable with (exciting though it promised to be). I would call the bag's owner as soon as I could get a signal and arrange to return the bag and its dubious contents at the very earliest opportunity. I needed shot of it. I needed a strong drink and the comfort of a re-assuring cuddle. I needed to get back home quickly to discuss this with clearheaded

Mr Rational, my all-so-perfect Henry, boyfriend-in-residence. He'd know what to do – I was clueless and couldn't handle this kind of madness alone.

Sadly, when I got back home to my flat in Deptford that evening, I found another kind of madness.

'You're what?' I was incredulous

'I'm going to India for a year,' Henry said.

'No you're fucking not.'

'Yes I am, Claire. And please calm down.'

'Calm down? Calm down? I'm completely fucking calmed down.' (Looking back on it, I wasn't.)

'It's not as if I hadn't mentioned it…'

True. He had been talking about overseas voluntary work for ages and ages, but then he was all talk, wasn't he? No fear of action surely. For all the nights down the pub righting the world's wrongs, we all knew he was never going to skim the waves as an environmental warrior for Greenpeace saving whales from the evil Japanese, didn't we? Henry was 100% mouth but a big zilch in the trouser department. But now this? Desertion! I was not happy.

'A fucking year?' Every time I swore he winced.

'Twelve months, with a review possibly extending it a further twenty-four.'

'Three fucking years?!' Louder. I think Henry was starting to worry more about what the neighbours would say rather than what I was saying: I was not being quiet.

'Possibly yes.' Every time I moved towards him he backed away

'And what does that mean about us? What about me? What am I supposed to do whilst you're saving the third world?'

'I think we should see it as a break,' he said.

'Like Ross and Rachel? A "we were on a break" kinda thing?'

He was mystified. I don't think he'd ever seen *Friends*. Not cool enough for his sensible sensibilities no doubt.

'A break. A time to consider things and where we're going in this relationship,' he said.

'I don't want to consider things – I thought we had a good thing going. But it's quite clear where you're going, at least. India! What the fuck for?'

'It's that voluntary placement we've been talking about.'

He may have been talking and talking and talking about it but as I say it had never been remotely real to me. Just talk. My brain knew I needed to take it down a notch or three but the message was getting lost before it got to my mouth. If anything his reasonableness was winding me up more and more.

'No break,' I declared.

'What? You're coming with me? That's great!' It was his turn to be surprised.

'No, we're finished.'

'Oh.'

'Done. Kaput. No more.'

'I thought you might think that.'

'But that didn't make you stop and think? Three fucking years?'

'As you always say, 'If a job is worth doing…''

'Don't use my clichés against me.'

'You're not being rational.'

'I know. Mark it down as Tough Love.'

'Oh. Okay.'

I didn't know what to think. What to say. Too angry. Too shocked. Too heartbroken? Possibly. It hadn't been great but it had been good and sometimes good was good enough. Already with the past tense…

'When are you leaving?' I asked.

'I have to be in Paris on Monday for Orientation.'

'Then you'd better get packing,' I spat.

'Can I leave my stuff here?'

'No you fucking can't. Put it into storage if you can't take it with you.'

'Will you help me? Nice bag by the way – is it new?'

'No I fucking won't and yes it fucking is.' I couldn't take any more of this. I stormed into the bedroom and slammed the door behind me.

I didn't want him to see any more tears.

Chapter 2

It took an hour or two but by the time I got around to calling the mobile number printed on the back of the rucksack I had calmed down to the point where I felt I could talk to a complete, possibly unstable stranger about his bag without the sobs getting in the way. There was an outside chance that I might even make some sense. So far, nothing else had made any sense whatsoever that day.

I guess I had always known deep down that things with Henry were never going to be permanent. Sometimes relationships stumble along more on hope than judgement, don't they? We weren't a perfect fit, we were simply too different on so many levels (I've never bought in to that 'opposites attract' nonsense). My absent family may have found his worthiness and charitable nature endearing, it was not something I empathised with. Besides, what did they know? They'd only met him the once so most of their judgement was based on hearsay rather than personal experience. Mum may have referred to him as 'a keeper' but for me, once the initial thrill of waking up with a grown man in my bed had lost its novelty (snoring can do that) it was never going to be the real thing. It had become strained and forced, and recently there had been more to complain about than compliment. Henry's permanent benevolence and righteousness was tiring and irritating. He was just too earnest, too *good* for me.

I tried to rationalise my shock, wrestling the rampaging emotions into some semblance of order. Him going was a good thing, an acceleration of the inevitable, an acceptance of the obvious. Let him piss off to India and help the genuinely needy, flee our First World trivial distractions to make a better hash of the

Third. That was for him and most definitely not for me. I had no desire whatsoever to experience a life tougher than I was already living first hand. Life was too short. Comfort too important. Henry could tackle those charitable challenges very much on his own as far as I was concerned.

It didn't make me a bad person, didn't necessarily make him a good one. At least I was about to demonstrate that I had the virtue of being shamelessly honest; that bag wasn't going anywhere without me making that call and returning it to its rightful owner. Having a gun in the flat was not something I could cope with, and I'd decided it all had to go, elegant luxury rucksack and all.

I made the call. It was brief and business-like. The man who answered the phone said his name was Barclay, and I agreed to meet him the next day at some pub nearby. He sounded calm, cold even, not a gun-toting nutter but not exactly gushing with gratitude either. I was a little put out that my virtuous, honest gesture was being taken completely for granted. Maybe he was one of those quiet psychos, the madness going on behind the eyes. I would soon find out.

He said he needed the laptop for some work he was doing. He didn't mention the gun. Neither did I. It didn't seem to be the right moment. I just wanted to be shot of the damned thing. 'Gun'. 'Shot of'. Hilarious.

My nerve started to fail me as I approached the pub. It was just a short bus hop from my flat in Deptford. It didn't look like a rough place, nestled in Greenwich's sophisticated Victorian residential streets rather than some dodgy factory wasteland. This would be safe, I thought. Safer, at least.

It was a small Shepherd Neame pub situated a short meandering walk from Greenwich High Road. 'Britain's oldest brewery' the sign boasted proudly and it looked welcoming enough, its livery recently painted in a bright red, gold and tasteful cream, a handful of unoccupied wooden tables and outdoor chairs neatly arranged on a front yard, a couple of empty pint glasses still sitting there from the previous night. Some underdressed builders opposite were noisily throwing bricks into an almost full skip, spoiling the back street tranquillity.

I was suddenly in two minds whether to call the police about the gun or not, especially given all that stuff on the news about some weekend street fights in Lewisham centre just down the road. 'A gun! I've found a gun!' I wanted to shout, but more out of childish excitement and bravado than out of any civic duty. I had been rational little Claire MacDonald for every second of my twenty-five years on this planet and it had done me no favours whatsoever in the 'exciting' game of life, but that was probably insufficient to justify me doing something as foolhardy as stealing a piece of luxury luggage then arranging to meet the guy who had lost said bag and its bloody not-so-safe contents.

I was not doing the right thing. I was not being sensible. Was this a new, post-Henry Claire? Was I being reckless? Did my actions seriously lack 'reck' (whatever that is)? The truth was that I was exhilarated by the bag and its contents, my humdrum life was about to have a much-needed jolt of possible thrills and surprises, I was going off-script and stepping out from my cosy comfort zone into the great unknown.

I walked up to the pub door then pulled away, indecisive, then turned to retreat and then turned back again, my courage ebbing and flo-ing. It did not go unnoticed – the builders opposite laughed at my impromptu hokey cokey. Sod it. Grow a pair, Claire. In.

I pushed open a heavy door and entered what TripAdvisor would inform its American audience was 'a quaint traditional British pub', all polished wooden furnishings and tasteful William Morris print wallpaper, some faint jangling indie music creating a welcome warmth from the winter chills outside.

The lounge area was almost empty, just a student barmaid dressed all in black, an assortment of piercings adorning her ears and nose, and a lone guy leaning against the bar, nursing a half-empty pint of something or other.

Was that him? Barclay? My god, he was gorgeous. Very tall and well built, his shoulders and strong muscled arms were barely contained by his tight white designer tee shirt. He had pale blue eyes twinkling out from a fading summer tan, his hair shaved fashionably at the sides but topped off with an expensively cut oiled hipster wedge.

Down girl.

'Mr Barclay?' I asked, barely able to contain my excitement. I couldn't believe my luck.

'No, I'm Barclay,' said a voice behind me. I turned and saw another man had followed me into the pub.

His voice was deep and resonant, rich in timbre like that guy who played Snape; a 'voice for late night radio' you might say. But he was not beautiful himself (unlike that hunk at the bar) – his face had character rather than conventional beauty, strong cheekbones and curls of black hair falling in an unruly manner over small, intense dark eyes. He was tall, slender, immaculately dressed – his dark double-breasted overcoat looked ridiculously luxurious (much like his rucksack that I had over my shoulder), the suit underneath probably Italian, the white shirt something out of the pages of Esquire rather than off the racks at M&S. He wasn't bad looking, it was just that the other guy was so jaw-dropping that my standards had momentarily been elevated to new heights. There was an authority about him, a sense of privilege and certainty. I'd hesitate to define it as charisma, but there was definitely something about him. I just couldn't put my finger on it.

'And it is just Barclay,' he said, straight-faced.

I held out my hand which he shook lightly. 'I'm Claire. We spoke on the phone. Claire MacDonald.'

'And you have my bag, I see. Good. What are you drinking?'

'What?' I hadn't planned on staying a second more than was absolutely necessary. 'Oh, that would be nice, thank you. A Diet Coke please. Lemon, no ice. Thank you.' Even the newly morally questionable Claire was still impeccably polite. To be honest I was still rudely distracted by the other guy.

Behave, girl.

I didn't immediately warm to Barclay but he didn't strike me as a brutal terrorist or manic gang member; I had been right not to panic and call the police. Probably. Maybe he even was police, undercover? Or maybe he was secret service or a spy? MI5? MI6? MI7? Is there an MI7? There was certainly a whiff of Old School, expensive education, a twist of Cambridge perhaps. My Deptford Green education had not prepared me for this kind of company. I was moving up in the world.

He got the drinks while I found us a table with an excellent view of The World's Most Perfect Man; I needed that assurance that he was just a few steps away if I needed saving.

Barclay joined me, my crass Coke in one hand, his sophisticated whisky (a solitary ice cube) in the other.

'I suppose I should say 'thank you' for calling me about my bag,' he said, placing the two drinks on the table, removing his coat and carefully folding it before placing it on a spare chair. 'I was concerned when I realised it went missing. I believed it had been stolen.'

'I'm not surprised you were concerned...' My nerves had returned and my voice sounded strangely unfamiliar. I instantly felt guilty for having explored its contents. 'I had to open it to find the owner,' I murmured, almost inaudibly.

'My number was on the label on the outside.' There was a flicker of a smile. He seemed to be amused at my embarrassment.

'It was lucky you had written it on the tag.'

'It is what the tag is for. They print it on there when you order one. My bag is important to me.'

'Yes.' I was staring at my glass. 'It's a nice one.'

'If one is going to have a bag, it is important one has to have something decent. You cannot be seen to compromise on the important things in life.'

'No, of course not.' I kicked my own handbag further under my chair. It was from H&M, knocked down from 19.99 in the summer sale, just a small step up from a Lidl plastic bag. There was no point in drawing attention to it. If he had noticed it he hid it well.

'I expect that you are anticipating a small reward for ensuring my bag's safe return?'

What? I looked up. I hadn't expected that.

'I thought so,' he said. 'Unfortunately, I don't have any cash on me at the moment.'

He clinked my glass but still didn't smile. 'Cheers,' he said. 'Here's to acts of kindness.' I couldn't say if it was with sarcasm or not – he was impenetrable, a face and demeanour too complex to read.

'Cheers,' I said, excited by the prospect of a little windfall to cover the month's rent.

The Diet Coke was warm and I should have asked for ice, its cloying sweetness was sorely failing in the refreshment department.

'I assume that all of my stuff is as you found it?' he asked.

'Yes.' I decided against mentioning that elephant-in-the-room handgun. 'Nice laptop.'

'The Air? Yes, a little underpowered but it does the job. Light on storage but that is what the Cloud is for. The eight oh two eleven AC is essential.'

His laptop had air conditioning? I had no idea what he was talking about, but smiled and nodded. 'Absolutely,' I agreed.

'Like I say, there is no point in compromise.'

'None whatsoever.' My own computer was a seven-year-old laptop from Curry's, still running the old version of Windows I had used in Sixth Form, more 'in a state' than 'state of the art'. I was out of my depth. Why couldn't that guy at the bar have been Barclay? The conversation would have been easier and the view spectacular. Sadly, he was finishing his drink and making a move, my bodyguard-in-waiting had tired of waiting. Another lost opportunity. Story of my life.

'What do you do, Miss MacDonald?'

'Do?'

'Work. Are you a student at the Uni?' Oh my god, he was attempting small talk. This was going to be painful.

'No, I work at Marshalls Design. We do web stuff.'

He raised an eyebrow. 'You are in technology?'

'Barely. I'm an Intern. Minimum pay. Maximum tea making and post distribution. But my stapling skills are second to none,' I babbled. 'The greatest challenge is staying awake. Spreadsheets, y'know?' I rolled my eyes, all too aware how colourless and mundane my life was sounding.

'And you enjoy that?'

I laughed. 'What do you think? Finding your gun was the most exciting…' I froze. I'd spoken of the unspoken.

'It may not the wisest thing to mention that in public?' he said under his breath.

'Sorry,' I mumbled. It was hardly 'in public' – the barmaid had disappeared and we were alone, but he had a point.

'But you work in technology. That is interesting.'

I could have pointed out that my technical prowess was limited to turning a computer off and on again, but not necessarily in the right order. I decided not to go into details.

'I dabble,' I lied. 'It's the future, apparently.'

'Actually, it is very much the present I think you will find.'

'Are you in technology, Mr Barclay?'

'Barclay. Just Barclay. I…dabble'

I smiled. 'Dabble?'

'Yes, I am *in* technology, as you so succinctly put it.'

'I'm told it's where the opportunities are.'

'They most certainly are.'

We were treading water. If the conversation shrank any smaller it would disappear completely. 'You mentioned a reward?' I ventured.

'What? Oh, yes. That. Sure. But you've got me thinking.'

'I have?'

'Yes. Let me check a few things but I may have something more interesting to offer you than tea duties and stapling.'

'Really? I'm not that kind of girl.' My nervous attempt at humour fell flat.

'Behave. Let me make a few enquiries this afternoon and I will get back to you.'

Interesting. He said he would call me before the weekend.

'Whenever,' I said, hoping to appear nonchalant.

'If it turns out there is something, are you around on Saturday to discuss some details?'

Saturday? I should have been helping holier-than-thee Henry get his stuff packed up for the Big Orange Storage or whatever the company is, I should have been pretending to share charity worker Henry's excitement and listening intently to his nervous planning of the un-plannable. I should have been doing my bit for His Great Benevolence's selfless adventure.

But I'd had enough of doing what I *should* have been doing. It was time to stretch my wings and fly into my own great unknown. I wanted to see what this Barclay character had on offer. It couldn't be less interesting than the life I was currently living, could it?

'Sure,' I said. 'I'm free Saturday or Sunday. Give me a call if there is anything.'

He rose, downed the last drops of his whisky (presumably an oak-aged malt, nothing second best for Barclay), collected his handsome overcoat, and gave me a curious little salute with his left hand.

'Until next time,' he said.

I smiled and saluted back. 'Until tomorrow?'

'Good girl,' and, as I bristled with being called 'girl', he left.

'What's going on?' I asked myself. One thing for certain, I was not going to accept compromises any more. No sir.

I finished my sickly warm Diet Coke and left.

Chapter 3

The bus ride home was my thinking time, my opportunity to weigh up the seismic shifts of the previous 24 hours. What did I actually know about this guy Barclay? Would I really put my future in the hands of a guy who I knew absolutely nothing about except he had a gun and an expensive taste in clothes and accessories? It was the most un-Claire thing imaginable.

The double decker was one of those ugly, bulbous scarlet monstrosities that the ugly, bulbous scarlet Mayor of the day had foisted on an unsuspecting London public. I had taken a seat upstairs and at the back. Normally I attracted the nutters on a bus like a powerful nutter magnet, but mercifully on that particular day they stayed away.

Maybe reckless Claire had scared them away?

So what did I know?

The obvious thing, and the biggest, was that I needed a serious change. My life, at twenty-five, was going nowhere at a pace that would have the guys at Guinness World Records taking an interest. My internship, contrary to the initial promise of high tech training and unlimited opportunities, had matured into endless tea brewing (my office nickname was 'Two Sugars Sweetie'), casual (but hurtful) sexism, and day long trips to Reading to drop off or pick up brown padded envelopes that always weighed a little more than you would have thought. Was I being used as a drug mule? Should I have been grateful they were at least using padded envelopes and not considering other, more personal hiding places? No, of course not. I didn't know exactly what was in them but you've never seen a company more straight laced and straight faced than BORING Marshalls Design. It may have boasted it did 'web design' but in the fast moving super highway of the Internet they weren't just in the slow lane, they were parked permanently on the hard shoulder. I had to move on, tell them to stuff their 50p more than the minimum pittance and call it a day. The days of stewing rather than brewing needed to come to an end. Stewed tea's loss would be my gain.

And what about Henry and my tattered, broken attempt at an adult relationship? Now that the shock had passed and the emotional tsunami had quietened to be less choppy waters, that was really a good thing, him going, not something to get angry about. I could only have feigned interest in his self-interest for so long. I'm not a charitable person I'm afraid. Like the men I'm attracted to, I'm too self-centred and self-absorbed to win any popularity contests. (Don't be shocked – I'm just being honest. More people should be. We're all in it for Number One, aren't we?)

Whisper it quietly, but I'm not even sure Henry is genuinely genuine. I mean is he really, truly, deeply, in it for anything more than improving his own social standing? 'Everyone loves Henry', 'he's so giving', 'always thinks of others, never considers himself', etc.

Bollocks. It's all about how others perceive him, not what he's doing as much as what he's *seen* to be doing. I give this India thing three months max. A couple of bouts of Delhi belly and some painful bloating and a Malaria scare or two and he'll be out of there. Once everyone's noticed and congratulated him, once the 'good old Henry' cheering has subsided and life returns to normal he'll quietly come back and pick his next Do Gooding exercise of self-importance. I guarantee it. Three months. Or sooner.

I had to get on with my life and forget him. It wasn't going to be difficult for me, but Mum would be upset (I would have to steel myself for the inevitable 'how's my lovely son-in-law?' questions before I let her down gently). My know-all of a little brother for once had been right – that guy was a loser. At least Dad would understand. Assuming he even noticed.

I had the opportunity of a clean slate on the relationships front then. Not that this Barclay would be a contender – simply not my type, too cold, aloof, distant. I sometimes play a game with my Mum where you have to sum up a person in three words. Three for Barclay; Cold. Aloof. Distant. No, I'd say 'Dangerous' would be a better fit than 'Distant'. At school I had always insisted that my three should be 'Amazing', 'Funny' and 'Pretty' but no one ever agreed and little kids could be so cruel. 'Dull', 'Boring' and 'Plain' were about as good as it got, and that was from Polly Dee, my best friend when I was growing up. (We used to call her 'Dolly Pee'. Like I said, kids can be cruel like that. I'm sure it made her cry when we weren't around.) I could be a little bitch at times. I wondered what Polly was doing now? One day I'd track her down on the web and see whatever happened to that little tightly-wound ball of premature neuroses.

But I digressed. This wasn't about the past; this was about my future. No more 'Dull', 'Boring', 'Plain'. What did I want in life? And how did I get there? Maybe this Barclay would open a few more doors, provide a bridge to a different life.

I bloody hoped so.

Home was not where the heart was. It was bloody uncomfortable. Charitable Henry ('Earnest. Worthy. Fake') was doing a fine impression of someone who was expecting the world to be at his feet, helping him pack all his immaterial material goods into a large stack of cardboard boxes he'd half-inched from out the back of the local Sainsbury's. That it had been raining hadn't helped – a number were damp and likely to burst if tested with any significant weight.

Henry would have liked that – even the elements conspiring against him. If he had believed in God he would have taken it as a sign, but he didn't (although he professed to be 'a christian with a small C') and so he muttered and cursed his way through the packing process.

'Need any help?' I reluctantly asked from the doorway. I don't think I've ever uttered three words so insincerely.

'No. I'm fine.'

Fine then.

I decided to take him at his word.

'Okay then. Want a cuppa?'

He huffed and puffed, heaving a pile of unread Hemingway paperbacks into an already over-filled cardboard box, previously the home of 48 Pampers. Somehow, it seemed appropriate seeing how full of shit he was. 'Two sugars,' he said.

'Yeah. I remember. I'm good like that.'

As I made the tea, dripping out the last drops from a carton of semi-skimmed, I wondered briefly if I should make the peace with him or let him, much like my tea, stew. On the one hand, I hated leaving things messy (although it was him doing the leaving). On the other, I didn't want to spend my weekend helping him pack and reminiscing about what a wonderful three months we'd had since he moved in (we hadn't but memories are often deceptive when warped by departures).

I decided to go for the middle ground. The tea was a start, even if it did look a little on the strong side.

'You're still going then?' I was asking the bleeding obvious.

'Yes. Of course.'

'Where in India, exactly?'

'Bengaluru.'

'I've never heard of it.'

'It's the real name of Bangalore. You've heard of that?'

'Southern India. Lots of people. Just below the malaria line. Most of the population working in Western call centres for the hard-of-paying.' I was good at geography at school and we'd done India and an hour or two on Bangalore as a project. Only it sounded like it wasn't called that any more.

'Eight and a half million people – more than Wales and Scotland combined. Most live in abject poverty. Horrible. And the divide gets worse every year.'

'I'm sure you'll make a tremendous difference.'

He grimaced at my cruel sarcasm and I almost felt ashamed. Almost. 'I'll do what I can, which is more than most.'

I let that hang in the air. No point in getting into an argument about the futility of his gesture (because that's all it was, a gesture).

'I will be gone on Sunday morning,' he said. 'Flight to Paris from City, a week's training and orientation, and then the direct Air France flight next weekend.'

'You've never been to India,' I said unthinking, as if he may not have realised.

'Nope. About time I lived it for myself.'

'Nothing going on in Africa caught your fancy then? Peckham poverty not good enough for you?'

He gave me a weary look.

'We're not a good couple, are we?' It was like the penny had finally dropped for him.

I sighed. 'No. This is good for both of us.'

'I think you're right.'

It was one of the very few times in the recent weeks we had agreed on something and we chinked our mugs of builders' tea in recognition of that. I wouldn't miss Henry, we had irritated each other from the very moment he'd moved in, after the limited 'thrill' had gone. We hadn't eaten the same food (he was Vegan, I liked my meat, the more processed the better), read the same books (my passion for tacky thrillers and real life crime out of place on his Guardian-recommended shelves), enjoyed the same classic films (how could he not fall in love with Butch and Sundance?) – we were Matthau and Lemmon, an Odd Couple best de-coupled.

Forget it being a break, this needed to be the real deal, a full break-up.

There were to be no half measures. No compromises. New Claire was taking over.

Chapter 4

Saturday had been my last night of sharing a bed with Henry but there had been no final throes of bedtime passion. We were both uncomfortable with him staying in the flat over our last weekend now that things were ending so he had made arrangements to stay with his bestest buddies Dominic and Sam for the Sunday; they had a van and were going to pop over to move out his worldly goods when I popped out to Tesco. Dom and Sam were a couple I'd miss them tremendously – they were originally Henry's friends and I knew whose side they would go to once we split. But it was time for the change.

The bed was cold that night, as it had been most nights in recent memory. We had never been a passionate couple, Henry was not a great or even competent lover, and that night we slept as we did normally – back to back, to minimise the impact of his window-rattling snoring. I was not going to miss that. The more I thought about it, the easier this separation was becoming.

Barclay hadn't contacted me though. Broken promises already. But then no one but Mum ever called me to be honest – Vodafone probably wondered why I even bothered with a phone. Poor, lonely Claire. I managed to fall asleep quickly and stave off the threatening melancholy. It had been a particularly arduous afternoon at Tesco after all.

I woke and rose early the next morning but Henry had already risen and was finishing the dregs of his packing. Good man. I hate goodbyes, especially potentially emotional ones. I was more upset when Dom and Sam arrived – I'd miss those guys hugely, we'd had some good times together, sometimes even with Henry, and we all knew that this was the end of the line for us as friends. There were tear clouds gathering and my voice broke as I helped them pack the last of the boxes into their old rusty van. Henry probably thought all the emotion was for him and he strode forward to hug me, but I was stiff in his arms to avoid any doubt.

And then so quickly they were gone, Henry was gone, and I was alone to make my own mistakes in this world.

It was Monday and Barclay still hadn't called, despite my hopeful glances at my Nokia every hour, on the hour, all weekend.

It all felt like a massive anti-climax, and my life seemed to have forgotten the exciting promise of the previous Friday with Barclay.

Work. Marshalls. Same old same old.

But no. When I got to my desk it looked odd. As in 'where's all my stuff gone?' odd, a lone Post-It in the centre, curling to hide its message.

'Please see me in my office. Peter'. That was not good. This was signed 'Peter', my boss's more formal corporate ego, not the less clenched, more approachable everyday 'Pete' I normally worked for. As I approached his door I saw him look up from his laptop. He was dressed in his best Top Man grey wool suit, a white button down Oxford and subdued red silk tie. Management personified. Suddenly I felt leaden in my step and dry mouthed. This wasn't looking good.

'Ah. Claire. Do come in and please shut the door behind you.'

By the book. No 'how was your weekend?' though, so he wasn't following the HR script 100%, but definitely not good. I quietly closed the glass door (a sound barrier only – so much for privacy). I figured I could always slam it on my way out for extra impact.

'Feeling any better?' he smarmed. He did insincerity very, very well. It probably featured highly on his LinkedIn profile. At least he'd noted I had been off on Friday.

'Not really,' I croaked, a final play for sympathy.

'Now Claire, sorry to catch you as soon as you walked through the door but it's best to get these things sorted as soon as possible I always say.'

"These things'?' I put on my best confused look, but I was pretty sure what was coming.

'As you know,' he continued, ignoring my attempt at a furrowed brow, 'things have been a little tough of late for us at Marshalls Design and we're going to have to make a few economies to be ready to kick off in the New Year from a sounder base, peel the onion on those costs and take a helicopter view of the operation. Some potential hot prospects for us to warm up for but we need to be fitter and a little flatter to gear ourselves up for the challenges ahead and...'

Uh oh. No doubt now where this was going.

'I'll save you the words,' I interrupted. 'You are going to tell me that my year as an Intern is coming to a close and you have reviewed the option of making my position permanent but at a time of commercial austerity and difficult trading in the web game and the threat of off-shore outfits outpacing and undercutting us, etcetera etcetera. Sorry to spoil your speech but I'm sure we both have better things to do with the day so just tell me how much I'm getting and I'll go.'

That hit him slap bang in the middle of his mono brow.

'Er well yes, exactly Claire. How very perceptive of you. Thank you for your understanding and your contribution to ...'

'Marshalls Design. Yes, got that. How much?'

'We'll pay you up to the end of the month. Including the holidays of course.'

So generous.

'Perfect. That's my first round sorted out.' I held out my hand for a final shake from the most ineffective man-child it had ever been my misfortune to encounter. 'Good luck and all that. It's been a blast.'

It hadn't been, but if I'd learned one thing from Peter Marshall it was insincerity that could be vaguely convincing. I didn't slam the glass door on my way out – what was the point? – and I wasn't in the least bit surprised to see a younger, cheaper, prettier prospective Intern standing outside his office waiting for a few minutes of his valuable time.

'You're next,' I smiled, and left without another word.

Chapter 5

Barclay finally texted me that lunchtime. It was succinct and to the point:

Ashburnham Arms. The quiet table at the back. 2pm. B.

How did he know I would be free today? Did he just assume he could click his fingers and I would come a-running?

It was the same pub as before, so it would be safe neutral territory and I did have the afternoon to kill, the rest of the week now. Rest of my life even. At least I was going to meet a dangerous man in a non-dangerous place – that pub was the kind where you couldn't imagine people getting even slightly tipsy, let alone a fight breaking out. The landlord probably considered calling the police when someone went 'tut' under their breath just in case all hell broke loose. I got to Greenwich and the pub a little early. Barclay was already there, sitting at the table furthest from the front door as if hiding from an imaginary throng of fellow customers – the place again was completely empty, not even any bar staff although there was the sound of someone moving crates of empty bottles out in the rear garden.

'Good afternoon,' he said, not rising to greet me. He was wearing a wonderfully cut jacket – pale grey, with a black shirt underneath. I felt underdressed in my best discounted Gap combo of jeans and overwashed bulky wool jumper.

'Hello,' I said, taking the seat opposite him.

'Would you like a drink?'

'I would like a coffee if that's possible.'

'When Kevin gets back I'll ask him to do you an espresso – they do a decent Nespresso here, better than that High Street rubbish.'

I don't like espresso – far too strong for me. But that day was now all about new Claire, maybe even Nespresso Claire, rather than boring old Nescafe Claire, so I let it ride.

'With milk on the side please,' I asked.

'You mean cream, surely?'

Of course. Cream. No compromises with Barclay. He had a glass of something clear and fizz with a slice of lime and ice. Possibly a G&T but I couldn't read the guy at all.

'So you have something for me? Are we talking a job?' I asked.

'Did you classify your work at Marshalls as 'a job'? That was paying below minimum wage, you know.'

'I thought it was little more, but close enough.' I was taken aback that he had somehow found out my salary and appeared to be aware that I was no longer working there, but then this guy seemed to know everything.

A barman (presumably this was Kevin) appeared and Barclay got his attention with a nod and held up two fingers, in the polite way. Kevin nodded and noisily began dissecting the coffee machine.

'I need an assistant, someone who can drive,' said Barclay.

'I…I don't have a car,' I said.

'I know. A car comes with the job. You have held a clean licence since you turned eighteen and that is all that is required. I have a new car coming for you.'

'You've already done that? What if I said 'no'?'

'You are not going to turn this down.'

'Apparently not.' The arrogance of the man. And how did he know about my driving licence and no car status?

I remembered the car keys I had seen in his rucksack. 'It must be expensive to insure an Aston Martin,' I said.

He raised his eyebrows. 'It is. But I don't drive that anymore. There were…complications. This work requires a more anonymous car.'

'That's good,' I said. 'I don't think I'd be comfortable driving something that costs more than I've earned in my entire life. I thought you said this work was going to be technical?'

'But you're not particularly technical, are you?'

'Not massively, no.' Rumbled.

'The work I do does involve mobile phones and computers, but it is the driving that is the pressing problem for me at the moment. I've been…' He hesitated, what was to follow was causing him some embarrassment. 'I've been banned for six months.'

I laughed. 'Banned?'

'Speeding. Parking. Driving while suspended, that kind of nonsense. Nothing major but it all totted up. I probably should have gone to the court thing about it but I had something else on that day. They weren't happy about me being a no-show so they hit me where it hurt. It has left me with a problem you can assist me with.'

Our coffees arrived, tiny half-filled white cups with a thimbleful of espresso in each. Even adding the cream made barely a mouthful.

'I just need to go to the loo,' I said. 'Need to make room for that.'

He nodded, but still no smile. Maybe he was shy and slow to warm up with beauties like myself. I left my handbag with him and made my way to the Ladies. When I returned, Barclay was rifling through my bag.

'What are you doing?' I asked.

'You went through my bag,' said Barclay. 'So, predictably, I am clearly going through yours.'

'Put that down!' But I wasn't quick enough and he had it open, the contents tipped onto the table.

'Calm down. Fair is fair. Now, what do we have here?'

He picked up my mobile phone. It was not going to impress Mr Barclay, that was for sure.

'Nokia? An early Nokia?' he sneered. 'I think my late grandmother had one of these. Do they still work in the 21st century?'

I made a desperate grab but he pulled it away, easily avoiding my lunge.

'It's all I need.'

'Really? Interesting.'

I felt like a sub-species. Was it too soon to call him cruel? After all, I'd only met him a few days before. 'At least you won't find a gun in there,' I snapped.

His eyebrows arched. 'No. Nothing so interesting. Oh my, what is this?' He held up my Kindle, pinched between thumb and forefinger. 'This really is the lowest of the low. A Fisher Price toy. There's no excuse for such a device you know – I would rather have an Etch-a-Sketch to read on. You can have too much technology – paper will always be superior. And more secure.'

I dropped my head at his cheap put-down and he continued to rifle through my possessions. I was too shocked to stop him. He ignored my lipstick, mascara and blusher; when you carry a loaded handgun in your own bag, the everyday contents of a nobody like me must make boring fare.

And then he found them. He held them up to his nose and took a deep breath.

'Ah, disappointing. They're a fresh pair.'

'Bastard!' I lunged, but again he easily evaded me. He balled my flimsy spare knickers in his left fist.

'Care to explain?' he sneered.

'I'm going,' I said, rising to my feet. 'And I'm going to report that gun to the police.'

He laughed. 'Sit down. And what will you tell the police, about stealing my bag at the railway station and then rifling through its contents before bothering to contact me? Why didn't you hand it straight to the police?' Ah. He had me. 'And what on earth did you do with my wallet and cards? I swear they were in the bag when I lost it but you appear to have failed to return them.'

My mouth made the motions but nothing came out. The gall of the man. 'Your word against mine,' I said, deflated.

'Good luck with that – my father is a high court judge.' (He wasn't, I later discovered and his father despised him.)

'Oh.'

'And a lovely pink umbrella, a Hello Kitty purse – what are you, twelve? – and some chewing gum. Scintillating. Here, have it back.' He threw the bag across the table at me. 'But I'm keeping these.' He shoved my knickers into the pocket of his coat.

I hated this man. But I couldn't move, his gaze didn't waver and I found myself transfixed. I drank my coffee in a single gulp. It was delicious. I needed four more.

'Now then, after that little distraction, let's talk about payment for the driving work and the reward for the return of my bag.'

'You are assuming that I want anything to do with you,' I said, surprising myself; I'd seemingly 'grown a pair'.

'Of course you do. This is exciting for you.'

'And how do you know so much about me?' I asked.

'I know more about you than you know about you. The internet may be a dangerous playground but it is a fascinating one.'

'Such as?'

'Well, let me cover the basics first,' he appeared to be enjoying himself, enjoying my discomfort and all too aware of the hold he had on me. 'Name; Claire MacDonald. Age; 25, birthday September 13th. Born just down the road in Greenwich Hospital, sadly an institution no longer with us. Parents; Desmond and Deidre MacDonald, now resident with your brother Paul, in Edinburgh. You went to school at Deptford Green High School but never went to college or university after Sixth Form. You have eight GCSEs but did not excel at any single subject. You live in a rented flat at 13 Dutton Road in Deptford. Your rent is £750 a month, which is going to be a problem now that your Ex, Henry has run away to India. But you are undoubtedly better off without him as it will give you the opportunity to work for me. Your closest friends were originally Henry's so they will leave you, too. Sad.' He pulled a sad face. I was not amused. Going through my bag was a very bad thing but this man had seemingly gone one step further and worked his way through my entire life.

'You were paid weekly on Thursdays by Marshalls Design as an Intern (Temporary), but the work and pay are both desultory, insulting, so them making you redundant this morning was no bad thing,' he continued. 'You complained bitterly about the company and your work colleagues on Facebook to anyone who will listen, but you do nothing about it. And no one listens, no one reads what you post. Did you know that? No one.' That was cruel – I didn't need to hear that. 'Shall I go on?'

'There's more?'

'You are very public online. Like I say, I know more about you than you do yourself. Do you know how much is in your current account? Or, more to the point, how much you owe NatWest?'

My jaw went slack. I'd heard about this kind of privacy intrusion on Watchdog and the like, but that happened to old people, the hard of thinking, surely, not real people. Like me. Who was this guy?

'No. Let's not go there. I don't need to hear any more, thank you very much.'

'The reward then, and a little retainer for your services as my driver and assistant. Shall we say five thousand pounds?' He pulled a pen and cheque book from his jacket pocket.

Suddenly I needed a drink. A strong one. 'That...that would be welcome,' I stammered as he scrawled the necessary on what would be my first ever cheque from a bank called 'Coutts'. That would raise a few eyebrows at the bank when I paid it in. He slid it across the table and rose from the table.

'I suggest we celebrate with dinner at Dion by St Paul's this evening. I have booked a table for two at eight.' He held his hand out and I surprised myself by rising from my seat to shake it.

'8 o'clock,' it was all too fast. 'I'll meet you there.' I was operating on automatic, damn near speechless as he left. I went to the bar. 'A gin and tonic please. Double. Light on the tonic.'

'Sure. Are you going to settle up Barclay's tab, too?' the barman asked.

You bastard, Barclay...

Chapter 6

I surprised myself and managed to arrive early, a whole half hour to wait for his majesty before I told him where to go. Or not. But that business with the spare knickers I keep in my bag had really riled me and I was favouring the easy option.

The restaurant he had selected for our 'celebration' was possibly the best I had ever been to. Situated right on the door step of St. Paul's, it had the kind of floodlit views of Wren's cathedral that would impress all but the most travel weary tourist. The place was crowded with noisy, opinionated City types in their dark pinstripe uniforms and pressed white shirts, the only women either staff or demure arm candy. Not the company I usually kept, of course (I have higher standards) but excellent for people watching nevertheless. I played Mum's old 'Three Words' game and found that I was applying the same three words to everyone there: Wealthy. Opinionated. Loud. Junior managers were lording it over their silent subservient worker bees, deep privileged tones were occasionally rising above the hubbub and spouting macho nonsense to the masses, inevitably punctuated with an overdramatic laugh.

I ordered myself a Diet Coke and pretended to read something on my mobile. It looked even more out of place than I did in this land of shiny smartphones and tablets.

So this man, this Barclay, what to make of him? The facts at hand: he had left an expensive bag (very expensive: I looked it up online and they go for around a grand and the laptop was worth even more) that I had picked up and, admittedly a few dark thoughts later, I had returned to him, intact, as any good, law-abiding citizen would. He had then undertaken a detailed, possibly illegal, certainly exhaustive online investigation without permission on yours truly and by all appearances he had harvested what felt like every online detail about me, including stuff that I probably don't even know about myself. School reports? Credit history? Medical records? My so-called friends bitching about me on Twitter behind my back? (Is that called 'twitchering'?) Had I been hacked? Had he hacked my bank, my email, my doctor? Did it matter? What could I do about it?

So many questions. And what did I know about him? Only what I found in that bag. I didn't even know his full name – was 'Barclay' his first or surname? Was it his real name? What was his line of work? Why did he require a gun? All I had to go on was his mobile number and a cheque, which had his bank account details and that was about it – the account name was simply 'Q. H. Barclay'. 'Q'? That sounded more like a name from a James Bond movie than real life. I couldn't even think of a male name that started with Q.

And why me? Was it my honesty in returning the bag, or my dishonesty in taking it that appealed to him? And who pays a stranger five grand for returning a bag? Was he buying my silence over the gun? Was I now an accessory after the event (or whatever they call it)? What was happening? Maybe I should get up and leave while I still had the opportunity. And yet…Barclay arrived a few minutes after eight, dressed in almost exactly the same costume as the City clowns (minus the pinstripe – not Barclay's style) but carried it off with pure panache. You could criticise him for many things (and I was assembling a pretty long list myself already) but you had to admit the guy had style. The head of the restaurant knew him, they exchanged pleasantries in French, and we were moved to a different table right at the back, away from the main crowds. Cosy. So much for my thoughts of possibly making a rapid exit.

'This is not a date.'

'It is not a date. We have been very clear on that,' said Barclay.

'It's just a getting-to-know-each-other meal.'

'Exactly.'

'We are not celebrating, more clarifying.'

'If you say so.'

As you can tell, the conversation was uncomfortable at first. We discussed the menu and its expensive dishes which seemed individually to cost more than my weekly shop. We ordered, me keeping an eye on the prices just in case. Barclay however seemed to be pushing the boat out. Surely he couldn't leave me to pick up the bill again?

Suddenly, without warning, he said; 'Sorry.'

'What?'

'That foolishness with your bag. That was stupid and childish of me. Not a good way to start things. Sorry.'

Disarmed, I said 'S'okay' under my breath.

'Forgive me?'

'Maybe.'

The starters arrived almost too quickly: the curse of ordering from the set menu.

'Tell me more about this work then. Where's your office? What are the hours? What will I be doing? I haven't said 'yes' yet, you know.'

'I've got a little mundane, boring stuff, and some not-so-mundane-stuff that's not strictly, exactly one hundred per cent…' He paused and looked around – there was no one listening. '…

that requires that you display a degree of moral flexibility.'

I knew it! I smiled. He smiled. 'How illegal?' I asked.

'Justifiably illegal,' he answered cryptically. 'You have my word that no one gets hurt. I will always have your back. You will sleep soundly at nights, I can assure you of that, and I'll take any heat if things get too...' He let that one drift, probably realising that he was saying too much.

"If things get too…' what, exactly?'

'Claire, you've got to ask yourself what exactly do you want from life,' he said. 'Do you really think the best that life in this wonderful town can offer you is a nine-to-five existence as an underpaid, overworked junior for some anonymous bunch of losers too stupid to hack it at Google or Facebook?'

I picked at the rocket in my diminutive avocado salad with my fork. I didn't know what I wanted, but he was right – I was starting to know what I *didn't* want. I didn't want to work in an office for anonymous people who didn't appreciate me, didn't talk to me, didn't even see me the majority of the time.

'You work with me, Claire,' he emphasised the 'with', 'and you'll never be bored again. I guarantee it.'

I had no answer to that. I was bored with my life. Twenty-five and already dreading the morning alarm, the sardine squash of the commute, the monotony of the blinking cursor on my screen, the pile of meaningless paperwork I had to complete and file for no one to read, the trip to Starbucks for everyone's latte but mine. Only another forty plus years of this to go – it will just fly by – and then I can curl up in front of my one bar heater with a mug of Horlicks waiting for the minute of conversation with that nice young man from Meals on Wheels. Bliss.

Barclay was smiling at me, knowing he had me. I tried not to smile back, but it was almost painful not to.

'And a car?' I asked.

'One appropriate to the work we will do.'

My mind started racing. Obviously something classy if I was to chauffeur him around for his meetings and engagements. This guy wouldn't be cutting corners with his wheels, that was for sure. A Jag? Beemer? Bentley? This could get very interesting.

'Do I get a chauffeur's cap?' the child in me asked.

He chuckled and shook his head.

'And my salary? I'm looking for thirty k,' I suggested.

'Then in that case I think you will be looking at a Job Seeker's allowance as I can't cover that,' he responded.

'And you're looking at Uber or an Oyster Card.'

'Touché. Twenty.'

'I'm sorry?' I cupped my hand to my ear, suddenly hard of hearing. Hilarious, I know. 'Twenty-five k.'

'Twenty-two. Done.'

'Twenty-five.' But it was too meek: he knew I was beaten.

'Twenty-two. And a cut of any extras we make together.'

I had no idea what that would amount to but I found myself grinning. I couldn't help myself.

The deal was done and there we were. Barclay and MacDonald. Partners in something or other.

Once we'd eaten and opened the second bottle of red:

'An excellent wine list here,' Barclay boasted. 'Makes up for the so-so food.' I wasn't complaining: those were undoubtedly the best salmon and crab fishcakes I'd ever eaten (on account of them being the only fishcakes I'd ever had not made by Birdseye. I thought it best not to mention it.)

'So tell me more about this Barclay guy,' I don't think I was slurring but maybe ordering a second bottle hadn't been a great move.

'What do you want to know?'

'Full name for a start. Is Barclay a first or second name?'

'It can be either.'

'Yes, but with you?'

'It is my surname.' He hadn't answered the original question but I let it pass. 'Born in 1986, to Mr & Mrs Barclay of Berkshire residence.'

'Do you see mum and dad much?'

'Only at Christmas. Torture.'

'Brothers and sisters? Cousins'

A small shake of the head

'Significant other?'

'No.'

'Ever?'

'No.' He shifted uncomfortably in his chair and took another sip from his glass. For the first time in our short acquaintance I felt like I had him on the ropes.

'Friends?'

'When I need them. I don't need them often. They are more like acquaintances, colleagues even. You?' He had switched the focus – had I hit a nerve?

'You know all about me.'

'Only what I found online. Surely that is not everything?'

'It seemed pretty extensive from what you said the other day.'

'That is not Claire MacDonald, the person. That is Claire MacDonald the online persona. I assume the two are very different – I would certainly hope so. And before you say anything I did no more than any employer would do when assessing a prospective job applicant. Surely you don't really think all that stuff people post on Facebook is private do you?'

I hadn't really considered it. I knew there were privacy settings, much like there was also all kinds of legal stuff, Terms & Conditions and other pages and pages of legalese that you were supposed to read before clicking 'accept', but who had time to look at that? No one I knew, that was for certain.

'I guess not,' I said.

'So Horrible Henry has gone?'

'He's not that Horrible, but yes. He and all his worldly have moved out and are scattered globally. His body is now in Paris, his mind already suffering in India, his boxes of books and other shit are deposited in some anonymous damp, rat-infested warehouse out Woolwich way. Good riddance.'

'You do not mean that so callously, surely?'

'I do. We weren't a good fit. He wants to help the world, stop global warming, feed the hungry, free the oppressed, clothe the naked, house the homeless…'

'Busy man.'

'Ha! If he spent less time talking about it to his mates and their girlfriends and more time actually doing something that would be a start.' I was sounding bitter, but the truth was I genuinely didn't care at all. He was gone. End of.

'So little Claire is all alone now in the big, dark city?'

'Hardly. I've got loads of friends.' It sounded like a boast.

"Good for you.' He didn't sound convinced. Neither did I.

'But most are away at the moment.'

'Not good for you.'

'That's the great thing about Facebook and…' I paused,

remembered that he'd been so dismissive of my Facebooking; apparently no one reads my stuff. No one cares. I was posting to the un-listening. That hurt. 'I find it difficult to make new friends, like I'm being disloyal to absent friends,' I said.

'I do not have that problem.'

'You make friends easily?'

'No, I meant I have no loyalty issues. I am not very loyal to anyone.'

'But you'll be loyal to me?'

'If you work with me? Yes. Of course. But loyalty has to be earned.'

'You'd make a rubbish dog.'

'Don't mention dogs,' he scowled, uncomfortable for some reason.

'You don't like dogs?' He shook his head but I couldn't say I was that surprised. This man's idea of a best friend was probably an Italian sports car or an expensive vintage cellar. Or a Prada rucksack.

Before I could stop myself I said, 'I get lonely sometimes, especially the evenings when Henry's out saving the world.' Uh oh. The alcohol was doing my talking for me. It just slipped out. Damn that second bottle.

'Who doesn't?' Was he being sympathetic or sarcastic? I couldn't tell.

'You don't strike me as the lonely type.'

'Everyone is lonely. It's just that some of us find it difficult to admit to it. Money doesn't always buy happiness. I would like to think I'm a loner but sometimes…'

And he left it there, hanging, unclarified. In time I would get used to it, but it was surprising that evening. Later I realised that with Barclay it was all front, all bravado. But deep down, further down where he didn't let you dig, there was a lonely, unhappy little boy. Spoiled rotten, unprincipled, sad even. The bugger just wouldn't admit to it. One minute it felt like he was opening up, only to slam that door shut with the next breath. Infuriating.

The restaurant had emptied out almost completely by the time we had finished our food so I figured I was on safe ground to mention the unmentionable.

'Can I ask you something?' I ventured.

'Sure.'

'The gun.'

'Ah.'

'What's it for?'

'I don't have it on me if you're worried.'

'I appreciate that,' the wine made it sound more like 'happreshiate'. 'But what's it for when you do have it?'

'Encouragement. Deterrent. The usual.' His voice drifted away as if that wasn't the whole story.

'Will I need one?'

He laughed. 'No.'

'So you've never shot anyone?'

'No.'

"No, you have' or 'No, you haven't'?' I pressed.

He sighed. 'It was in my bag because I had to meet this guy who was being difficult over some money he owed me.'

My eyes widened. 'You threatened someone with that gun? Shot him?'

'No. Of course not. What kind of man do you think I am? Even I would not do that just for money,' said Barclay.

'Good,' I said.

'But I may have killed his dog.'

'You shot a dog?'

As Barclay was getting quieter I was getting louder. The restaurant was now empty except a few staff well out of earshot. Just as well.

'Keep it down. No one can claim to be perfect. Not even your Ex. Look at you – you stole a bag,' he replied.

'No I didn't. I picked up a bag that some idiot had lost. I gave it back.'

'Eventually. I didn't shoot a dog. I shot *at* a dog. And I missed. Deliberately. The dog had a heart attack. It was not my fault.'

'You believe that you are completely blameless for its death?'

'Pretty much.'

'And you did this because this guy wouldn't pay you?'

'He owed me money.'

'So you shot his dog.'

'*At* his dog.'

'For money?'

'Why else would I do it? I like dogs.'

'You have a funny way of showing it.'

'Look, he owed me money. A lot of money. Fifty grand. That is a lot of money. And he was refusing to pay, so I needed to shake him up a bit and remind him of his obligation.'

'Bang. Dead dog.'

'Actually it was bang bang bang, woof, topple, dead dog. I am not very good with guns.'

'Evidently. But effective nonetheless.'

'So it would appear. Look, Claire, I do hope this will not come between us…'

'There is no 'us'. I'm not sure I want to work for you anymore.'

But my eyes were smiling

'But we have a deal. 22k.'

'I thought we'd agreed on twenty-five? So if I now say 'no' you'll shoot me? Sorry, I meant 'shoot *at* me'?'

He smiled. Damn it, I found myself smiling, too.

'It's going to be fun,' said Barclay.

'No guns,' I said.

'No promises,' he replied, and ordered another bottle.

Chapter 7

He had probably answered all of my questions. I had possibly asked all of my questions. Sadly, the large quantity of quality wine consumed meant that I could remember nothing with any certainty, so I was none the wiser. The following morning all I had to show for the evening with Barclay was a Saharan mouth and the dull, unrelenting pounding in my forehead. Oh, and a business card that had just BARCLAY printed on it. On the reverse he had scrawled his mobile number, a Docklands address (presumably an office?) and a time: 11am.

It was 10am when I read it. Despite my head screaming that I was in no fit state to rise I forced myself out of bed and dressed with the clumsy, lethargic motions and lack of care of the truly hungover. I decided to skip the shower and make up and my breakfast consisted of a mouthful of Colgate foam.

So much for making a good impression on my first day.

Mercifully the sky outside was dull and grey – I don't think I could have coped with any brightness that morning. There was a dampness in the air that wasn't quite drizzle that softened the hard lines of the buildings as I made my way to the local Docklands Light Railway station. At least the commute would be easy – Barclay's office looked like it was about half an hour away. Plenty of time to sober up and start feeling human again for my first day in my new life.

But it wasn't an office. The building was a sharp-cornered modern glass and steel tower of an apartment block, built for a sparkling future that still hadn't quite arrived despite the promises of the developer's brochure. My doubts returned and I still wasn't quite sure I was doing the right thing. I was going to his flat? Even newly liberated Claire wasn't wholly comfortable with that particular step into the unknown. But it was too late to walk away, and I was pretty confident I could take this Barclay character in a fight. Even so, my hand reached into my bag for the calming assurance of my attack alarm key ring, though going on previous experience it was as likely to deafen me as much as any attacker.

And then suddenly there was my prospective 'attacker', holding open the building door for me, beckoning me inside. And … smiling? Was that a smile?

'Good morning. You look…tired,' he managed, about as polite as I could have expected in the circumstances. In stark contrast Barclay looked like he had spent the last few hours with his personal barber and tailor – if I said he looked 'immaculate' I'd have been understating it. Even his teeth looked newly polished.

'I work from home,' he explained. 'But you won't need to come here very often. Everything will be on the laptop I've got for you and the car's being delivered this afternoon.' We had walked to a bank of lifts and entered the one he had presumably just descended in. He pressed the button marked 'Penthouse' and we started our ascent.

The giddy girl in me I had tried so hard to contain was easily impressed and quite excited. I was going up in the world, both literally and figuratively.

'Make yourself comfortable over there at the desk. I'll get some coffee on – you look like you need it.'

Barclay disappeared behind what was presumably a kitchen door and I was left alone to take in the eye-watering views of

Docklands and the almost-as-stunning apartment. I tried not to look too awestruck, but it was bloody difficult.

So this was how the other half live.

It was a large monochrome high tech flat, the furnishing was sparse: a designer recliner here, a matching sofa there, a state of the art work desk and chair all chrome and glass and leather sparkling under the halogen lights set deep in the ceiling.

So was this Barclay's home? Wow.

Barclay's deluxe lifestyle trappings weren't limited to the contents of his rucksack. The polished steel of three TV-sized computer screens jostled for dominance with laptops, iThingies, keyboards and mice on a smoked glass desk that was more like a futuristic work bench than a table.

The entire far wall of the room was obscured by three of the largest televisions I had ever seen, effectively they *were* the wall. Boys and their toys, huh? All the gear and no idea.

But curiously the room was stylish but without style, a show home lifted from the pages of *Wallpaper* magazine or *Esquire*. There were no ornaments or plants whatsoever, cables had been tucked away out of sight and it all felt artificial and false, the result of either chronic OCD or someone desperate to impress. It was very much a personality-free zone. Polished but seemingly unloved, there were no feminine graces. This was a cold room, almost antiseptic in its detachment from a personal touch. The only softness in the entire room was from a single grey fake fur rug that leaked out from under the work bench, concealing the cables presumably for all that technology piled up on top.

All I could learn about Barclay from this room was from what wasn't there rather than what was. There were no pictures on the walls, no family photos, no newspapers or magazines or CDs or

DVDs or books or paperwork or even post.

The more I looked the less I found. Few cupboards, one set of (locked) filing cabinets, not even a coat rack. Presumably everything was crammed into the bedroom, which I had no intention whatsoever of visiting.

How long did it take a man to make coffee? I needed a drink and felt like I could pee like a grizzly coming out of hibernation. There were three doors leading out from the main room. Barclay had gone through the one on the right to make coffee, so presumably that was the kitchen. The one on the left, which would presumably share the stunning views of the main room, was likely a bedroom so I guessed the one in the middle, slightly ajar, would be the loo.

I pushed it open and clicked on the light and entered. The bathroom was five-star hotel spotless, a shining example of just how sparkly chrome fittings and white tiles can be. Mr Muscle would be so proud. My eyes did not appreciate the additional jolt of polished surfaces and tungsten brilliance. I did my business and helped myself to a glass of water. It really was like a hotel – the glass was in a little plastic bag.

When I went back into the lounge Barclay was sitting at the table, two tiny clear glass cups of espresso proudly sitting before him. Oh, for a cup of instant.

'Sorry it took so long. Kitchen's a bit … untidy,' he apologised.

'Nice place,' I said.

He nodded but said nothing. Instead he pushed one of the laptops towards me as I sat in the other chair at the table.

'This is for you,' he said, lifting the lid of what looked like the Apple laptop that had been in his bag. I spotted the scratch I'd made on its perfect skin while on the train and my cheeks reddened.

But it was like being reunited with a lost love. I'd swear I could feel the tears welling in my eyes.

'Thank you.'

'Unfortunately the work I need you to do on it today is far more mundane. I need help completing my Self-Assessment tax return and ... actually, I don't need help as much as I need you to do the whole thing. I've got to go and sort out your car at the dealer, so let me just get the receipts and stuff and I can leave you with it while I get the car.'

I'd noticed the Audi dealership on the train over. Or maybe it was that Jaguar place opposite? I wouldn't mind filling in his boring old tax return while waiting for the keys. Besides, a man's tax filing can reveal all kinds of things about an individual, surely?

He went into his bedroom and emerged with a small box file and his coat.

'Okay if I leave you here? I'll be a few hours.'

'Sure,' I said.

'Ciao,' he said, pulling on his coat and whipping a Paul Smith silk scarf around his neck.

'Ciao'? Had he really said that? How totes Eighties...

Barclay's tax return was a massive disappointment. Sorting through a nominal handful of receipts and bank statements yielded precious little information about the man and, much like his apartment, it was what was missing that spoke more about the man than what was there. It wasn't going to take a massive amount of work to complete it, but at least there were a couple of surprises that made it more interesting to do than my old job's paperwork.

Surprise number one: his full name was Quentin Horatio Barclay. Quentin? So that was the 'Q' on the cheque. Mystery solved. Hardly a name to be ashamed of these days – old

Tarantino had done the world's Quentins a massive favour, even if it would never quite be cool. I'd been thinking more along the lines of 'Quincy' or 'Quigly' or even 'Qatermass'. 'Quentin' was disappointingly conventional, and I couldn't for the life of me see his problem with it.

(But I guess 'Barclay' fed his ego better, of course.)

Surprise number two was that his taxable income for the entire year was eighteen grand. Eighteen! And his sole employer during that period appeared to be a local coffee shop where he worked as a barista. Seriously? The coffee he'd made me that morning was okay but nothing out of this world – Barclay was a barista?

I sorted through the receipts he'd left me and poured over the bank statements. It was not what I'd expected, a man living pretty much on the breadline, a current account dipping into overdraft most weeks, topped up with tiny dribbles from the coffee place that barely paid off the previous week's deficit. He'd even asked me to put his home address as the same as the coffee shop rather than this high tech palace.

I looked around the flat. How could he afford all this? And the clothes he adorned himself in? And an Aston Martin (or whatever he'd sorted for me)? Something wasn't adding up.

I could only guess that his declaration to Her Majesty's Revenue puppets was at best a sleight of hand to keep them from his real lifestyle and earnings. I'd only been working for him a few hours and I was already guilty of filing a false tax declaration and fraud.

Oh Barclay, you're leading me astray.

I finished the online form and checked and re-checked my work. All in order. I pressed send and clicked 'yes' a zillion times and then it was on its way. Crime number one neatly wrapped up and delivered on day one. Imagine how productive I'd have been with a clear head?

The hangover had subsided a little and I'd calmed its temper with a succession of glasses of tap water from the bathroom. But having finished the main job at hand I needed something more, some food perhaps. He'd warned the kitchen was a mess but how bad could it be?

Bad. As I opened the kitchen door I almost retched. In contrast to the designer perfection elsewhere the kitchenette was a devastated disaster zone, stacked high with unwashed plates and cutlery and what looked and smelled like a week's worth of discarded takeaways. I instinctively held my breath: abandoned food was everywhere. The nauseating stench of several half-eaten stale curries competed with the sickly aroma of rancid sweet and sour chicken. A token pedal bin was overflowing – it hadn't been emptied in weeks.

Desperate for a drink I opened the fridge. Empty, except for an unopened, out-of-place bottle of Dom Perignon Champagne. It looked like it had belonged in someone else's home. (From what I'd already learned of Barclay, it probably had.)

I needed a drink but the coffee machine looked too complicated. Maybe he was a barista after all? Nothing around that looked remotely as practical as a kettle. I settled for another glass of tap water in the last clean glass, then ran from the kitchen before the combination of last night's excess and the cloying smells of Barclay's culinary depravity proved too much. I needed to get out and draw in a lungful or seven of fresh air. I grabbed my coat and bag. I'd leave the door on the latch – I'd only be gone a few minutes, I just needed to clear my head and, most importantly, my nasal passages.

*

'Oh. Hello,' he said.

For some reason I hadn't expected to meet anyone in the corridor outside the flat but I guess stranger things have happened, even to me. (Barclay, for one.)

The guy looked confused and a little lost. 'Is Barclay in?' he asked.

'Er, no. No one home I'm afraid. Were you after him? I was just leaving.'

'No. Yes. Are you… are you his girlfriend?'

I laughed. 'God no. Just a …' (friend? employee?) 'I'm Claire,' I said, holding out my hand in a ridiculously formal manner.

He was confused but amused by my business-like gesture and shook my hand nevertheless. 'Tom. Thomas,' he said.

"Tom Thomas'?' I grinned. 'Really? Did your parents think that would be funny or something?'

He laughed too. 'No. I'm Tom, but I'm trying to be 'Thomas' now and it's not quite working. Tom Pedakowski.' That explained the slight American accent I was picking up.

'I prefer Tom I think. Don't be a 'Tommy' though. It would make you sound about five years' old.'

'Tom it is. I'm thinking of cutting the surname back to something more British – it sounds too foreign and I end up spelling it out on the phone all the time. I've been test driving 'Thomas Peters'. Can't get used to it myself. I keep forgetting then correcting myself.'

'I like your glasses,' I said out of nowhere.

'They're Tom Ford's,' he said.

'Doesn't he miss them?' I cracked. 'It's amazing the prescription works for you.' Hysterical, I know.

He smiled again, revealing near perfect teeth, a credit to the great American dentist profession. I like good teeth. He had a nice smile. He was a little lacking on the height front (around my height) but he wasn't unattractive. Blondish hair, a little unruly, light stubble, probably late thirties, casually dressed but smartly so. On the old Claire-phwoar-meter (now back in use in the post-Henry world) he was an 'Interesting' but not in the 'Drop Dead G.' category. Close, but not quite.

Whatever. Maybe it was the dim light in the hallway or the relief of being away from the horror of that kitchen and back in the real world, but I suddenly felt myself relaxing, the day brightening up. I was in no rush to go and my head was feeling surprisingly clear.

'Why are you after Barclay, Tom Thomas?'

'I quite like that. I might go for that.'

'You're welcome. It's of no use to me.'

'I need to sort something out with him. We occasionally do business together but it's all gone a bit messy and I just wanted to straighten it out before it went too far.' He paused. I think he was considering how much to tell me. 'We had a bit of a disagreement.'

'You run the coffee shop?' I said, all innocent.

'No, not a coffee shop.' His bemused look was a firm indication he didn't have a clue what I was talking about. I moved on.

'A disagreement? He's quite a disagreeable sort. I don't know him that well but I can see how he rubs people up the wrong way.'

Tom nodded. 'He sure can. I think there's something faulty with his wiring, sometimes he seems to be oblivious to the way he makes people feel. Like that medical condition.'

'Asperger's? I don't know it's that extreme but I haven't known him that long. He doesn't seem to care what you think.'

'It's not an endearing quality,' said Tom.

'So shall I tell him you called by? I've just been tidying up some paperwork for him.' I thought it best to make it absolutely, 100% clear that there was nothing going on between me and Mr Barclay. 'He should be back shortly. He went to see a man about a car.'

'Another Aston Martin? Man, I loved that DB7, that was just beautiful.'

I grinned uncontrollably. Soon it would be mine.

'Shall I..?'

'Yes please. Actually, no. Don't bother. I'll catch him at some point. It wasn't important, just me wanting to tie up some loose ends and not leave things unspoken.' He pushed the button for the lift and the doors opened – it hadn't gone anywhere since his arrival. 'Going down?' he asked. I nodded and joined him.

The lift descended uninterrupted. We stood in silence, uncertain where to look. Instantly strangers again. As we neared the ground floor, he said:

'I was just wondering…'

'Yes?'

'I was wondering if you'd like to have a drink with me sometime?'

I didn't know what to say – it had been a while since someone had asked me out, and this guy was a complete stranger. I didn't know anything about him or…

'Sure.' The word surprised me but it had definitely come from lips. 'That would be nice. I don't live around here though – I'm over the river. Deptford.'

He hummed the theme from Neighbours. 'I'm in Lee. Maybe before Christmas? I've got this trip home I'm heading out on next week.'

'Home? America?'

'San Francisco.'

'Very nice. Yes, before Christmas suits me.' This was all going too fast for comfort but I wasn't resisting; it was just one of those days when things span out of my control. We exchanged mobile numbers and I held my hand out for another overly-polite shake. 'Nice to meet you, Tom Thomas.'

'Nice to meet you, Claire.'

He walked off towards a parked BMW and blipped the blippy thing as he approached it and it blipped back in recognition. I waved then took in a few deep breaths of the damp air I'd been so eager to consume just a few short minutes earlier.

'Well,' I said to myself, 'That really was quite pleasant.' A date? So soon after Henry? Things were looking up. Tom Thomas – it was growing on me, even if it wasn't his real name.

Two new men in a week. And it was still only Tuesday. A girl could get a reputation with that kind of hit rate.

Chapter 8

The car was not exactly what I had been expecting.

'It's a classic,' said Barclay, sensing my disappointment.

'Is it?' I was definitely not convinced. 'A classic what, exactly?'

'They don't make them like this anymore. Actually they probably still do, down in South America or somewhere. A classic never goes out of fashion.'

'Assuming it ever was in fashion in the first place. What exactly is it?'

'It's an early nineties Fiat Uno. Car of the year in its day. The first supermini. A racing hot hatch. 55 metric horsepower.' The words were English but he was talking a different language.

'I thought it would be … nicer.'

'This is as nice as you'll find a Fiat Uno these days. They're pretty rare. This is a great example of Italian style and engineering.'

It was like dealing with a second-hand car salesman, only this car looked distinctly fourth or fifth hand. Barclay was gamely trying to sell it to me but it was a pretty herculean task to convince me to even step closer, let alone step inside.

To describe it as 'boxy' would be unkind to boxes. For one thing, boxes look more solid and even a soaking wet box would appear more secure. It was square and angular in a way they just don't make cars these days, you could almost cut yourself on the sharp corners that had only been slightly softened in the interest of aerodynamics. It was as if it had been designed with just a ruler. At least the wheels were round, and, presumably, the now-missing hubcaps had been too. The wing mirror (there was only one, on the driver's side) looked like it had been glued on, a plastic afterthought added to scrape through an MOT.

It occurred to me that it may have been maintained as a failed school metalwork project, there was definitely some DIY welding on one of the rear doors and some of the rust had been painted over, possibly with household emulsion.

Colour? Well it had several in truth, even the rust came in several fetching shades. It was possible that in a past life it had been red and quite dashing in its youthful eighties' heyday, but now it was several dull, faded pinks, darker on the driver's side for some curious reason like an old Royal Mail post van parked under a blazing hot sun for a decade or two in exactly the same place.

I circled it to see if it had a better side, maybe the light was playing tricks.

Nope.

I reached to open the driver's door but pulled away sharply, as if my touch would confirm the new ownership.

'Don't be timid now,' said the used car salesman who also happened to be my new boss. 'It won't bite.'

I gritted my teeth and clasped the handle. With a sharp tug it was open, and a stale odour of mildew knocked me back on my heels. Involuntarily I tried to swat it away as if it were a cloud of midges.

Barclay laughed, but it wasn't an infectious laugh. I felt like crying.

'I thought…I thought it would be something special,' I whined.

'It is special Claire. A white one of these killed Princess Di!'

I had no idea what he was talking about. I made a pantomime dusting motion at the driver's seat then engineered my butt into the vehicle.

Actually, it wasn't too bad. No, I'd got further than that, it was quite comfortable, firm in support and the dashboard was clean and functional. It would have been out of place in an Aston Martin, but then so would I.

'And you want me to chauffeur you around in this thing?' It didn't make sense.

'Sure. A bit of retro chic never hurt anyone. Besides, it will be dark, no one will see us.'

'Dark?'

'Yes. Didn't I mention that?'

'No.' What else hadn't he mentioned? 'What exactly is this driving job, Barclay?'

'Nothing to be alarmed about. I just have some business deals I'm doing in the next few weeks and need a driver to help me…'

'Get away? Flee the scene? Do a runner? Are these dodgy deals you're doing in the small hours, Barclay?'

He gaped at me in surprise, hurt even. 'Dodgy is a strong word. At worst I'd suggest they're 'below the line'.'

'But I'm a getaway driver?'

He looked suddenly tense, concerned, unsure where I was taking this. 'I guess so, yes,' he said, doubt crossing his face for the first time. 'I've got it all planned, it's very straightforward and…'

'Cool!'

I was grinning, I couldn't help myself. 'When do we start?' I asked.

His relief was visible, his shoulders relaxed and the old Barclay arrogance immediately returned. 'I need picking up at three tomorrow morning. It's not far. You'll be tucked back safely in bed by five and you can take the rest of the day off.'

Generous. I turned the Uno's ignition and unexpectedly it bit first time, a little coarse, throaty even, but it hadn't misfired and it sounded surprisingly assured. I gingerly pressed down on the accelerator and the engine responded, making an almost manly growl. The cold hard plastic of the steering wheel felt good in my hands and suddenly this didn't seem at all bad. I'd never had my own car before and I had to start somewhere. Okay, so Barclay probably had been paid to take it off some crook's hands at a scrap heap, but it worked and felt curiously cosy once I was inside. Snug even.

'Take it for a spin,' he said, closing the door and patting the roof.

With a little too much effort I managed to get it into first and lifted the clutch. A jerk, a jump, and I was moving, a little nervously (I hadn't driven at all for a few months) but my confidence grew as I took it through the gears. I could get used to this, I thought. My initial disappointment was, much like Barclay, disappearing fast in my rear view mirror.

Claire MacDonald. Getaway driver. You heard it first here, folks.

I was in the Fiat Uno parked on the edge of an abandoned DIY store car park at just passed four in the morning on a freezing Tuesday in December. Ignoring Barclays' instruction I had left the engine running to keep the heating ticking over – he couldn't expect me to freeze, surely? I was bored out of my mind.

And maybe, just maybe, a wee bit scared.

'Ten minutes. Tops,' he'd promised. That had been twenty minutes earlier and to be honest I'd never expected it to be "ten minutes, tops", he didn't strike me as a punctual person. But now though I was unsure that this little 'below the line' caper of his was actually going to plan. He had disappeared around the corner of this shuttered not-so-super superstore to do the pick-up and there had been no sign of him since.

Maybe I should have turned the car off, but I was still nervous that it would restart easily on my command – 'reliable' wasn't one of the three words that sprang to mind when considering the Uno. The heating was hardly worth it, more noise than heat and Barclay could have been out there screaming for me for all I knew and I wouldn't have heard it. I know what I should have done. I should have turned it off and wound down the window and listened for him, that was what a professional getaway driver would do.

Mind you, a professional getaway driver would probably have demanded a better set of wheels than that little ageing Italian runaround, that I was actually quite taken with. He had told me that the most important thing in this line of work was that we had a car that nobody would look twice at. Well, with the Uno they might have, but the first look would have been shock and the second more like pity.

Despite my new confidence behind the wheel I was secretly hoping that I wouldn't have to 'burn rubber' and get involved in a high speed chase. The badge on the back proudly boasted that it was an Uno 55 –was that its top speed? It seemed nippy enough, shifting up through the tricky gears, but it did start noisily vibrating, almost straining when I got to thirty and I'd been reluctant to push it passed fifty in case bits started shaking off. That car may have been able to park on a postage stamp but I feared it would be a serious stretch of its abilities to reach 60mph. Going downhill. With a strong headwind behind it.

I turned off the engine. Instantly it was as cold inside as outside, but, I reassured myself, at least it wasn't raining.

Splat on the windscreen. Splat splat splat. Typical.

The high flying criminal life could be trying at times.

Where was he? Where was Barclay, the man who was supposed to be saving me from a life of office-tied tedium and evenings of DVD box sets and lonely bottles of Merlot for one?

I waited. And waited. And waited. 'Come on, Barclay, where the hell are you?' I muttered to myself. At least those first drops of rain didn't live up to their promise. I checked my watch and it was almost half an hour passed drop time.

Something had gone wrong. Something must have gone wrong. I lowered the driver's window, the cold air rushing in, instantly releasing the last vestiges of warmth.

Just the noise of faraway traffic. I heard a dog bark off in the distance and I noticed again the slight mildewy dog smell of the ageing fabric on the car's rear seat. Maybe the heaters had brought out the worst of it. It must have been a previous owner's pooch: Barclay never struck me as a pet person. At least he hadn't taken a gun with him – 'no animals were harmed in the making of this getaway'. Or did he have the gun? Why did I trust that man?

I was being stupid. That bark was from the wrong direction. There was no dog there to get in the way. Calm down. I had the easy job, sitting in a car, waiting. Well worth it for a few quid. And Barclay knew what he was doing, right? He said that he'd done this kind of deal without a hitch dozens of times before.

But had he? I only had his word for it of course. I was starting to have my doubts. I was tapping the steering wheel like I was waiting for my driving test result. Couldn't panic. No need to panic. It was just Barclay making sure everything was in order and…

And then suddenly he was there in the rear mirror, jogging gently, a large holdall in hand, something resembling a grin on his face.

I reached over and unlocked the far door. He climbed in, the bag down between his feet and rubbed his hands together.

'Why so cold in here?' he asked.

'You told me to turn the engine off to avoid attracting attention!'

'Are you mad? It's below freezing out there.' Incorrigible. 'Let's get moving.'

Suddenly nervous I turned the key and the over-confident engine coughed and revved into life. Go! First gear into second, third gear just minutes away now folks. I felt that the world record for fastest getaway was safely ours.

'All good?' I asked, gripping the wheel like Lewis Hamilton but driving more like Lady Hamilton.

'Yes. He was a little late. Sorry about that. He couldn't wait to give me the bag. Almost threw it at me. Then ran away. A dream pick-up.'

'And that bag's full of cash?'

'I haven't counted it but it looks and feels good. He looked like a nice guy.'

'Really?'

'No, not really. Didn't get a good look at him, and he didn't even glance at me, so we can … hey! Slow down!'

We were barely doing thirty, but already the Fiat's minuscule engine was straining.

'Don't need a speed camera ticket, do we?' he half joked.

He had a point. I had one thing to do and I was closer to panic than I had ever been in my life. It's a cliché but I could feel a pounding in my chest. Literally. I had never known a thrill like that before. This was the adrenaline-fuelled life I was destined for. Bonnie and Clyde! Barclay and MacDonald!

Fucking hell – I was a getaway driver! Woo hoo!

(At 29mph in a built-up area on a deserted street.)

He was rifling through the holdall, counting out the bundles. "Yes, all here. Easiest money you'll ever make."

But I was barely listening. The blood was rushing in my ears, my heart was racing, pulse throbbing in my wrists and I had a grin as wide as a psychotic clown's. We had done it and now we were heading out of town and on to whatever was next in my new life of crime. Our new life of crime. It would be dark for several more hours on that crisp, cold night, but already my day was brightening faster than the December sky.

I floored the accelerator. The Uno protested but was up for it. Barclay was gripping the holdall's handle. We were both smiling as a light fog enveloped us and we made our first getaway.

'Well,' said Barclay. 'That was something pretty special.'

My heart was still racing and I could hear the blood in my ears throbbing. "Yes." I was still out of breath.

'Exhilarating even.'

I nodded. 'Sure was.'

I clenched and unclenched my hands several times to try to calm myself down.

'I'm sorry if that was all a wee bit too fast for you,' I said.

'Isn't that supposed to be my line?'

We both laughed. I may have blushed a little; it was difficult to tell as I was still feeling quite flushed. Oh my god, we did it. We really did it.

'In my defence it was my first time,' I said.

'Could have fooled me. I felt like I was in safe, experienced hands.'

'Thanks.' It was an unexpected compliment. 'Felt a bit fumbly at first.'

'Didn't notice. You're a natural. This is going to work.'

I nodded, still catching my breath.

'And you sound like you enjoyed it?'

I hadn't expected to, I thought I'd be too nervous and would cock it up and let him down, let us both down.

'I was a teensy weensy bit nervous,' I confessed.

'Teensy weensy? Aren't they the Teletubbies?'

I hadn't expected Barclay to do funny. I also didn't expect him to know about the Teletubbies. This man could surprise for Britain.

Then he laid another one on me; 'I still get a bit nervy, too. I think the adrenaline is all part of this, part of the thrill. I'd like to think I'm ice cold and calm and James Bond-like, but that would all get quite boring after a while. It's that edge that makes it, losing a little bit of self-control every now and then.'

My eyes widened. 'So you're not as cold and heartless as you first appear? Not as manipulative as I thought?'

'Manipulative, yes. But I'm no Daniel Craig.'

'Your eyes are too dark.'

'And I don't have those ears.'

'Nor the hair?'

He snorted in derision.

'Nor the body?'

'Nor the body. Although I'm probably taller.'

He did remind me of someone famous though, but I couldn't for the life of me remember who. Certainly not Daniel Craig. Maybe someone off the telly?

He turned to me and fixed me with those dark, impenetrable eyes. 'What you're really saying is that I'm not as shallow as you first thought?'

'That's another way of putting it.'

He paused. Whether for effect or humour or genuine reflection I couldn't tell. Despite what had just happened, we were still two strangers. I was beginning to wonder if we always would be.

He sat straighter. 'No. I am pretty shallow. I might surprise every now and again but I'd say that what you see is pretty much what you get with me. No great hidden depths here to explore.'

He was drawing the Barclay blinds down. Show's over for tonight, folks. As if to emphasise the point he said 'Time to call it a night.'

It was actually nearer morning, but the streetlights would burn through the mist for a while yet.

We sat in silence. I was smiling, still enjoying the moment. He turned to the window and gazed into the distance, shutting me out from his thoughts.

Chapter 9

'So how old are you?' I asked Tom Thomas.

'Thirty-three.' A pause, a correction to cover his embarrassment. 'No, thirty-seven. Sorry, don't know why I said that. I'm thirty-seven. Bizarre.'

I picked up my glass of the overpriced Rioja and took a quiet sip to fill the yawning seconds. Shit, I thought, he sounds mad. The man doesn't even know his own age. This was a bad idea. Like the thing with Barclay, I was jumping in to this far too fast. The last few days had just been too …no. This was fine. He was just nervous, like me first date jitters, and we both needed to relax.

He smiled. 'Look. I'm thirty-seven. Honest.' He played the sympathy card. 'I'm a little jumpy. It's been a while since I've done this kind of thing.'

'Me too,' I said, smiling. It was only the smallest of white lies.

'It's a reflex answer I seem to have developed. Can't explain it. It's a bit like when you're a kid and someone asks you what your favourite colour is. I always said 'blue'. But I don't have a favourite colour – who does? – but I didn't want to sound odd or different, so I said I had a favourite colour and it was blue. I liked some blue things, – sky, the Pacific at the beach – but not everything blue. That would be odd, if you liked things simply because of their colour. I'm talking too much. Shut up, Tom.'

'Thomas,' I corrected him.

He smiled.

'Is the Pacific really that blue?' I asked. 'I've never seen it. Never been to America in fact.'

'It was in my childhood at least. Probably more grey than blue though these days, with a delicate sheen of spilled oil to add to its twenty-first century charms.'

'I was asked to name my favourite colour last week,' I said.

'Really? How old are you exactly, Miss MacDonald?'

I laughed. 'Thirty-three! No, I'm twenty-five.'

'So who asked for your favourite colour? Isn't that kind of question normally left behind in a kindergarten?'

'Maybe. It was some internet thing on my laptop. One of those security questions things that you always forget as soon as you type in an answer. I put 'blue'. I was buying some shoes. Boots, actually.'

'Good for you. We have something in common at least, albeit a lie.'

We both laughed and clinked our glasses in a silent toast. It was going to be all right after all.

The waiter arrived and took our order. He poured an unnecessary top-up into our glasses before disappearing into the kitchen.

'The pedant in me says that he's overfilled that,' I said. "What I know about wine can be written on the side of a fag packet but I know that red needs to breathe in the glass. More importantly, if you overfill, you can't do that pretentious swirly thing that makes you look like you know your stuff. Like you were doing.'

'I like the way it rides up the side of the glass. A little bit dangerous on a first date given that I have a propensity to spill it.

Wine talk. Small talk. This had doomed date written all over it.

'Is this a date?' I asked.

'Technically and mathematically yes. Socially…maybe. Let's play First Date Questions,' he suggested.

'Okay,' I was cautious. 'Fire away. But keep it clean.'

'Of course. Right, where were you born?'

'Greenwich. The London original, not the village in New York. America's probably got hundreds of Greenwichs.'

'A few I know of, no doubt dozens I don't. I was born in San Diego, but my folk now live further north, outskirts of San Fran.'

'Mine live in Edinburgh. The family abandoned me when my grandmother died and left us a huge house in the cheap part of the city. I've got to go back up there next week for Christmas.' I pulled a face, suggesting it was the last thing on earth I wanted to do.

'You have my sympathy. Okay, let's move to easier ones. What's your favourite film?'

'Easy. *The Notebook*.'

The look on his face told me that Tom had never heard of it.

'Oh, that one with whatsisname?' bluffed Tom.

'Ryan Gosling,' I tried to help.

'Yes, him. I preferred him in that other one, *Green Lantern*.'

'That's Ryan Reynolds.'

'Burt's brother? I'm not very good with my Ryans.'

'There aren't a lot of Ryans to get confused by.'

'I still struggle with my Ryans.'

'He was in *Deadpool*, too.' Another blank. 'So what's your favourite movie?'

'*Green Lantern*.'

'Isn't that supposed to be shit?' I'd never seen it.

He laughed.

'It is shit. I paid good money to see it and it was a disastrous date, probably the last one I'll own up to, and I'm still trying to convince myself it wasn't a waste. I tend to fall asleep in superhero movies – an understandable habit but not exactly endearing on dates. Let's never go to a superhero movie.'

'Deal.' We were both relaxing, the wine was helping.

Maybe a cinema date next?

More questions followed. Favourite book? I said mine was *Gone Girl* (I'd made it through the first fifty pages before shelving it); he was a Stephen King fan. Favourite music? I admitted to my soft spot for Adele but spared him my impression. He predictably cited the Beatles. Uh oh – my Beatles-bore warning bell started to ring but it was a false alarm, and we quickly moved on, like he could see my eyes glazing over. Quite different from the odd conversations I'd been having with Barclay where I could never be sure if the man was actually listening to a word I said.

We politely small talked our way until the food finally arrived and we made the appropriate noises of delight. Once the waiter had left I said: 'That looks good. Mine is somewhat spectacular though.'

'Agreed. I don't think I've ever tried soufflé – it looks like an omelette on steroids. Makes my sole look…' he lifted the fish with his fork, ' … a little flat.'

Ho ho. Tom didn't do pretentious by the sound of things, such a contrast to Barclay, such a welcome change.

(Get out of my head, Barclay.)

The soufflé was delicious. I found Tom's company charming. We ate in silence, the odd murmur of contentment as we relaxed into the evening.

The waiter cleared away the dessert plates and brought our coffee. Proper coffee in a mug, none of that espresso nonsense that lasted seconds. Tom suddenly looked serious, which was a shame after such a nice meal.

'Barclay,' he said.

'Barclay?' I asked. 'There's nothing to it, honest, just a work thing.'

'Of course, but he's dangerous. How much do you know?'

'I only started on Monday. I know he's … interesting, fun even.'

'He's not fun, he's dangerous. You need to get yourself out of that thing.'

Two 'dangerouses' in quick succession. Tom looked stern. There was an awkward silence.

'I can handle myself,' I assured him. 'I'm thirty-three, remember?'

He smiled but his eyes had turned cold. 'I'm not joking, Claire. You need to get out of whatever's going on with him. It'll end in tears. Or worse.'

'I'll be fine.'

He didn't look convinced.

'Please don't get hurt, Claire.'

'I'll be fine,' I smiled, patting his hand. 'Shall we go?'

Outside it was a little chilly, a cool wind had picked up while we had been eating and I only had a light jacket, fooled into it by a late burst of winter sunshine at the end of the afternoon.

'Would you like my coat?' he asked

'I'm fine.' It was my word of the evening, a poor, insincere word that rarely gives anyone the assurance it promises.

'Let's get us a ride home,' he said, waving down a black cab that had freakishly materialised south of the river. Where was home, I wondered. Mine or his?

I was not an 'easy' first date but I'd have been happy if we had gone in either direction. Henry was barely gone forty-eight hours and this dirty trollop Claire was already considering taking another man between the sheets.

And I didn't care.

'So how do you rate our evening overall?' he asked.

'Oh, definitely an eight.'

He started to pull me closer then stopped, squeezed my hand and kissed me quickly on the lips.

'That was … nice,' I managed, our noses still gently touching.

He kissed me again, a little longer this time but still chaste, affection rather than passion.

I squeezed his hand. 'Maybe a nine?'

'It gets a ten in my book.'

'Does it need a nightcap to elevate it to a ten?' I asked.

Before Tom could answer the cabbie interrupted: 'Where are we going then?'

Good question, sir, an excellent question. I had no idea.

Chapter 10

The morning text from Barclay was succinct and to the point:
Pick me up at 3pm. B.

No 'please' or 'if you'd be so kind'. Really, the manners of some people make you despair. At least it was a 'pm' this time – much as I had enjoyed my first driving job, that early hours-of-darkness start had not been appreciated and a similar early rise the night after the night before was not what the hangover doctor ordered.

The late afternoon time suggested that it wouldn't be another getaway featuring a bag stuffed with used twenties taken or stolen (but certainly not voluntarily donated) from god knows where. Which was a little disappointing but presumably a tad more legal.

Ho hum, how innocent was I?

As I dressed after a much-needed shower my mobile rang. It was Mum, checking that I was still heading 'home' to Edinburgh at the weekend for her family Christmas. I loved my Ma more than anyone on Earth but boy she could chat for Britain. This proved to be yet another one of those conversations where I managed to contribute one word (usually 'uh-huh') for every thousand or so of hers. She was a great talker, possibly the greatest, but not so big at the listening thing. Worryingly, Mum seemed to be getting worse and sometimes she even had to stop herself after a few minutes (that felt like hours), unable to remember who exactly she was talking at. She was harmless enough and probably a wee bit lonely and it was, after all, her phone bill she was running up. Resigned to losing the rest of the morning I tucked my phone under my chin and tidied the flat as she droned on and on about my errant brother Paul, her best friend Sharon, my dad's job security, and that nice boy down the road at number ten. I think she was referring to the Prime Minister. I thought of pointing out that he was neither nice nor living down the road, but it was all one-way traffic and I wasn't going to take the risk of lighting the political debate touch paper.

After an hour I'd had enough. With no little skill I somehow managed to engineer the one-way conversation to a close and was able to make my escape. Parents, huh? Can't live with 'em but you can never really move out of their lives either. I couldn't waste the entire day. I had work to do.

The sudden noise had stopped several passers-by on the street in their tracks. I could understand their sudden distress.

'That's unusual,' said Barclay, emerging from his apartment building and climbing into the Uno's passenger seat.

'A little surprising, I agree,' I said. 'I haven't used it before. Must be the Italian heritage.'

The Uno's horn had proven to be deafening yet surprisingly melodic, shattering the office hours' calm of the street where I was collecting Barclay. There was no modest toot or peep from my little runaround, oh no; some previous owner had added a powerful two-tone klaxon under the rust-encrusted bonnet of my Eighties' marvel and the car was now very loud and extremely proud. I wouldn't be using the horn again in a hurry –the last thing we wanted was to draw attention to ourselves as we went about our business.

Or, I should say, Barclay's business. I was just the driver, and his reluctance to give me any useful details about the nature of said business was rapidly becoming irritating.

'I need to go to Eynsford in Kent,' he said, sharing the bare minimum with his woman-servant. 'Something I need to check on. I'm a little concerned.' He was wearing some snazzy designer sunglasses so I couldn't read his eyes. Barclay, concerned? Really?

'Okay,' I said, hoping to learn more. But he wasn't forthcoming and I was out of luck. I crunched the Uno into first gear and we pootled south to the Garden of England, the bright, low winter sunshine pleasantly warming in my steadfast Italian chariot.

It had been a beautiful day but the sun was setting fast and I figured it would be almost dark by the time we got there. As we joined the queueing traffic departing London early for the evening, I asked;

'Barclay. Your tax form. Was that all in order?'

'Yes. Nice job.'

'But it said you worked in a coffee shop.'

'Yes.'

'And that you earned eighteen thousand last year. Just eighteen thousand?'

'Yes.'

'And that it was your only employment?'

'A little white lie.'

'As is the eighteen grand?'

'You're a fast learner.'

'I take it that anything else is pretty much 'cash in hand'?'

'It's difficult to define it any other way.'

'Isn't that illegal?'

He yawned. 'You didn't seem to mind when I gave you that cheque the other day.'

'I didn't say I minded, I asked if it was illegal.'

'I'm not a lawyer,' he said. 'They can't tax what they can't see.'

'But it's a crime.'

'A very small one. Best they focus on the Amazons and Googles and the big boys. Why bother the baristas?'

'What if everyone did it?'

'But they don't.'

'But they could?'

'But they don't.'

'I could do it.'

'But you don't. Or, I should say, didn't.'

He had me. I decided to let it rest. I had a feeling that tax evasion was the least of Barclay's crimes.

To describe Eynsford as 'picturesque' is an understatement, on a par with 'that Taj Mahal, it's okay for an old building'. Take a right just before the turning for Brands Hatch and follow the road down the slight dip and round to the left. You can't miss it: a short high street lined with colourfully quaint higgledy-piggledy terraced cottages and shops from some bygone era, packed shoulder to shoulder in a disorderly fashion as if in denial of modern planning laws. It was like we had turned a corner and travelled back a century. 'This is lovely,' I thought to myself as I dropped to a pedestrian ten miles an hour to take in the view. Barclay didn't say a word. He hadn't spoken since I had questioned his tax legality. He may have fallen asleep.

A Volvo honked in annoyance as I squeezed passed it. Barclay's eyes snapped open, startled.

'Nice kip?' I asked.

He frowned and for a moment didn't look himself.

'Bloody Volvo drivers. Something on your mind?'

'I am … concerned, as I said. This man I want to check on has just gone silent and that's not like him. He has not been responding to my emails, texts, calls, he's posted nothing on social media, I rang and he hasn't been seen at his office for over a week. Nothing.'

'Is he a friend?'

'Hardly. He's the guy with the dog I mentioned.'

'The dog you shot?'

He had woken grumpy and wasn't amused. 'At. I shot at.'

'Yeah, right.'

'He still owes me the money.'

'What for?'

There may have been tumbleweed rolling in the deafening silence.

'Eynsford's pretty' I said, keen to change the subject.

'His house isn't. It's one of those ugly monstrosities up there on the right, just before the station.'

The cute little lost-in-time high street petered out after a few hundred yards and was replaced by a small but perfectly-inappropriate housing estate, a shocking modern day eyesore after the tranquil rustic idyll we'd just passed.

'Urgh,' I said, unable to conceal my disgust.

'Not so pretty, see?'

I nodded in agreement.

Barclay pointed at a small detached red brick house at the far end of a cul-de-sac, away from the main street. Its driveway was dominated by an enormous, ostentatious white BMW 4x4 that dwarfed its surroundings and made the house behind appear undersized by comparison. It was a testosterone-enhanced brute of a car, bought to impress and intimidate the simple minded.

Tutting under my breath I parked my Toy Town car in front of it, blocking the drive in case it decided to steamroller its way out.

'I'll be ten minutes, tops,' said Barclay, exiting and striding up to the front door of the house. He rang the bell.

Nothing. He tried again, this time following it with a firm percussive knock, then hammering on the door with the side of his clenched fist. Still nothing. He peeked through the letter box, then peered through the downstairs window, the room behind unlit despite the darkness.

He turned to me and shrugged. I shrugged back. He walked up to my side of the car and I unwound the window.

'No one in by the look of things, and the post is pretty stacked up in there. I'm going to see if I can get in around the back. You stay here and keep watch.'

'What do you mean 'see if I can get in'? You're going to break in?'

'Sure. Think of me as a bailiff, collecting what's mine.'

'And I'm your look out?'

'Someone has to be.'

'What if someone shows up?'

'Then you honk that macho horn of yours. I should be able to hear it in there.'

'And wake up the whole of sleepy Kent? You're joking, aren't you?'

'Okay. Maybe not. Come and get me if you see anyone heading directly for the house.'

'And then what will we do?'

He nodded at the Uno.

'Another getaway?' I asked.

'If we are walking calmly so as to avoid suspicion I'm sure we'll get away comfortably. Stop being so negative.'

"Walking calmly? Are you serious? But…'

He turned his back on me and disappeared down the side of

the house.

Brilliant. More hanging around waiting for Barclay. The opportunities just kept on coming.

Moments later there was the distant sound of a grown man foolishly trying to shoulder his way through a locked door. Thud. Grunt. 'Fuck'. That hadn't worked. A slight pause for him to gather his composure then the sound of a small window being broken, only slightly softened by what I assumed was Barclay's coat. Another pause, then he appeared at the front window and waved before drawing the curtains closed. I looked nervously around the street – no one, not even a solitary dog walker. And the ridiculous BMW tank was proving a blessing in disguise, concealing much of the front of the house from any prying eyes.

Long seconds stretched into long minutes, the sky grew darker and the street lights blinked into dim, early life. I stared at the dashboard clock and drummed a nervous, erratic rhythm on the steering wheel. Come on Barclay, get a move on.

Barclay had worked his way upstairs, pulling the curtains across before turning on the lights. I was getting cold with the window open but needed to keep an ear as well as an eye open.

In the rear view mirror I saw a silver car, one of those Japanese save the planet things, pull up at the far end of the road, its silent electric engine catching me unaware despite having my window open. I turned around too quickly and ricked my neck. Ouch. Fortunately, it was a good fifty yards or so from where I was parked so I saw no reason to panic Barclay. A couple of uniformed school kids jumped out the back, and a woman clambered from the front seat, struggling with armfuls of school bags as she juggled with her keys. She stumbled to the front door and let the excited kids into the house before slamming the door shut on the outside world.

As an afterthought, the car's lights flashed orange as she locked it from inside the house.

I turned back to see Barclay peeking through the curtains – he'd seen the Prius, too – then he pulled back and I guess resumed his search.

What was he doing in there?

What was he looking for?

What was I doing outside?

As if to answer me another car, a bigger one this time, sort of sales exec Mondeo-y I guess, turned into the cul-de-sac and drew up about twenty yards away, pulling into the drive of a house just three along from where Barclay was fucking about. Too close. Its headlights dimmed slowly but nobody got out. I could see the driver just sitting there. I gave it a few minutes but still no movement, nothing.

Not good. I needed to warn Barclay.

I unbelted and attempted to look composed as I left my car. No bleeping locks with my bleeping relic from the last bleeping century. A few cautious glances left and right before I stole down the side where Barclay had disappeared. There'd still been no movement in the newly arrived car.

It was even darker around the back of the house but I could just make out that the back door was ajar, a small glass pane by the handle had been smashed by Barclay.

My mouth went dried and I swallowed hard as I entered, adding breaking and entering to my growing charge sheet alongside tax fraud and aiding and abetting. I was willing to bet that the Uno's MOT was probably dodgy, too. Not a bad list for a few days' work.

'Barclay?' I whispered as loudly as I could, pointless I know but it seemed wrong to shout. 'Barclay?' A little louder.

There was a scrambling noise from upstairs and the banging of wardrobe doors. I made my way through the dark kitchen, tripping over a dog's water bowl by the door. That was sad. Barclay had killed that dog.

On tip toe I hurried through the shadowy sitting room, too nervous to have a nose around. There was a light from the top of the stairs and the sound of Barclay hunting for whatever he'd come for.

'Barclay!' Still whispering, but very, very loud whispering.

'Claire? I'm in the main bedroom.'

'There's another car pulled up but no one's got out yet.'

'I know. I saw. Odd.'

'Barclay, what's that smell?'

I pushed open the bedroom door and screamed.

The wardrobe was half open and there was a naked man hanging from a belt pulled tight around his neck. He looked like he'd been there for several days. He smelled like he'd been there far longer.

'Shhh!' said Barclay, calm as you like.

I couldn't say anything, just shoved my fist in my mouth and stared at the naked body. It was heavy set and ugly and the folds of flesh had a pale, waxy texture. If I hadn't known better, I'd say it was still sweating, like old cheddar left in the sun. It also seemed to be entirely shaven, not a hair on it. It's strange the things you notice when in shock. But the smell, the smell was unlike anything I'd ever experienced before.

'Yes, I was a little taken aback I must say. Try to control yourself, Claire.'

My voice spluttered back into life. 'Taken aback? That's a dead fucking body!' I couldn't blink, couldn't breathe.

'Like I said, odd.'

'Odd? ODD?' I grabbed his coat and pulled him towards the door. 'I'll tell you what's so fucking odd – us still being here is bloody odd. Let's go!'

'But I haven't found what I came for.'

'I don't care. We need to go. Now.'

He resisted at first but my persistence got the better of him and he reluctantly followed me down the stairs, I lost my footing under his weight and almost fell.

A body! What the fuck was that all about? I tugged him down after me and, with no small effort, dragged him through the house and out into the back garden. He stumbled over a watering can as we made our clumsy exit.

So much for 'walking calmly so as to avoid suspicion'.

The new car had gone. We were alone again.

'What...what was that all about, Barclay?'

'It was his thing, his sexual peccadillo. I didn't expect him to go all Kung Fu on me but he liked the old erotic asphyxiation thing and it was only a matter of time. Poor guy. Anyway, it's not like he's going anywhere soon. I'm going back in,' he said, pulling away from me, and disappearing once more into the gathering late afternoon gloom.

'Fuck,' I muttered. No way was I following him. That was his funeral. And what did he mean 'go all Kung Fu on me'? It felt like were were speaking different languages at times. I got back into the car and angrily crossed my arms. I like to wallow in a good sulk, although I was not sure what I was actually sulking about. Why hang yourself in a wardrobe? And completely shaven from skull to toe? That's just plain weird. Well, weird to you and me, but Barclay seemed to be taking it all in his stride, like it was all in a day's work for him.

Barclay emerged after another ten minutes. He waved a carrier bag at me then trotted over to get into the car.

'About time, too,' I harrumphed. 'Did you find what you were after?'

'Not exactly, no. Some cash in the house but probably only a few hundred quid. I did pick up some cans of Coke from the fridge and some crisps in case you were peckish.'

'No thanks,' I murmured. I didn't think I'd ever feel like eating again. Certainly not cheese.

I started the car and we pulled away, re-joining the main street and the traffic heading north. After a few minutes I asked;

'Seriously, what … what was that all about?'

'Looks like he just pushed it too far. Been gone a few days, much like the milk in his fridge. I thought he might make a run for it but...'

'He must have really loved that dog.'

Barclay nodded.

'So he hung himself?'

Barclay turned to look at me, shaking his head.

'Can't pretend to understand that. I knew he was into all kinds of kinky stuff but that's not something I know anything about or can easily explain. Different strokes and all that. Wasn't there a rock star in the nineties who went the same way? Most peculiar. It was quite cold, you know, to touch I mean. The body.'

I shuddered. 'You touched it?'

'Couldn't resist. Back of my hand though, so no prints.'

I was shaking my head. I just couldn't process this.

'What did he do, that guy?'

'He is … was… a Financial Advisor, believe it or not,' Barclay said. 'Very quiet, as corrupt as sin but so clever and cautious with it.'

'And how did he owe you money?'

'A long story. Maybe later,' he said, and turning away from me stared out the window at the dark street as the car gently shook, straining to make the sixty I was demanding of it. I needed to get out of Kent pronto.

'Should we tell the police?' I asked.

'Tell them what? That we found a body hanging in a wardrobe when attempting to rob a house?'

I really should have given that 'thinking' thing a go before asking those kind of questions.

'Maybe not,' I mumbled.

We drove back to London in silence, neither of us absolutely certain what the fuck we had just witnessed.

Chapter 11

Tom was distracted. The cherry tomato was doing its third lap of his salad plate, looping around the inner rim propelled by his fork. He hadn't looked up for five minutes.

'You're not listening, are you?' I said.

'What? No, of course I am,' he lied. 'Something about going to Edinburgh for Christmas?' It was a shot in the dark and we both knew it.

'That was ten minutes ago! I was telling you about my family. Mum, Dad, brother Paul.'

'Right.'

'What's up?' I kicked him playfully under the table.

'I've got work stuff I'd hoped to sort out before flying home, and it has kind of gotten more complex, rather than sorted.'

Didn't I know that feeling!

'Bummer,' I said. I liked talking American to my new American friend. He looked up and smiled.

'It happens. I don't like taking work home over the holidays but I'll have to make some calls I guess, and that's not easy from the West Coast.'

We had decided to have a quick lunch before he jetted off to the US and I got on my train to Edinburgh; him for 'The Holidays', as they call them over there; me for good old fashioned Christmas.

It was a nice little bistro cum patisserie Tom had suggested, on a side street just off Great Marlborough Street and its non-stop traffic. Later that evening I would be heading to Kings Cross, he'd already be on a United flight to California. I know which trip I would have preferred to have been doing.

I was deliberately not mentioning Barclay and our Eynsford escapade to Tom but it was never far from my thoughts that lunchtime. After Tom's warnings about Barclay it was a strictly taboo topic of conversation as far as I was concerned, so I decided to play it safe and keep things civil and a little dull.

'What is it you do again?' He'd said something about being a consultant but we hadn't gone into details.

'I told you. I'm a consultant. In law enforcement.'

My fork dropped and bounced noisily off the bistro table onto the floor. Several other diners turned to see me open mouthed and possibly going into shock.

'Really?' said my smallest voice.

Tom laughed, and it was a genuine laugh. 'Yes, really. I didn't expect you to react quite like that – let's get you another fork.' He signalled to our waiter and a replacement was quickly brought over.

'Got something to hide, Ms MacDonald?' he laughed. I laughed too, suddenly nervous, playing the innocent fool.

'When you said 'consultant' I just assumed it was finance or IT or strategy or something like that. Do the police use consultants?'

'Everyone uses consultants, it's the grease that oils the wheels of industry these days, the costs you can hide under the bottom line of the spreadsheets as 'Other Expenses'. With this government's budget cuts the police need them more than ever. Besides, I'm a specialist, an authority even.'

'What in?' I was almost too afraid to ask but my voice still sounded composed, mercifully.

'Cybercrime. Computer fraud. Hacking. I've been working here for a few years now. It's a growing industry, which is good for me but pretty shit for everyone else.'

Did that explain how he knew Barclay, I wondered? Barclay who 'dabbles' in technology? I wasn't going to ask and ruin our lunch date, but that would make some kind of sense.

'How's your work going?' he asked.

'S'okay, I guess. Done some paperwork. Got a company car. Been running a few errands.' For some reason I neglected to mention the tax fraud, speedy getaway driving from God knows what and…oh yes, how did I forget? Finding a decomposing body of a sex pervert in the bedroom of a house we'd broken into.

'Good. Steering clear of Barclay now, I trust?'

I looked down at my plate as I nodded. As lies go it wouldn't have convinced me, but Tom seemed to buy it.

'Hours not too demanding?' he asked. I started to wonder how much he knew.

'The odd early start, but the new boss is quite flexible with the time in lieu thing.'

'Good stuff,' he said, finally piercing his tiny tomato and popping it into his mouth. 'Why does your family live in Scotland? You don't sound Scottish.'

Thank god. No more work talk.

'I'm not. Obviously. They moved up there five or six years ago. I grew up with them in Deptford and we had a little two up, two down for me to charge around in, but then Mum had a few hospital things, the usual stuff, and they decided to slow life down and get out of the city and move up to a quieter life.'

'Edinburgh's quieter?'

'Everywhere is quieter. Edinburgh's cheaper. Or at least it was then, not so much these days. I never fancied it so I stayed here, first planned to go to art college or university but that never really happened.'

'Lucky for me.'

'Lucky for me too, I think,' I said, smiling as I polished off the last of my cheese toasty and salad.

'And your Mum – she's all well now?'

'She has good days and … less good days, but generally is okay. If it got bad Dad would give up work but he hasn't mentioned that at all so I guess it's all fine. They need the money from his job really – I've a younger brother, Paul, who arrived unplanned and keeps the expenses running high.'

'How young?'

'Twelve.'

'Almost a teenager.'

'Already a pain in the arse. Sorry, I meant 'pain in the ASS'.'

Tom laughed. 'I have two sisters in the States and haven't seen either since Thanksgiving last year. They'll be there this weekend, with their Ivy League husbands and pictures of their palatial houses, boring us with talk of their perfect lives of suburban prosperity. All money and equity talk, can't wait.'

'You're not going to get any sympathy out of me. Christmas in San Francisco sounds brilliant to me.'

'It's okay. Just about bearable. My folks are good fun. You'll like them.'

He was thinking of me meeting his parents? Wow. Second date and that was the way his mind was working? That man was fast.

'Maybe one day,' I said.

'Let's hope so.' He looked at his watch. 'What time's your train?'

'Oh, it's not until this evening. I'm getting the sleeper up there. I've not even packed yet.'

'I'm going to have to make a move,' he said, signalling for the bill by signing the air with his forefinger.

'It's a shame we're going to be apart for a week,' I said, a little bubble of emotion getting caught in my throat.

He grinned and took my hand across the table. 'Time for a quickie?'

'Out the back by the toilets?' I joked.

'No. In the kitchen. Let's give the staff something to talk about. Sure beats tipping them.'

'You romantic, you.'

It wasn't even amusing but we both laughed hysterically as if it was the funniest thing either of us had ever heard. Oh, to be young and … in love? Too early. Oh, to be young and hysterical? Maybe. That would do for now.

The bill arrived and he tapped his contactless card to pay.

'That's so cool,' I said.

'The wonders of technology. Pretty easy to hack though – you have to be careful in crowds with it.'

'You're the expert.'

He winked. 'I've seen things you people wouldn't believe.'

I clapped my hands together in delight. '*Blade Runner*! I just knew you'd know a decent movie or two.'

'I've even downloaded *The Notebook* for my flight.'

He remembered. He was so sweet.

'We can compare notes,' I said.

'Count on it.'

Outside the bistro it had just started to rain and umbrellas were being raised as lunchtime crowds were quickly making their way back to the office.

'So see you in a week,' he said.

'Enjoy *The Notebook*.'

He pulled me close and we kissed a long, sad goodbye kiss. It was delicious. I can still taste it.

'I will see you later then,' I said, clutching at the moment.

'Enjoy Scotland,' he said quietly. I nodded and reluctantly turned and left him in the rain with his suitcase on wheels. I only turned to wave three times. Four, maybe. I was still grinning when I headed down the steps at the tube station.

Chapter 12

Thank the lord Christmas only comes once a year. I love my family, I really do, but like all relationships that affection can rise and fall with the tide of conversations and circumstance. The annual pilgrimage from Kings Cross to Edinburgh was getting harder every time, a solitary reminder on my calendar of the life that left me behind.

Ah, 'twas the season of family embarrassment and tedium, the hallowed time of me recalling every tiny detail of the previous twelve months for my over-enthusiastic mum, barely-there dad and whatever uncles and aunts were dropping by for the free scotch and G&Ts and bowls of leftover-from-last-year nuts. In the past it had been difficult to drag out anything of any note from my boringly monotonous life to fill the painful, prolonged silences, the airless gaps in the chit chat when conversation just died on everyone's lips and you could hear the mice scurrying around under the floorboards. But that year it promised to be even worse, I wanted to tell them everything, boast even – but I could say nothing. Torture.

I had been dreading the conversations with Mum in particular. I didn't sleep much on the train journey up as I played out over and over what she would say, what I would say, how I would keep 'mum' about Barclay and Tom (funny girl; ho, ho and a seasonal ho for luck).

So much had happened in the last week, so much that I would normally turn to Mum to for advice and comfort, but I couldn't face the prospect of tipping her out of her cosy, comfortable world of tickity-boo Claire. Dad had been suggesting for some time that Mum's forgetfulness and the one-sided conversations were symptoms of a bigger problem, possibly even an early onset of dementia, but none of us were brave enough to take it any further, and Ma was so terrified of doctors and tests that it was never openly discussed, least of all with her.

I did consider telling her about Tom, but it was still too early, too unsure. Knowing Mum, she would instantly be working on finalising the wedding gift list and the reception seating arrangements before I even got to pronouncing Tom's real surname. 'Claire Thomas' I could fantasise over and possibly live with but 'Claire Pedakowski' was a non-starter. A nice, orderly life for nicely ordered Claire is all Mum wanted for me, and no loving daughter should ever go out of her way to dampen that hope.

Before I knew it I was sitting there at the kitchen table with Mum updating me on Paul and that he was twelve now of course and it was his last Christmas before he became a teenager and how we won't see him for days on end and he will be lost in his Xbox world and… on and on she went, fretting about kids these days and how dangerous it is out there (if only she knew) and how she was worried that he will be led astray by those video games and that horrible Internet and he won't turn out nice like me…

I couldn't tell her. Not a word.

'And can you please make an effort this year, Claire, to be nice to him?'

'Me?'

'Yes you, dear. None of that backchat and sarcasm. Do it for me, dear.'

'Of course,' I kind of promised. It would not be easy and I was sure he would not reciprocate. Little bastard.

It had been different with Mum when we talked on the phone,

where I could hide behind a silence or quickly move things away from talk of the 'new job' with a random digression. But once I was in the kitchen with her, once she had me in her truth-seeking steely gaze over our 'catch-up coffee', all milk and too many sugars, once there was nowhere to run or hide and nothing to distract, I was convinced I was going to slip up and she would know immediately something had changed, that this new boss certainly wasn't like the old boss and that there was something different going on with her sweet little Claire bear.

I could hardly tell her about my new employment as a small hours of the morning getaway driver, the afternoons of tax evasion and burglary, could I? How would that have gone down on Christmas Day as we prodded the over-cooked sprouts and unpleasant sage and onion and the driest turkey that no amount of her watery gravy could moisten? That would have been a real choker. And that was assuming that every one's heart would keep ticking merrily along after the shock of learning that their eldest, dearest offspring had now opted for a life of crime with some posh wide-boy ne'er-do-well.

'How's Henry? Mum asked.

I stared at my mug as if hoping that it could answer the question for me. Stick or twist?

'He's okay. I guess.'

'What do you mean, 'you guess'?' She could still be as sharp as a paper cut when she wanted to be.

'He's gone to India for a few months. It's for work.' Translation: He's left me and run to India for a few years to ease his moral conscience and make a futile gesture he can bore his friends with when he finally deems to return to our lives.

'Oh, that's a long way. I hope he writes regularly.'

'He texts when he can get a signal. It's different out there.' I hadn't heard a peep out of him. I doubted it was a signal problem but I didn't feel like discussing it – Mum had such a wonderful, if somewhat naïve, view of relationships and didn't like the idea of things not following her preferred "and they all lived happily ever after" script.

Besides, I just couldn't mention the other guys now on the scene, the heart stealer with his bewitching schoolboy charm and the intriguing boss, all devil-may-care attitude, conversational eyebrows and steepled fingers.

'I like Henry.' She wasn't making this any easier. 'He's a keeper.' Thanks, Mum. Somehow I was expecting that one.

'Yes.' It was easier to keep up the pretence; I saw no point in causing her world to come crashing down with reality on Christmas Eve, that would just be cruel. Almost Barclay-esque.

'And how is that new job working out?'

'It's okay. Not as boring. I've been doing some of the work in the evenings and the pay's a lot better so I'll see how it goes in the new year. I haven't decided yet completely if it's for me.'

'Oh. You should talk to your father about that. You shouldn't give a job up on a whim.'

'I will,' I assured her.

There had been some culinary disaster in the kitchen ('it's okay – your mother is fixing it') and we found ourselves sitting at the table in a state of muted apprehension, awaiting our overdue dinner as Mum wrestled with whatever tragedy had struck with such unfortunate timing. The comforting aromas of roast turkey, sage and onion from the kitchen appeared to be slightly tainted by a faint odour of charcoal.

Paul, Dad and me: an unholy trinity at any time of year, but somehow in this season-to-be-jolly a particularly mismatched trio, not a wise man amongst us.

Dad wasn't good at small talk. He didn't excel at big talk either. Silence, apart from the odd grunt or clang from the kitchen. Dad's unease was proving infectious; the thunder clouds gathering behind the kitchen door adding to the tension.

'So,' Dad began, then paused as if the sound of his own voice breaking the silence had surprised even him.

'So?' I asked. 'A needle pulling thread?' They didn't get it – Mum was the only film fan and she was locked away performing unspeakable acts with a cumbersome dead bird.

'So your mother tells me you've started another job. I take it it's better than the last one?'

Yes, I'm a getaway driver cum apprentice burglar for an egocentric, self-centred misogynist who does god knows what, who is obviously breaking the law in a thousand ways ... oh, and he randomly kills dogs.

'S'alright,' I actually said. 'A bit of paper pushing, spreadsheet stuff, a bit of evening work, gets me out and about and pays the bills. Irregular hours. Moving money around, that kinda thing.'

'Boooooooring,' yawned Paul. 'Boring boring boring. What's the point of living in London if all you do is stare at screens and shit like that all day?' Little twat – what does he know about real life? What would he make of his big sister living a life that makes his world of Grand Theft Auto look pedestrian? I was old enough to know better, but...

'It's not dull,' I said through clenched teeth. 'It's actually very interesting. And I'm not office-bound any more – I'm out on the road for much of the time, meeting new people, even changing their lives in some ways.'

'Gripping.' His sarcasm was galling and I found myself rising from my chair, my balled fists tightening. Every time he did it. Every time I fell for it.

Dad attempted to calm things, aware that a catastrophe was pending in the kitchen. 'Hey, Paul, no need for that. I'm sure Claire is a better judge of how interesting her new job is than you are.'

I sat down. Two against one. My kind of odds.

Bravely, Dad attempted a digression. 'And how's your man Henry? He's a keeper.'

'He's in India. Doing some work there.'

'What a loser,' said Paul.

Get back up to your bedroom, child. Don't rise to it, Claire. Keep a lid on it.

'He's a good man,' said Dad.

'He's a twat,' said Paul. It was the happiest I'd seen my evil brother in years. 'India. What a sucker. Fucking A!'

Dad and I both stared aghast. Swearing was strictly taboo in this house and this was a first from Paul. He was growing up too fast.

'Fucking shit bastard bird!' came Mum's cry from the kitchen.

We all burst into laughter, the paralysing tension finally released.

The meal was overcooked and we all knew it, but still the compliments flew Mum's way ('great spuds, love'; 'I love these puréed sprouts, Mum') and she batted them away with false modesty as she helped herself to another slice of bread sauce.

Most families drink their way through the Christmas pain but the MacDonalds are not a boozy congregation regardless of the occasion; the lone bottle of M&S sparkling white was still only half empty by the time we all slouched in front of the TV for whatever feasts Auntie had scheduled for her license-paying devotees to sleep through in their stupor.

Mum didn't last five minutes, and soon her full-on snoring was competing with the telly for our attention. Sadly, the remote could only temper one of the competing sonic forces. Dad made a motion with his head – he wanted a quiet word with me by the look of things. Either that or he was developing a frightening tic.

We quietly left Mum to her unquiet slumbers and Paul considering his own escape options and returned to the kitchen, where every encrusted pan and plate and bowl my family owned was stacked high and unloved in and around the sink, the baked on, burnt on food demanding our immediate attention. It didn't get it.

'It's about your mother,' he said, and my heart grew heavy.

'How bad?'

'Nothing big, but I thought you should know that she's struggling again, getting forgetful and angry with herself.' This wasn't easy for him to articulate nor for me to hear. The great unspoken was being spoken of.

'Will she see a doctor this time do you think?'

'I've tried to raise it but she's not listening,' he said, his eyes suddenly looked bloodshot and tired, as if he'd been crying for hours. I put my arms around him and hugged him tight, an action sadly all too unfamiliar to both of us. He relaxed into my embrace and we stood in silence, afraid of the words that remained unsaid.

'What can I do? Do you want me to see if she'll talk to Claire Bear?' I whispered.

'No, I don't think she'll listen. I'm going to talk to Sharon next door and see if she can help Mum see some sense. If it works, it might be easier to go private than get her down the doctors – she's always thinking she's going to run into someone she knows down there and word will get around.'

'That won't be cheap.'

'Any chance that you could help in ...' He couldn't finish the sentence.

'Of course,' I said, pulling him tighter. 'Not a problem, Dad. I'll do a cheque when I get back to town.'

Chapter 13

I was struggling. Chivalry was truly dead. Despite the hurrying crowds there was absolutely no one at Kings Cross to help the poor maiden with her mum-packed, bulging suitcase and collection of overstuffed plastic bags off the train. Could no one see how overloaded I was, how much distress I was in? Worse, I now had to bustle my way down the stairs onto the packed tube platforms and wrestle my way onto the packed holiday carriages. I suddenly had renewed sympathy for the bag ladies of this world.

Just when I thought it couldn't get any worse my Nokia rang and I jumped in surprise, dropping a Top Shop bag and spilling its contents under my fellow traveller's trampling feet. Shit shit shit.

'Claire?' I don't know why he asked, it was not as if there was anyone else likely to answer my mobile.

'Hello, Barclay.'

'I need your services again. Tonight, pick me up from the usual place. Three am.'

None of that nonsense chat. No 'How was your Christmas, Claire?' 'Very nice thank you, Quentin Horatio, and how was yours?' palaver. And it was only December 27th, so no extended holiday for me this year. No rest for the wicked, they say.

'Same car? Please tell me you got a new car for Christmas.' I was only half-joking – the Fiat may have had its own, curious charms but was in all honesty an accident waiting to happen, even doing twenty on a quiet side street.

He sighed. 'I have already explained this, Claire.' The tone, the tone – it was if he were talking to a five-year-old. 'It is important that your car is anonymous. We simply cannot have something that stands out. It has to look like it belongs to the streets of South London, not newly escaped from some Porsche showroom or something hot-wired for an early morning joy ride.'

'I suppose so.'

'Tonight then. Same time. Same car. And we will be going to the same car park. Be ready on time if not a little early.'

'Okay. Got it. See you later. And Barclay?'

But the line went dead. No fear of a long, drawn out goodbye with Barclay.

When I got home I was knackered. It's funny how sitting on a train motionless for hours on end can do that to you. I could have gone straight to bed but needed to keep going for a few more hours, so I spent my time clearing out the last physical remains of Henry from the flat – he said he'd taken everything but I'd found some neglected underwear at the bottom of the laundry basket, a lone shoe under the bed and he hadn't even bothered with his CDs. His loss was to be Oxfam's gain, although I thought the chances of them taking soiled underwear were pretty slim. Even charity only goes so far. After that I thought I would try to get a few hours' kip before the late night/early morning start with Barclay, but I half expected that the adrenaline would kick in and I'd struggle to get even twenty of the prescribed forty winks.

I woke at three am. I had, for the first time in a long time, slept like a babe. It was a good job I'd set the alarm on my Nokia or I would have fucked it up completely. Four hours, a solid four hours. Brilliant. I was ready for anything.

I trotted to the bathroom and splashed my face with a shock of ice cold water to clear the last remnants of sleepy Claire, brushed my teeth and hair, then dressed in my blackest outfit. Black jeans, black shirt, that tight knit navy polo neck jumper from Gap, even my undies were black. Getaway drivers can never be too careful when doing night work.

I picked Barclay up from outside his building in the Uno. He was right – it was as anonymous a car as you could possibly imagine. Not one of those funky little new Fiats with the bright colours and the cheeky styling. Not quite. For me this was the car that took the word 'super' out of supermini and firmly trashed it. A car so anonymous even its mother wouldn't recognise it. Maybe I should have considered cleaning it – I felt dirty just looking at it, and touching its failing paintwork made me want to scrub my hands with a Brillo.

It was another particularly cold night and even inside the car I could see our breath forming as we spoke.

'Good morning.'

'Hiya,' I said. 'Hop in.' I'd kept the engine running, still not sure if turning the motor off was going to prove to be a final, fatal act. I'm sure the Italians make some excellent engines, objects of breath-taking engineering beauty and stylish mechanical efficiency. This was not one of them.

'Shouldn't take long tonight. This is normally pretty straightforward.'

'Good.' I still wasn't ready to ask what exactly was going on with these 'jobs' involving picking up large amounts of anonymous cash at four in the morning in desolate car parks on the edge of town. Chances were that it may have been a wee bit dodgy. Who was I kidding? I knew from the off that it was, without question, highly illegal and probably morally suspect, too. But it was one hell of a thrill and the shy, grateful coward in me figured that the less I knew the easier everything would be, so I didn't ask any questions and just did as I was told. I was being paid to 'do', not 'think'.

We pootled through the Blackwall Tunnel and around the quiet night-time streets of South London, the last dregs of late night humanity shuffling out from desperate looking all night takeaway dives. Even through the Fiat's windows I could hear the distant howls of police sirens competing for trade with those of emergency ambulances. It was not pretty. This area didn't do 'pretty' at this hour. Or any hour, come to that.

True to form, we drove in silence. I wanted, desperately wanted, to ask about the hanging body, but just couldn't find the courage to raise it again, so to speak.

The car park was deserted. The wayward anarchist in me parked badly over two bays at an uncomfortable angle.

'Right,' said Barclay. 'I will be ten minutes. Tops.'

'You said that last time. I reckon you'll be twenty at least.'

'Not tonight. Too cold to hang around out there.'

'Too cold to hang around in here, too.' There was no way I was not going to have the almost-heating running tonight – it was close to freezing outside and there were wisps of a light mist gathering, already threatening to blur the orange of the distant street lights. I should have worn gloves. Maybe I could buy some of those ridiculous leather driving gloves with this week's money? Mind you, woolly mittens may have been more useful that night.

He was gone just five minutes. He suddenly appeared, sprinting around the corner, a jumping sports bag strapped across his back. Panic? Barclay? Maybe this time. I'd never seen him run before and it was not exactly poetry in motion, flailing arms and uncoordinated legs. Tall men can't run. Official.

I threw the passenger door open for him. He hurled the bag in the back and jumped in.

'Drive!' he barked, eyes wide and staring.

I stamped on the clutch and fumbled the gear stick into first. We lurched off, jumping almost into a stall, then I dragged it into second and third in one of my more impressive gear changes. I didn't stop to check the exit, just shot out onto the A2, heading west.

'Fuck fuck FUCK,' said Barclay.

Into fourth, the Uno's engine surprisingly coping with the urgent call to action. Thirty. Forty. Fifty. No other traffic. The lights at the foot of the hill were mercifully green as we shot across the junction. Barclay still hadn't put his seat belt on. Deptford sped by. New Cross and its one-way congestion nightmare loomed. I slammed on the brakes, dropped into third, much to the disgust of the engine, and threw the Fiat down the sharp left at Goldsmith's and we shot up a quiet residential street. I started to slow – there were no lights in the rear view mirror and I guessed that whatever had shocked Barclay was gone.

'Why are you fucking slowing down?'

'What?'

'He's on a bike – he'll easily fucking catch up!' Suddenly there was a single headlight growing in my mirrors and the sound of an accelerating motorbike. But despite Barclay's sudden panic I was thinking calmly – surely he wouldn't know Barclay was in this particular car?

Almost nonchalantly I slowed further, indicated left and parked on a yellow line next to an overfilled skip. I killed the lights as the speeding motorbike roared passed us and raced up over the hill.

Sometimes I surprised even myself.

Barclay was breathless but I was calmness personified. I wanted to nonchalantly light myself a cigarette and look like I'd done it a hundred times before. If only I smoked. I hadn't smoked since that coughing fit behind the school garage with Dolly Pee. For just a moment, I needed a cigarette to look as cool and collected as I felt.

'That…' he panted, 'That was…good.'

I smiled. 'That's what I do.'

'Yes. Excellent.' His breath and composure were slowly returning. He took a minute, taking deep, meditative breaths. That had not been a Barclay I had seen before. Panicked, even fearful. I found it quite unsettling.

'What exactly happened?' I asked.

'It wasn't a set-up but not to plan. He had second thoughts and wouldn't let go of the bag. Idiot. We wrestled with this,' he motioned to the bag, 'and it all got a bit ugly. Bastard.' I noticed Barclay's trousers were torn and there was blood, as if he'd fallen clumsily. 'I whacked him with the bag. I ran for the car and saw he was going towards a parked motorbike I just hadn't seen. Lucky you were ready.'

I gave him a knowing smile. 'Nothing lucky about it. You're in safe hands, Mr Barclay.'

For once, he didn't correct me.

We sat in silence as I drove us back to his building, but I was far from uncomfortable. Who was the Muppet now, eh Barclay? He should have spotted the bike. He shouldn't have panicked. Thank god for Claire MacDonald, her serenity in the face of adversity.

Smug? Me? Too bloody right.

I pulled up outside the building. It was 4.30am, not a soul around. Barclay had been counting the bundles of notes in the sports bag. He dropped a handful in my lap.

'Here. Half tonight. You deserve it.'

I couldn't speak – there must have been over a thousand quid there, even some of those oversized fifties you hear about but never get from the cashpoint.

'Thanks,' I managed to say.

'And don't read anything in to this, but I need to ask a favour of you.'

'Sure.'

'What are you doing over New Year?'

Was this really Barclay sitting next to me, or some defective clone who'd come out in his place? Was he asking me out on a date?!

'It's not a date,' he clarified hurriedly. 'Not a real one. I need a … companion when I go and visit my parents for their New Year's Day lunch, it eases some of the pressure, you know, and I was hoping, if you didn't already have plans, if you would join me? No funny business, it's only the lunch so no 'whoops, we need to share a bed' nonsense, no obligations…'

I was taken aback but the adrenaline was still pumping. 'It'll cost you,' I chanced.

'I…er…I thought it might. But I've just paid you and…'

'…a new set of wheels.'

'What?'

'Barclay, if we are doing this seriously we need a more reliable car. This is great, I love it, we're really attached and everything, but it's a sick, sick motor and it will let us down when we really need it. I thought it may have died on us tonight but we got by, but it will cough its last any moment and, it may well be anonymous, but we have to be driving something better.'

He was silent.

'We cannot outpace a motorbike in a thirty-year-old Fiat Uno,' I campaigned. 'Let alone a police car. It doesn't have to be a Porsche or anything flash, but it does need to be sound and reliable and trustworthy. Keep it as anonymous as you like, but we can't rely on this rust bucket for another getaway.'

I'd made my point, set my price. He nodded in reluctant agreement. 'Okay,' he said. 'Let me see what I can sort out. But you're good for New Year's?'

For some reason, that seemed to be so important to him. 'Yes, I'm good to be your beard for the day,' I said.

'It is not like that. When you meet my family you will understand.'

I was sure I would, but nothing was going to take anything away from my triumph that night. He got out of the Uno.

'I'll be in touch,' he said with a wave.

I grinned and waved back without thinking.

I was too high to sleep. Instead, I did what every right-minded criminal would do with their ill-gotten gains: I sat at a table and counted out the cash. I had never had so much.

I made myself either the last coffee of the night or the first of the morning. It was mix of notes; fivers, some tenners, just a few twenties, so counting it was more of a chore, albeit a pleasurable one. There was a little smile on my face when I'd counted out the first hundred, an even bigger one when I got to three, a quiet 'fucking hell' when I reached six and a hysterical laugh when I got to nine.

I had never held so much cash, let alone owned it. Counting it was an obsession and my coffee had cooled. I put the mug into the microwave to warm it back up. In all there was £980. I guess we had been short-changed by twenty quid? I didn't really care. Just twenty-four hours earlier twenty pounds had been a lot of money.

Suddenly it was small change. I couldn't have been happier.

I started to consider the commitment I'd made Barclay. Was I really going to play the part of 'faux-girlfriend' for this man just to meet the family that spawned him? It seemed like a small price to pay, especially as I'd managed to add in the promise of a better car into the deal. I would do it. Besides, I might even enjoy myself.

Chapter 14

Barclay had said that the traffic might be bad, so he wanted to make an early start. I said I'd be ready 'whenever'. He suggested 10am to miss any drivers who were still pissed from the night before, which made sense. I said 'whatever'. He suggested I make 'an effort' to look nice for his parents. I said 'fuck off'.

As you can see, we were developing our witty rapport.

At ten to ten I was ready. I hadn't made a spectacular 'effort' but my recent investments in the shops around New Bond Street had certainly paid dividends, and the dark skirt complemented the white silk shirt and linen-mix cardigan. Hark at me – H&M girl makes good. I'd had my hair styled too, after one quip from brother Paul too many. I went to somewhere really expensive on Oxford Street and instantly felt like I had walked into a different reality. Funny people, hairdressers, not like us humans at all. All that conspiratorial giggling and looking distracted and far too much interest in my holiday plans for my liking. Nice haircut though – I don't think I'd ever felt so fab. I was sure it wouldn't survive me washing it with my all-in-one Superdrug shampoo then blasting the style out of it with my bargain basement drier.

Maybe I had made an effort, but it was very much for my benefit rather than Barclay's.

I couldn't believe we would be rolling up at the Barclays' family estate in the rusty old Uno, but there had been no word from His Lordship about the new car he had promised. I pulled the Fiat up outside his building, parking behind some boy racer's pride and joy that was hiding under a protective tarpaulin cover. Bastard.

Some guys have all the luck.

I woke the neighbours with a honk of my too-proud, too-loud Italian horn and, moments later, Barclay appeared at the door. He was grinning. It was unnerving.

'Good morning' he said, a spring in his step as he strode over to the concealed car in front of me. He grasped the tarpaulin in his right hand and pulled it majestically away like the flamboyant conjuror he evidently imagined himself to be. 'Ta-daaa!' he beamed.

Oh. My. God.

I had stopped breathing. Was I dreaming?

I couldn't stay in the Uno a second longer. For me? This was for me? There were tears in my eyes as I clumsily clambered out of my humble shit heap of a car.

It was a 1962 Volkswagen Karmann Ghia. Of course I didn't know that at the time, I only knew that it was undoubtedly the most beautiful car I had ever seen. Every curve, every line was handsome, perfect, and it shimmered with an almost feminine glamour. It was a vision in sea blue and cream steel, its polished surfaces lustrous in the sunshine.

'Oh, Barclay,' I whispered as I timidly reached out and stroked its aquamarine contours for the first time. It was, possibly, the most erotically-charged moment of my life. I staggered back a step. Bloody hell. I'd wanted new wheels and the man appeared to have listened.

'Just for today,' said Barclay, but even that disappointment couldn't kill my new ardour. 'Are you ready?' he asked.

'I...I certainly am.'

He threw me the keys and I opened the door, only to notice that the steering wheel was on the other side.

He laughed. 'Left-hand drive only, I'm afraid.'

I frowned. 'I can see that.' My self-esteem took a stumble but at least no one else had seen me standing on the wrong side like an idiot. No one except Barclay. He'd enjoyed my seconds of embarrassment but I just didn't care – let him have his pathetic humiliation. Today was my day. Our day. Me and Karmann's day.

I dropped slowly down into the cream vinyl driving seat, lower and softer than I was used to. The interior was, if anything, even more basic inside than that of the Uno, but what was sparse and stark in the Fiat was charming and delightfully considered in the VW. The dashboard was shockingly bare, just three unpretentious dials for guidance. A fragile knitting needle of a gear stick poked proudly erect from the bare floor, accompanied by a cold steel handbrake rising from an ageing, wrinkled fake leather skin. It was all that was needed – anything more would have looked crude and ostentatious.

I had met a new world of sixties glamour and was smitten. Damn you, twenty-first century and your technology-driven complexity.

Barclay opened the passenger door and joined me, clearly delighted with my reaction. I inserted the key and, at the second time of asking, the VW announced itself with a bark and a splutter.

'Oh my.'

'Good Christmas?' he asked.

I couldn't answer at first – that world seemed a million miles away and I was tightly gripping the hard plastic of the outsized steering wheel, scared I'd wake from the wonderful dream, still lost in my rapture.

'What? Christmas? Oh yes, we had a good Christmas I guess, thanks. You?'

'Later. Shall we go?'

I shuffled my feet on the pedals, pressed hard on the clutch and wrestled the gear stick into first. The engine gave a throaty splutter as I gently revved the accelerator and we jumped away from the curb. At last, at the tender age of twenty-five, I had fallen in love. I loved that car from the moment we met.

Barclay said something but I didn't hear it. I was driving with a fierce concentration as I negotiated the quiet Bank Holiday streets. God, I hoped Barclay's parents lived a thousand million miles away and it would take us forever to reach them.

We sailed through the West London streets towards the M25 and the countryside freedom beyond. Sitting so low in a sports car was not something I was familiar nor 100% comfortable with, the other traffic felt overbearing and monstrously large, passing buses and vans seemed to thunder overhead as the engine maintained a steady forty. For once I was a cautious driver, the car feeling delicate on the road amongst the twenty-first century beasts surrounding it.

We were still travelling in silence. Barclay's casual conversations were painful at the best of times, and I was still savouring the car. But he was bored, so:

'And things were all good up in Glasgow?'

'Edinburgh. Things were fine. Things were normal. Mum asked after Henry. I didn't tell her we were finished, just said he was in India for a bit.'

'Have you heard anymore from him?'

'There were a couple of missed calls on my mobile but no texts. Are we going far?'

'Gloucester, so a couple of hours. Just outside Stroud. Traffic's not too bad by the look of things.' Bliss. Even though the engine felt like it would hit its limit at fifty I was happy to take my time. Can cars saunter? If so, we were sauntering.

A few more minutes passed, then he said:

'There's something I didn't tell you about my family.'

Uh oh. That didn't sound good.

'I have a sister, Dawn. She can be a little … odd.'

'Is that 'odd' like as in 'Barclay odd', or is she in a different league of odd?'

'You think I'm odd?' He looked quite pleased with my description.

'I think you're one of a kind. Are you saying your sister means that there are actually 'Barclays' blessing us with their presence?'

'We are … not similar.'

'Why didn't you mention her when I asked you about the family before?'

'I forgot her.'

'You forgot? You forgot you had a sister?'

'Sometimes I forget I have a mother and father, too. It's not that unusual. Everybody does it.'

'No they don't.'

'If they were more honest, they would admit to it.'

I really didn't know what to say to that. I guess there was maybe a small element of truth to it, after all, families are funny things and who hasn't wished at some point that they would all just go away? And if there's a list going I would like to volunteer my brother for it right now. But has anyone else ever really *forgotten* they have a family member? What a bizarre thing to say.

It wasn't worth an argument, but I was more intrigued than ever to meet his father, mother and, new addition folks, sister

Dawn at stately Barclay manor.

I had pictured the Barclay family home as some kind of minor royalty palace. Maybe it had a pool? Huge expansive gardens that were prime for fracking? Nothing could have been further from the truth. As we left the A roads behind and I coaxed the VW around winding country roads I slowed at the turnings for each isolated, wind-swept mansion, only for Barclay to wave me on, 'not yet, not that one,' he muttered. His earlier chirpiness had quietened as we neared our destination, and when he finally said 'here', pointing to my left, my astonishment no doubt added to his embarrassment.

It was no five star hotel. It would barely have rated two. It was a modestly-sized and somewhat shabby pre-war detached house, three or four bedrooms at most, desperately in need of some TLC and a slathering of paint to protect it from the elements that had clearly taken their toll. I doubted if it had ever been impressive and, stranded in the middle of an overgrown, unkempt garden littered with long-abandoned childhood swings nestling in the weeds and wildflowers it looked sad and unloved, almost derelict.

This was 'stately Barclay manor'? Bugger me.

'What's that then?' asked Barclay's father. He waved a glass of seasonal sherry at the snowy drive out the front of the house where our decorous German classic was parked. He didn't seem to be surprised that we had arrived in a car oozing style and class. Maybe the Aston Martin keys I'd found in Barclay's rucksack had been genuine after all.

'A 62 Karmann Ghia,' said Barclay. 'Not many around these days, but worth the hunt. A bit tight now I'm a couple.' His arm had somehow worked its way around my waist and he gave me an 'affectionate' squeeze. Not happening, mister. I pulled away, but surreptitiously so as not to cause a scene. 'But I may be looking to trade it in soon. I may go for something more modern – the new Aston's due in the spring.'

'Boys and their toys,' tutted Barclay's mother, shuffling into the room with yet another bowl of dry roast peanuts. 'Nut?'

I noticed that Barclay almost instinctively put a little distance between himself and the bowl of nuts, and I suddenly remembered the adrenaline Epipen I'd found in his bag a few weeks back and wondered if he actually had a nut allergy. And his mother didn't know about it? How strange. Were they that distant?

Nothing was going to surprise me though about this family – 'odd' was the word Barclay had used to describe his sister (who I still had not met) and it was very much a family trait. The Barclays' house had several large rooms that could have been referred to as the lounge. They even had a room that only seemed to be referred to as 'The Other Room', as if it were inferior or secondary for some reason. Needless to say it seemed perfectly adequate and normal to me.

The room we had settled in was decorated with a peculiar nostalgic mix of Seventies and Eighties furniture, presumably salvaged from the various Barclay family homes over the decades; a sagging leather sofa, a wicker throne that wouldn't have looked out of place in a corny porn video; a low mahogany coffee table whose sole purpose was to support a collection of unread coffee table books; one of those oversized American recliners parked in front of a television that must have been many decades old. And what a TV – only junk shops stock ones like that these days. It was in an enormous dark wood cabinet with shutter doors pinned back, revealing the antique marvel within; a telly as deep as it was high, with what by anyone's standards was a small screen, curved slightly with rounded corners. Underneath was an ancient VHS video recorder with large clunky buttons for playing, rewinding and FF-ing. Like something from the ark. As was the small library of video tapes in their cases; *The Far Pavilions*, *Brideshead Revisited*, *Jewel in the Crown*. Programmes from before my time but I'm sure my Mum knew them. Mrs Barclay ('call me Jean, dear. After all, you're almost family already!' she had said) and Mum would get on well – they shared a common place in the home (the kitchen) and in time (the eighties). They'd never meet of course – we were playing a game, Barclay and I, and doing it quite convincingly. We certainly had Mrs B. convinced, but that hadn't proven particularly difficult.

Mrs B had curious tastes that wouldn't have been out of place on an edition of *Antiques Roadshow*. There were the ornaments; a collection of cutesy-pie Hummel figurines sitting uneasily with his father's ancient darts trophies on flimsy ancient stained pine shelving. The little ceramic children were in classic Heidi-esque lederhosen and chequered dresses, Swiss oddities that somehow looked dated and timeless simultaneously. They were possibly worth an absolute fortune, or had cost one but were now sadly worthless. I made a silent resolution to myself to look them up on the web when I got home. (I never did.)

There was snow on the ground outside and temperatures were around zero, but there was no excuse for the thermostat being turned up quite that high. Even stripped of my coat, scarf and woolly hat I was still baking.

'And you're sure you don't want a sherry?' his father asked me.

'No thanks, not really my drink,' I said. 'A glass of cold water would be nice though?' Mr Barclay nodded and waved his hand at Mrs B, who disappeared at his command to fetch one from the kitchen.

'And you?'

'No thank you,' said Barclay. 'You know I'm not a sherry drinker. Do you have any of that Chablis we had last year?'

'Of course I do, but I'm saving that for a special occasion,' his father said.

Right on cue his mother returned from the kitchen.

'And Quentin's only visit of the year isn't special enough?' she asked. Barclay visibly flinched at the mention of his hated given name. 'No,' answered his father.

'Oh.' Head bowed, she shuffled back to the kitchen to fuss over some other unwanted side table snacks. It seemed to be norm, her husband belittling the poor woman and putting her firmly in her place. He didn't show any sympathy for her and her oppressed life as unappreciated cook, cleaner and housebound servant. I felt for her. No one deserved such scorn.

'How is London life?' Barclay's father asked him.

'As exciting as always. I've got a new opportunity, just needs some seed capital and…'

'If you can afford to replace that bloody car, I'm sure you don't need to ask for anything from me.'

I didn't have a clue what Barclay was talking about, but he couldn't have it both ways; pretend he was loaded (the car, the clothes, me on his arm in all my new finery) and then ask for a loan.

Muppet.

'Would you at least like to hear about it?' Barclay chanced.

'No.'

That killed the discussion stone dead, a welcome chill suddenly dampening any illusion of joy at this tired, tiring family reunion. With impeccable timing, Mrs Barclay reappeared.

'Nuts?'

The late New Year's Day lunch had proven almost unbearable. As the enmity between Barclay and his father developed further they descended into a succession of prolonged uncomfortable silences, only broken by Mrs Barclay's imploring for us to 'eat up – there's plenty more'.

Barclay's 'forgotten' sister Dawn had proven to be a no-show. No mention was made of her and every time a car passed outside I looked at the window in curious hope, but there was no relief from our unspeaking quartet.

I wasn't sure Christmas Day leftovers were still good to eat a whole week later, and I was even less sure that they'd been anything special when they'd been fresh. For someone who appeared to spend an inordinate amount of time in the kitchen Mrs B didn't appear to be particularly gifted in the culinary skills department. At least the wine was good – excellent in fact. A girl could get used to this taste of luxury at least.

I needed to get out of there, even it was just for ten minutes. It was suffocating and I think my credibility as Barclay's 'girlfriend' was hanging on by a rapidly unravelling thread; Barclay was neglecting to play his part and I was buggered if I was going to make up for his shortcomings on that front. If the subterfuge was going to last the visit I needed a break.

'I need some air,' I said. 'Okay if I pop out the back?'

Only Mrs B showed any concern – Barclay was gazing at an old movie playing silently on the dining room's telly.

'Of course dear,' she said. 'The back door's open.'

'Thanks. That was delicious, Mrs Barclay.'
'Jean.'
'Jean.'
Like I say, suffocating.

Outside it was mercifully clear and crisp, refreshingly cold. The stars were already blinking in the darkening sky, a sight so unfamiliar to us light-spoiled city mice. If I'd been a smoker this would have been an excusable break, but I'd probably only have a few minutes to gather my thoughts and gird my loins for more of the same. How I longed for the solitude of my beloved Karmann.

'Hello.'

I jumped. I hadn't noticed anyone else out here when I'd stepped out but I could now see the amber glow of a cigarette tip and smelt its faint aroma on the light breeze.

'Hello?'

A girl, no more than sixteen, stepped into the light from the kitchen window. She wore a heavy winter Parka and was wrapped against the elements, hugging herself to keep warm. She was tall, probably taller than her brother, and slightly ungainly. Her hair was blue black and cut with a strikingly harsh fringe just above the pierced eyebrows. Her nose had a septum piercing, her ears resembled curtain poles, adorned with rings almost too many too count. She was thin, punky, gothic in her style and clothing. Probably tattoo-ed all over.

Even in the dim light I could see that her eyes were breathtakingly blue. She was confidently beautiful, quite exceptional.

'You must be Claire?'

'Yes. And are you...Dawn?'

She smiled.

'Bad in there, is it?' she asked.

'Horrendous. I had to get out. I couldn't breathe.'

'I've been out here for hours. Told Mum I was going round some friends but I wasn't. I just hate it in there. Christmas really is the worst time of year.'

'I can only imagine.'

'I wanted to see Barclay but I've lost my nerve. He doesn't visit often.'

'I can see why.'

'Him and the old man. It's horrible. I'm sorry you had to experience it. Must put you off him.'

Before I realised what I was saying I said, 'Oh, we're not a couple…'

Ah. My boo-boo. It just slipped out. Sorry Barclay.

'I didn't think so. Barclay can't do relationships. Not even friends.' She drew hard on her cigarette. 'It's good of you to come with him. I think he's a lonely soul, but I didn't tell you that. You seem too nice for him, but my parents won't notice that. Too subtle for them.'

That was nice to hear but we'd only known each other for a minute or so. 'Oh, you don't know me. I'm actually quite bad and Barclay makes me do bad things.'

She laughed. 'Yeah, I'd imagine he does if it's work. So you work for him?'

'Yes. I'm his driver.'

'I didn't know he had a driver. I wasn't even sure he had a car. That VW is a rental, isn't it? Just for the day to impress the old folk?'

Of course. Bloody hell, Barclay.

'He's done it before,' she continued. 'Asked some poor schmuck to be his girlfriend for these visits, to act as a parental distraction. Drives up in a flash car to impress. A few hours of empty, uncomfortable silences and then he disappears again for another year or two.'

Somehow I felt smaller, almost insignificant. 'I would imagine so,' I muttered, looking at my shoes and the patterns the heels had made in the light snow on the grass.

'Don't feel bad. He uses people. Always has. Always will. It's never personal. He gets it from Father.'

I was starting to feel the cold but I was warming to Dawn. She was the normal one in the family. Maybe that's what Barclay meant by 'odd', as in 'odd one out'.

'Are you still at school?' I asked.

'I'm older than I look. I'm at art college on my Foundation. Just home for the holidays.'

'Where's college?' I asked.

'Camberwell in London.'

I was stunned.

'I live in Deptford – we're almost neighbours.'

'I thought we might be. Barclay lives in Docklands somewhere but never makes the effort.'

'Do you live in Camberwell?'

'I wish. Too expensive though. I live in Peckham, a few miles down the road. A smelly bedsit above a smelly shop.'

Suddenly I had an idea. Unlike me I know, but I was already so far out of my comfort zone I couldn't stop myself. This was New Claire. Living dangerously. I was probably doomed to failure so what the hell?

'I don't suppose you're looking for somewhere to live?'

She looked at me quizzically, a smile playing on her lips.

I was speaking without thinking. Slow down Claire, before you say something you'll regret.

'I've got a spare room in the flat and my ex has just moved out. I need help with the rent and I'm looking for a flat mate and…'

Her face lit up. 'That would be brilliant! How much?'

Henry used to reluctantly contribute £750 a month.

'Five hundred?' I suggested.

'Wow that would be great!' Over-excited she hugged me like a long lost sister. I barely knew her and I had invited her to live with me.

'I'm getting too cold now,' I said. 'I need to go in. Let's talk about it later.'

'I'll join you,' she said. 'It'll be a distraction for them. Let's not mention the flat just yet though …we don't want it to become a discussion.'

'Agreed.'

I put my hand out and she shook it, laughing. (What is it with me and the hand shaking thing? Am I a closet business woman?) She stubbed out her fag on the paving – she had amassed quite a collection underfoot I noticed. She really had been standing out there all that time.

'No smoking in the flat,' I said.

'You're going to be as good for me as Barclay is bad for you,' she joked as I opened the kitchen door and we both stepped into our shared private hell.

'You what?' Barclay was genuinely surprised. Stunned even.

'I asked your sister to move in with me,' I said, calmly smoothing my coat as I climbed into the passenger seat. He swung my door closed, threw a cursory wave over his shoulder at his family (he needn't have bothered – they'd already gone back inside) and strode round to the driver's side. Once we were out of sight we would swap – the illusion was everything.

And Barclay was not happy.

'But you hardly know the girl!'

'I know her enough. Probably know as much about her as I know about you.'

'But I don't live with you!'

'Then I will get to know her better than I know you. I like her. She's nice. No wonder you find her odd.'

'I find you bloody odd,' he muttered, turning the key, stalling, then igniting the engine of the temporary Barclaymobile.

'And this is a hire car, isn't it?'

'Yes of course it bloody is.'

'And it's back to work in the Fiat when we get back I take it?'

'Of course.'

'You promised…' But he wasn't listening, preferring instead to pretend to be concentrating on his driving rather than talking to me.

'Fine,' I said, crossing my arms in another huff. 'So I did this for nothing?'

'You got a free lunch.'

'It *was* a free lunch…it was week-old leftovers.'

'And you got to meet my family, including your new flat mate.'

'And what a bizarre bunch they are, too. No wonder you're so fucked up.'

He glanced over at me, brow slightly furrowed. Hurt? Probably not.

He drove for a mile before he pulled up and we swapped seats, all legal now. The VW had turned ice cold from being left alone and unloved for most of the afternoon and it was taking forever to warm up. A hush descended again, uncomfortable but I wasn't going to break it. Damn him, I was going to savour my last moments with the car. I didn't care that my plans with Dawn had clearly rattled him – he didn't own me.

He didn't own anyone. He didn't even own the car I was driving.

About a mile along the M25 the Karmann coughed and spluttered its last and died an undignified death on the hard shoulder. It took a garage four hours to reach us; by then, my brief passionate affair was truly over and I longed for my Uno.

True love can be such a bitch.

Chapter 15

Dawn was looking for a corkscrew to open the second bottle she'd 'borrowed' from her father's cellar. The first had been the familiar screw cap and had been possibly the most delicious thing I'd ever tasted in my life. It had barely lasted thirty minutes. I couldn't recall if I'd ever used a corkscrew before – it's a generation thing now, I guess – so I didn't hold out a lot of hope for her finding one in the 'all the other stuff' drawer in the kitchen amongst the rubber bands, probably-dead batteries, wooden spoons and that curiously sadistic-looking thing for lifting the spaghetti.

I was wrong. 'Success!' she beamed, triumphantly holding a near-antique penknife-like object aloft. 'A sommelier knife!' These Barclays, they all spoke an entirely different language.

'A semolina what?' I asked, completely bemused.

'A sommelier knife. It's got a blade to cut the foil and a lever if you're feeling a bit feeble and even a bottle opener. One of the great inventions. It's an old one but will do the job I'm sure.' She sat back down with me on my sofa and went about attacking the top of bottle number two.

'This one's from some fancy place in Italy I think – a Barolo. Father's favourite and rather special. He'll be furious it's gone. We really should let it breathe first.' I nodded wisely in bemused agreement. 'Have you got a decanter at all?'

'I didn't know I had a corkscrew.'

'No worries, we'll let it breathe in the glass, but we can decant the next one now if you've got a clean Pyrex lying around.

That I did have, and collected it from the cupboard where it had been gathering dust since Henry's departure. She uncorked a third bottle (three? Was she expecting guests or something?) and splashed the contents into the litre sized measuring jug.

Back to bottle number two. 'Cheers!' she said, raising her glass.

'Cheers.' Was Barclay junior going to add to the life of depravity her errant brother had introduced me to by turning me into an alcoholic? I could think of worse paths of destruction to stagger and stumble down, especially if all the booze was this exquisite. I would never look at my Jacobs' Creek with quite the same lust again.

She had arrived shortly after five like Taz the Tasmanian Devil from Cartoon Network, a whirlwind of frantic activity and volley after volley of incessant chatter. Whereas Barclay himself would frequently withdraw into silence mid-sentence, his sister didn't appear to even draw breath and was non-stop energy. She arrived pulling a large bright pink suitcase on wheels and a battered wine carrier thing with half a dozen chinking bottles ('I can always ask them to send more if we need it,' she had half-threatened, half-promised). She certainly wasn't going to over-clutter the flat, which was a relief, but from the evidence of the first few hours she was still going to be more of a handful than I had been anticipating.

She was the antithesis of Barclay; in fact you could have called her the anti-Barclay. Her laughter was infectious and long, Barclay's was controlled and brief – a sharp bark at best. Where he was reserved and cold, she was warm and open. She thought aloud whereas he preferred silent contemplation. Did they really share common parentage? The immediate evidence suggested otherwise.

'And what exactly does 'driving Barclay' entail?' she asked, picking up our conversation from a few days previous.

'That's a good question. I'm not really sure, it's only been a couple of weeks. He's banned at the moment.' Her eyes widened. 'I just do the quick sprints around town in the Fiat Uno.'

She laughed and spluttered in her glass. 'A Fiat Uno? Whatever happened to the DB7 he had last year? The Aston Martin?'

'He's got some keys but I've only ever seen the Fiat Uno and Karmann. Endearing little rust trap. He's promised me something better but I'm not holding my breath. The Uno's not reliable for what we're doing…'

'Which is?'

'Tearing away from car parks in the middle of the night with a bag of cash.'

She almost dropped her glass. 'Seriously?'

'Yep.' We were both grinning like mad things.

'You're a fucking getaway driver?'

'I fucking am!'

'That is so cool!'

'I know.'

'And where does he get the bags of money from?'

'I have absolutely no idea.'

'That's even cooler! Don't know, don't care! I love it!'

'It's the new reckless me. Cheers!'

We chinked glasses again, instant BFFs.

'Can I come on one of these getaways?' She was hugely excited. I couldn't imagine Barclay welcoming a passenger – the Uno struggled enough carrying the two of us.

'Maybe. If he gets a bigger car. It would be a squeeze in the back of the Uno. We do seem to do this pretty early in the morning though.'

'How early's early?'

'Three, four.'

'Bummer. Okay. Maybe not.'

'Late riser?'

'Kinda. Certainly not that early. I don't think I've ever seen three in the morning, at least, not as a starting time. Looks all blurry as a finishing time though.'

I nodded in agreement and we started sharing stories of wild nights on the town we'd enjoyed. Mine were part-drunken recollection, part-fabrication. My wild social life had pretty much ground to a halt since taking the Intern position and attaching the ball and chain of Henry. Dawn's were epic – long, rambling tales of partying into the small hours followed by quest-like journeys home that even Frodo Baggins would have baulked at. She had certainly packed a lot of living into her eighteen years – heaven knew what she'd get up to when she was old enough to drink legally.

We talked long into that first night together. She was due back at college the next day, first day of a new term and she had said she planned to get in bright and early and bushy tailed. All three of those were looking a trifle ambitious by the time we hit the Pyrex of red, bottle number three.

'Tell me about Barclay,' I slurred.

'What do you want to know?'

'Oh, everything. Tell me everything.'

'Everything I know. Sure. But I don't know everything. I can't tell you where he's getting that money from for a start.'

'Whatever,' I said, waving my glass too casually and spilling a little of the red stuff. Didn't care. Beyond caring. Does red wine stain? Surely this stuff was too good to stain.

'Older than me by a good ten years or so. Wasn't around when I was tiny – they packed him off to some posh public boarding school. He got weirder every time he was back for holiday – even little me could see that. Never wanted to play, showed no interest in my best friend Tinky Winky…'

'Your best friend was called Tinky Winky?'

She laughed and playfully hit my knee. 'My best friend was a guinea pig – I was a lonely kid. Don't look so shocked. You've met the family. So that had been a big deal for me and my idiot brother disappeared into his bedroom at every opportunity rather than entertain his only sister. Then he just vanished from our lives completely. Mum said he'd gone to university to do something with computers. She didn't know what. Father didn't either. Neither seemed to really care and he kinda disappeared from our lives for a while, never mentioned, never seen. By the time I was at high school myself I'd pretty much forgotten all about him. I didn't get the posh expensive school they'd wasted their money on for him – they weren't going to be bitten by that one twice, and besides, money was suddenly a little harder to come by. Once father became 'Sir Desmond' and Mum was a Lady they instantly seemed to become less wealthy.'

'I didn't know your dad was royalty!'

'It's not royalty, just a knighthood.'

'What was it for?'

'I never asked. We never talked about it. All a bit embarrassing really.'

'So Barclay's as much of a mystery to you as he is to me?'

'Pretty much,' she said. 'We're not close and both prefer it that way.'

'Fair enough.'

We chinked glasses again. It didn't look like I was going to learn that much more just yet, which was just as well as she could have shared the secret of life that night but the vast quantity of quality alcohol would have ensured it still remained a secret for all eternity the following morning.

Chapter 16

Barclay and I were sitting in the Uno (yes, it was back) in a half-empty car park, but this time it was late on the Monday afternoon, with the supermarket winding down but still with a few people milling around, last minute shopping for dinner or emptying their recycling into the overflowing bins and so straight onto the floor (so much for saving the environment). Barclay had told me we were waiting for someone who was going to help him on the next pick-up, due later that week. Tom Thomas's warning was playing on an endless loop in the back of my head – he was coming back from San Francisco that night and I was desperate to see him.

'I know you think it's best that I don't know what goes on, deniability is the best defence and all that, but could you at least give me a clue?' I asked.

'I would rather not. Deniability and all that. I can tell you what it is not, if that helps.'

'It would be a start I suppose, something to chew over while I'm sitting in the eight by eight holding cell waiting for the judge.'

I was only half joking. I hadn't developed a guilty conscience or anything as extreme as that, but, as Dawn had pointed out earlier that morning, trust was not something Barclay had actually done anything to earn from me. I guessed it was illegal – otherwise he'd get the money through a bank transfer or cheque or something, so it must have been dodgy to require that the payment was untraceable and off-the-record.

'It is nothing to do with drugs, if that is keeping you awake at nights.'

Well, that was a relief. I didn't fancy getting tied up in anything as illegal as that.

'It does not involve violence. Not by design, anyway. Sometimes a threat of violence is required…'

'Like the dead dog?'

'That was most unfortunate, and more to do with the animal's existing health condition than any action on my part.' I didn't buy that but let it rest.

'It is not theft, burglary or anyone being robbed of their life savings. The money comes from people who can easily afford to give it without their lives being wrecked as a result. It is not fraud, counterfeit goods or that kind of activity. It does not harm people.'

I was checking a list off in my head. He'd got the obvious ones I'd thought of earlier and I was starting to run out of guesses.

'It's not murder is it?

'I said it does not involve violence by design, so obviously not.'

'Kidnapping?' I asked.

'And where am I keeping the kidnap victims?' He was enjoying this game of riddles.

'But it is illegal?'

'In most countries, well, yes. Actually, it is probably illegal in every country, but not punishable by the death penalty anywhere as far as I … ah, here he comes.'

I struggled to turn in the tight confines of my seat belt, only to see an absolute hulk of a man approaching the car. He was as wide as he was tall (and he was at least a six footer), the result of too many hours pumping iron and gobbling handfuls of steroids, a veritable goliath of muscle and brawn. His arms and chest were so horribly overdeveloped they didn't seem to fit together properly, his broad head meeting his broad shoulders with no obvious neck in-between. Despite the plummeting temperature, he had no coat, only a short-sleeved black tee shirt that was struggling to contain the distended, stacked muscles upon muscles beneath. He walked with a heavy, wide gait, almost a waddle, his formidable thighs uncomfortably rubbing as he moved towards us and I shrank down as low as I could manage. He was possibly even larger than the Uno.

This was a colleague of Barclay's?

I was simultaneously revolted, terrified and fascinated. I didn't know the human body could become that…that enormous.

He raised his hand to Barclay in greeting. There was no smile, no words. Barclay exited the car, holding his right hand out in welcome. I wouldn't have done it – that was not a handshake anyone who valued their fingers would attempt – but the man mountain gently encompassed Barclay's bony fingers in his own and they shook.

It (I wouldn't say 'he' – this was not a person in the conventional sense) grunted.

'Good of you to come,' said Barclay. 'Let me introduce you to our driver. Claire?'

I am not ashamed to admit that I was cowering, making myself as tiny as I possibly could in my seat. Barclay indicated I should leave the safe confines of the car and meet this shaven Kong. I pulled my bag up onto my lap and half hid behind it for protection, a little shake of the head to demonstrate my reluctance to join them.

'I'm fine here.' It was barely audible even to me.

'Claire? We have not got all day for God's sake.'

I swallowed hard and whispered a godless prayer. I unclenched my body and made a hesitant exit from the car, ensuring I kept the door open and vehicle between us. Not that it would have offered much protection if the guy made a hostile move.

'Claire, this is Thug Number Two.'

'What?'

'He prefers people not to know his real name. Thug Number Two – this is Claire,' said Barclay.

'What?' I was stunned. 'So it's okay for him to know my name but I can't know his?'

'Be realistic, Claire. It is only being sensible. It is not like you are on every European security service's Most Wanted list, is it?'

Not yet, I thought.

'What's he wanted for?' I couldn't address Thug Number Two directly, couldn't look at him in case – the horror! – he looked back. I felt if I could avoid the eye contact he'd not see me.

'Nothing with sufficient evidence to prosecute with any certainty that I'm aware of.'

'Well that's reassuring.' My voice sounded tiny.

'Thug Number Two will be joining us in our work this week. I wanted you to meet him and to see if he can get into the back of the Uno.'

He was joking, wasn't he? It was more likely he could swallow the Uno whole himself.

'I don't think so,' my quietest voice suggested. 'The rear axle can only take so much…weight.' I took a step backwards in case that offended it in anyway.

'Yes, I can see that now. Silly me. Number Two – it looks like we will need a bigger car after all. Do you agree?'

The mighty beast's head nodded slightly. Still no words. No smile. No relief from the relentless menace I felt just being a few yards away from it.

'Okay then. I will see what I can do.' Barclay turned to me.

'It looks like you'll get your wish after all Claire – we're going upmarket with the vehicle.'

I forced a smile. 'Thanks.'

Thug Number Two, or 'TNT as I preferred to think of him as – it seemed appropriate – turned and started lumbering slowly away. My relief was audible. Barclay smiled.

'Goodbye monsieur. We will pick you up on Tuesday, 2am. Please try to be on time.' The creature waved without looking back at us.

We climbed back into the Uno. I was shaking and tried, unsuccessfully, to conceal it.

'Yes, he can do that,' said Barclay. 'Quite magnificent though, isn't he?'

'Chatty chap,' I ventured.

'He is not one for small talk, I agree.'

'Is there a Thug Number One?'

'We don't talk about Thug Number One.'

'Oh.' Leave it, Claire.

I started the car and we set off.

'I felt after the last little episode that we needed a little… muscle…to help oil the wheels of commerce, to bump up the protection.'

'It looks like you've gone for more than a little.'

'True. I think he's been working out since I last saw him. I honestly thought he would be able to squeeze in the back of this… thing.' I was having trouble shifting into fourth gear, the clutch action was not the smoothest or quietest.

'So he will just be along for the ride?'

'Pretty much.'

We entered the streets of Camberwell and turned onto

Peckham Road. I wasn't particularly comfortable with the thought of meeting TNT again but I wasn't in a position to raise an objection. At least he would be on our side.

'That's Dawn's college over there,' I said, pointing out the Art College, an awful windowless concrete monstrosity that had been built in the most appalling Sixties manner. It was unspeakably ugly, even by Peckham standards.

'Charming,' said Barclay. He couldn't have been less interested. We hadn't talked about Dawn and I didn't even know if he knew she was now in town and my new flatmate. He'd made his disapproval of the arrangement perfectly clear on the drive back from his parents and it wasn't a topic I was going to raise again, especially as I was still coming down from the fight-or-flight endorphin rush of meeting TNT.

We drove on in silence, our earlier game of 'guess the crime' forgotten. I was starting to realise that this was getting serious and there was no turning back. It was exciting. It was terrifying. Would I mention my encounters with Tom Thomas and his words of caution?

I didn't think so. It was not the kind of thing easily explained, especially as I didn't have a clue what was actually going on.

Chapter 17

'What…the fuck…is that?'

It was a reasonable question, given the sight before me. It was early, 1.30am, on a particularly parky Tuesday morning and I'd not even attempted a few hours of sleep but I felt I was in a nightmare. My eyes were sharp and alert though thanks to late night Nescafe but still I couldn't quite believe what I was seeing.

Barclay had left the driver's door open and stood by it, beckoning me forward like an over eager car salesman once more.

'Your chariot awaits.'

'Fuck off.' I wasn't joking. It was quite simply the ugliest car I had ever seen in my life.

Barclay looked hurt, but fired me what he clearly thought was his winning smile.

'It is a Fiat Multipla,' he beamed. 'A design classic from the nineties. Stylish but practical. Winner of Top Gear awards many times over if I recall correctly.'

'It…it looks like a duck!'

'What?' He took a step back as if he hadn't really been looking properly before. 'A duck?'

'Like Daffy Duck's head. In the Looney Tunes cartoons.'

He shook his head. He wasn't seeing a resemblance.

'I do not understand you. You wanted, nay, you demanded a new car, and here it is, big enough for Thug Number Two and certainly a better runner than the Uno. There is no pleasing some people.'

'Sorry to sound ungrateful but it looks like a little car parked on top of a slightly bigger one. Whatever happened to us having an anonymous, inconspicuous motor? There'll be no mistaking this aberration on Crimewatch.'

'I hear your very small point, but needs must. It is wide enough for Number Two and that's the main thing.'

'Can the rear axle take his weight?' I was genuinely sceptical that this was a step up from the Uno, which was proving to be my dream car compared with the alternatives Barclay was sourcing.

'Of course. Do I look like an idiot?'

Best not to answer that one – if he was seated in the driving seat of the Multipla, my answer would definitely be a resounding 'yes'.

'Get a move on,' he said, walking around to the passenger side. 'We don't want to keep the man mountain waiting.'

He had a point – TNT was not a man to be left waiting by the roadside – he would be an obstruction to passing traffic for a start. I climbed into the car and was surprised to find it was even more like something from another planet on the inside, three seats across in the front like a builder's van.

'Ooh, roomy,' I said before I could stop myself.

'See? I know what I'm doing,' he smiled. But I wasn't convinced.

The dashboard was a very nineties idea of what a 21st century car would look like: not a straight line in sight and everything swelling against convention as if to prove a point that cars don't need to be practical … or attractive. Everything was curved and bulged at jaunty angles, more Fisher Price than Fiat, a child's delight. Even lit under the dim glow of the interior light it was breath-taking in its misshapen, warped ugliness.

'It's…what…how…' I just couldn't find the words.

'The gear stick is there,' said Barclay, helpfully pointing to a short, swollen knob that jutted out from the sea of plastic in a vaguely pornographic manner.

'I'm not sure I'm going to be one hundred per cent comfortable touching that,' I complained. Barclay laughed.

'Oh do get a grip, Claire,' smiling at his own joke.

I sighed and reluctantly turned the key. The engine caught first time but it shared the same rattling voice of the Uno, more grumble than purr, sounding like it needed a damn good cough to clear its throat.

I did a double-take before grasping the stubby gear stick and shifting it into first, a surprisingly smooth action after the faltering jerk of the Uno's.

Barclay belted up.

'Number Two lives over by the Dome. We'd better get a move on. I'm seeing the money at two thirty.'

'You're the boss,' I muttered. As if there had ever been any doubt.

After ten minutes' driving through the sleeping streets of Greenwich I was a little more appreciative of the new car. A little.

It still looked like it had been panel bashed by a particularly over-sized Ugly Stick wielded by a drunken blind man in a debauched Piñata ceremony. To its credit though it was surprisingly comfortable, like sitting in an elevated armchair, and it made me feel like I had a better view of the world around me, almost like riding at the front on the top deck of a bus. And Barclay was right – it was a better drive than the Uno, comparatively smooth although it tugged a bit to the left and the width made it difficult to judge the Blackwall Tunnel.

Barclay directed me through the maze of roundabouts and lights that surrounded Greenwich's own Yuppy backyard, the

Blair legacy that is the Millennium Dome and its ugly collection of unaffordable housing and apartment blocks, the Greenwich Peninsula. If this was modern living you could keep it – my home in Deptford was looking cosier with every turn of the wheel.

After a couple of mis-directions from Barclay we saw TNT ahead, waiting under a flickering streetlight. He hadn't lost any of his phenomenal bulk and could have easily been mistaken in silhouette for a small gathering rather than just a lone individual.

'There he is,' said Barclay, unnecessarily. I flipped the wipers by mistake before flashing the headlights at our companion. It was as friendly as I was willing to get with Mr Intimidation. He waved. No smile though. Not his style.

TNT opened a rear door and climbed in. It may have been my imagination but I swear the car reared like a bucking bronco, front wheels rising with the dramatic shift of weight. And something cracked – I'm sure something cracked in the Multipla as it accommodated his immensity. He filled all three rear seats and was touching both sides of the interior.

Timidly, I moved into first gear, half expecting the car to surrender and die, but somehow it took the extra weight in its inelegant stride and we eased off without a hitch, none more surprised than me.

Barclay had said that this was to be a drop-off rather than a pick-up. Why that meant bringing TNT I wasn't quite sure, but the more questions I had the fewer I raised. I really was happier in my ignorance.

The drop was a few miles further south, yet another anonymous, dimly-lit car park Barclay had selected from a seemingly endless list of dodgy rendezvous destinations he had. I was too frightened to speak as I got to grips with the bizarre car's steering and uniquely personal eccentricities. TNT's mouth-breathing was loud and unsettling and I put the radio on to try to drown it out. After a burst of Thin Lizzy's 'The Boys Are Back In Town' I thought better of it. A shame we hadn't brought any cassettes with us to ease my tension. Not only could I hear TNT's breathing, I could smell it, taste it, like a foul dashboard air freshener it filled my every pore.

'Here. This is it,' directed Barclay, much to my relief. Another car park, abandoned, its pot-holed surface, wet from the earlier rain, littered from the overflowing bins that had been stuffed by the daytime January sales bargain hunters.

I engineered our Noddy car over a couple of parking bays and turned the engine off.

'Ready, Number Two?' asked Barclay. The response was a guttural grunt. The rear door opened and I felt the suspension bounce in relief as he exited.

'We will be ten minutes, tops,' said Barclay. 'Should be less drama this time with Number Two here.'

They disappeared around the corner of a darkened warehouse with a sports bag, presumably full of cash, and I was alone. I turned the car's electrics on to keep the car warm and decided to try the radio again. The subtle melody of Dusty Springfield's 'Look of Love' wrapped me in its sexy embrace and I instantly wanted to see Tom again. Never mind, just a few hours and we'd be together again. I love that record, and it put a smile on my lips, even in my nervous excitement of waiting for Dastardly and Muttley to return from another escapade.

I didn't have to wait long. As the fading strings signalled the end of Bacharach and David's song the familiar figure of Barclay jogged back into view, another rucksack slung over his shoulder.

TNT followed, walking rather than running, despite Barclay's protestations to 'hurry along'.

'All good?' I asked as they re-entered the car and I started the engine.

'Yes. He was surprisingly agreeable. No need to shoot off this time. In fact...' Barclay paused, thinking through an idea by the look of things. 'Actually, let's hang around for a few minutes. I'd like to follow him.'

'Follow him? But we're not exactly inconspicuous in this thing are we? Surely he's bound to notice this balloon car crawling up behind him with the world's largest man sitting in the back?'

'Oh, Number Two can hunker down, can you not, sir?'

TNT grunted in agreement but I couldn't see it myself. Just wasn't going to work. Oh well. Who was I to argue?

We sat in uncomfortable silence for a few minutes then Barclay did a condescending little wave of his hand and I pushed the phallus into first.

We inched out of the car park and I turned in the direction where they'd disappeared just a few minutes earlier. Up ahead, scurrying under the bright streetlights of the high street, was a small figure, furtively glancing from side to side as he scampered from the rendezvous.

'I take it that's the guy?' I asked.

'Yes. That's him. Stop here and let's see where he goes.'

I pulled up on a double yellow. Our target was heading straight passed the closed shops and looked like he was heading to the all-night supermarket on the corner. Despite the bright lights of the High Street I couldn't make him out much. He had skinny jeans and a hoodie up over his head, topped with an inflated puffer jacket. At that hour he looked like just the kind of guy the police would want to call upon when rounding up the usual suspects. And to think I was worried about us looking conspicuous…

'Jumpy,' noted Barclay. 'That's good. He's been a pain in the arse recently. Very good. Go passed him and we can take a final look. Number Two: make yourself small.'

It was never going to happen, but TNT gave it his best shot and tucked his head down into his Olympian shoulders. Fail. I still couldn't see out the rear view mirror.

I moved the car forward and we picked up a little speed in second. As we neared him he threw his hood back and, as we passed, I glanced and got a quick look at the nervy, agitated guy Barclay and his massif had just been doing something dirty with.

The air left my chest. I recognised him. What the hell?

It was Tom Thomas.

Chapter 18

Was it him? Had I really been falling not-so-slowly but definitely-surely for a man Barclay was exchanging bags of cash with? Had my exciting new world of Crazy started taking the dubious blue pills to elevate its status to Even Crazier Totally Fucking Nuts World?

Driving back to the flat (having deposited the incredible hulk and infuriating sulk off at their respective homes) I replayed that quick glimpse of the guy over and over and over again. Tom Thomas? Seriously, that nice, witty Tom Thomas? But he had been so nice, so easy, so natural, that little twinkle in his eyes, the smile, the teeth — Jesus, I found myself grinning just thinking about him. He'd warned me off Barclay but I'd ignored him, pushed the thought away, figured I could cope with any supposed danger. He said I should make sure I didn't get hurt. How much did he know? More than me, no doubt, but that wouldn't be difficult. Why had he been hanging outside Barclay's flat when we first met? What had he said — that he and Barclay used to be business partners? And then there was the investigation thing? I was tired and couldn't think straight, and I'd kept schtum about Tom with Barclay, just in case. Barclay doesn't share so why should I?

When I got home and had parked the Multipla in a space where I prayed the neighbours wouldn't see it, the temptation to wake Dawn and tell her what had just happened was almost irresistible, but resist I did and lay on my bed covers, fully dressed, eyes wide.

Suddenly that evening's date with Tom wasn't looking like such a good idea. I needed time to think, to talk to Barclay. Had it *really* been him? It was a split second glance, a blink-and-miss moment.

It could have been just a similarity – everyone in hoodies looks the same, don't they?

I was all over the place and not thinking straight, straying dangerously into implausible explanations and my exhausted mind was racing with doubt after doubt. I really needed to get an hour or two of sleep and maybe it would all be right in the morning.

Hell, it was morning already, wasn't it?

Was it him? Nice Tom? Tom Thomas, the Green Lantern fan? What if it was?

'Please don't get hurt, Claire.'

(It was the 'please' that stuck in my heart.)

Over and over I played it, replayed it, asking questions, answering questions but lacking conviction, asking them again, answering them again, round and round and round. I must have fallen asleep eventually, but it was a fretful, almost painful slumber. So much for Barclay's promise that I'd sleep well at nights.

My phone woke me with a start. Fumbling in the darkness I stared at it as if for the very first time. Shit. It was five past ten already. Fucky shit. It was Tom Thomas calling.

You know the guy; 'Please don't get hurt, Claire' Tom. That's the one.

Do it, Claire, just talk to him. This was the time for to-the-point, no bullshit Serious Claire, and Serious Claire was going to have a serious conversation she didn't really want to have.

'Hiya,' he said. 'I'm back. Are you still on for tonight?'

'Depends,' said Serious Claire. 'I need you to be straight with me.'

I could hear a deep breath at the other end.

'Straight?'

'Yes. It's about Barclay.'

'Ah.'

'Yes, "ah" indeed.'

'You've talked to him?'

'Not about what you said, no. But I can't get your 'Please don't get hurt, Claire' and 'he's dangerous, Claire' out of my head and it's fucking me up, keeping me awake. It's seriously … fucking me up, Tom.' He could hear I was close to tears.

'Sorry.'

'Dangerous how? Hurt how?'

'I'm just warning you. All I can tell you is that…' he paused, hesitant, as if he was about to talk before thinking. 'Look, Claire, this isn't easy, I shouldn't tell you anything, shouldn't have mentioned it.'

'Tough. Too late. You did.' Serious Claire was a serious bitch.

'He … Barclay … he's involved in the investigation I'm working on, he's heavily involved, and it's highly confidential. I wish I'd not mentioned it.

'But you did.'

'Yes, I did. Not my finest hour. But I don't want to see you hurt.'

'Hurt how?'

'I can't tell you. It's not nice.'

My heart felt leaden. 'Drugs?'

'God no. At least I don't think so.'

'So not drugs. Does it involve animals? Dogs?'

'What? Dogs? Why dogs? What makes you think…'

'Okay, so forget the dogs thing. So if you're involved it's a hacking webby internet thing.'

'That's part of it but I'm not really the best person to talk to about this…'

'So who is?'

'Barclay. You need to find out from him what he's up to, get it from him. Leave me out of it. Make your own decisions.'

'You want me to be an informer?' I shouted.

'God no. But I want you to be informed, to know what you've gotten yourself into.'

'But you won't tell me?'

'I can't tell you. And please don't mention to Barclay that you know me. That would get me into trouble with my superiors if it got out.'

'Does he know you? Have you met?'

'He doesn't know as much as he thinks he does. Talk to him. I'm not important.'

'But I'm asking you.'

'But I can't…'

'So if you can't, you shouldn't have said anything. He's my boss. He pays my wages. I need the money for Mum. And he clothes and feeds my imaginary children, cares for my fictional ailing grandmother in her fictional convalescence home, he … I need him, Tom!'

'Sorry but…'

'Don't 'sorry but' me, Tom, I need more than 'sorry but' and a vague warning.'

'It's unpleasant,' he whispered. 'Blackmail.'

'What?'

'He's blackmailing people. Dangerous people.'

'Blackmail? Over what?' I was faltering.

'Like I said, I can't share the details. It's not good.'

Blackmail? Suddenly it all made some kind of sense, it explained the untraceable bundles of second hand cash, the nervous pick-ups, the need for a fast getaway in case of … what? Police? Vigilantes or…

'I'm not fucking about, Claire, he's playing a dangerous game. People are unhappy. It won't end pretty.'

'Well, maybe people shouldn't have done whatever people did to make them so blackmailable.'

'Sure, there's maybe some truth in that, but it doesn't make what your Barclay is doing acceptable or right.'

'Very much depends. And he's not 'my Barclay'.'

'But you are 'his Claire'.'

'Only for work.'

'That's as may be, but it's still something you should end now. He's an extortionist, Claire. And if you're an accomplice, that's a custodial sentence if you're caught. When you're caught. And that's assuming it's us that catches him and not one of his targets or victims or whatever he calls them. These people aren't happy and I don't know how far they'll go to sort this and Barclay out. It never ends well for someone like Barclay and he'll drag you down with him. Steer clear, Claire.'

Easier said than done. (And not that easily said, come to that.)

My moral high ground was starting to crumble beneath my feet. Tom was caring, looking out for me with kindness and concern and I was arguing with him like the heartless, amoral monster I appeared to have become. I needed to calm down, think this through. I needed time.

My silence wasn't welcome.

'Let's talk about it later,' he suggested. 'We still on?'

'I guess so' I said, almost under my breath. Lost for something to say I said, 'Mum's not well.' It came out of nowhere, a play for sympathy to signal the departure of Serious Claire.

'Oh Claire, I'm sorry.'

'Dad says she's showing all the signs again, forgetting things that happened just hours before, not making sense. There've been a few falls…' I was close to tears again – suddenly saying it aloud brought the latent emotion to the surface that caught in my throat and took me by surprise.

'Oh Claire…'

'So I need the money… I need Barclay.'

'No you don't, Claire. You're better than that. Better than him.'

'Maybe I'm not,' I said, and hung up the phone.

Blackmail? So bloody obvious really. I suppose it could be worse.

I'd have been more worried if it was drugs or something that was hurting people or robbing the poor, but as crime goes blackmail isn't all that bad. For a start, it can only happen if the blackmail-ee has done something really bad and naughty that they're ashamed of to be blackmailed over. If anything, it's almost like a middle man operation, Barclay finds someone getting away with whatever and makes a few quid that they'd rather pay him than pay a judge or do the time behind bars.

Barclay, judge and jury, though. That logic had more than a hint of vigilantism about it? But it's a crime based on shame, I tried to convince myself, so if they have nothing to be ashamed of, there's no crime.

I wasn't assuring anyone, least of all myself. I needed to find out more. I needed to talk to Barclay.

'Claire? Pick me up at noon. I have an …'

'No.'

'… appointment with an associate who…I'm sorry, what did

you say?'

'I said 'no', Barclay.'

'What do you mean, 'no'?'

'I mean 'no, I will not pick you up at midday or ever again come to that unless you tell me what the fuck your game is.'

He paused. 'I take it you didn't sleep well?'

'I slept fine thanks. Stop playing games with me Barclay, I need to know what you do, what we're doing. And don't give me any that 'best you don't ask any questions' shit.'

'Ah.'

'Does Thug Number Two know?'

'He doesn't ask questions.'

'He doesn't say anything, so that hardly counts.'

'True. Okay, Claire, so let me try this again. Pick me up at noon and I will answer your questions.'

'That's more like it.'

'And what do you think it is I do?'

'I think it's blackmail.'

He paused for a second that felt like a minute, and then said 'smart girl,' and the phone went dead.

'So I'm right, it's blackmail, is it?' I saw no point beating around the bush as he climbed into the ridiculously inflated Fiat.

'What's blackmail?' he said, combing his hair with his fingers. 'Nice to see you, by the way.'

'Blackmail. You blackmail guys for vast quantities of cash.'

'So?'

'So...why didn't you tell me?'

'The less you know the safer for you.' He was smiling. 'Are you going to try blackmailing me over the fact that I am a blackmailer?

Ooh, the irony.'

I remembered how he gathered all those details about me from the web when we first met and realised that he had resources beyond the ken of luddites like myself.

'What do you blackmail them about?' I asked.

'Pretty much whatever they have to offer,' he said.

'Such as?'

'Financial improprieties. Affairs. Non-mainstream sexual preferences. Illegitimate offspring. You would be amazed how easy it is to find once you control someone's computer or phone.'

'And that's what you do? Hack them?'

'Pretty much. Ever heard of phishing?'

Even I knew what that was. 'People opening a dodgy link in an email?'

'Exactly. Or a tweet or text or anything else. People are stupid, you know. No matter how many stories they hear or how many times they are told, they still do it without a thought. They deserve everything they get.'

'And you don't draw a line?'

'No two are alike, each target is different. Unique. And so are the principles I apply. I do have a moral code, but it's …' he hunted for the word, 'flexible.'

'So the guy last time for example,' I ventured, meaning Tom Thomas. 'What had he done?'

'That one was slightly confused...'

I was desperate to know more but didn't want to alert him to my interest in Tom so I let it lie.

'One I'm currently working on is quite different though,' said Barclay. 'A young married schoolteacher having an affair with a 15-year-old boy. I will not be needing the services of Thug Number

Two for that one: she should be fairly compliant.'

'She's a 'she'?' I was surprised. To date the targets had all been men.

'Yes. Newly married but still carrying on with him. Husband a City millionaire, her career would be on the line. She's already agreed ten k for me to keep that one from her husband and school.'

'And what guarantee does she have that you will do that?'

'Why wouldn't I?'

'So she just has to trust you, a blackmailing stranger?'

'Basically, yes. But what you may find surprising is they actually do trust me, and, unless I find them a particularly irksome individual, I am good for that promise of it being a one-off demand. Maybe they find some odd comfort in knowing that their secret is out there, albeit just with me, and it acts as some kind of release for them. I don't know.'

'So you never go back? Unless you need more money I suppose.'

'Why take the risk? They just want me out of their lives and I'm not greedy by nature, everything's small scale, below the police radar. Occasionally, if I get a sense that they may try to resist, I have to involve additional assistance.'

'Such as your rather over-developed thug of a friend?' I asked.

'Yes, he is quite the charmer, isn't he? Depends on the target. I'm not the most intimidating chap, hence I sometimes have to call for Number Two.

'And what if they don't pay up?'

'Like I say, sometimes I have to call Number Two. But he's all bark and no bite – I don't think I've ever seen him actually hit anybody. He's not the violent type.'

It all sounded too easy. Too innocent. Surely there was something in this that didn't make sense otherwise everyone would be doing it.

But I couldn't think of it. It looked like he had thought it all through, had all the bases covered. It may not be legal but as these kind of things go, it seemed pretty fool proof.

'Why me? Why did you rope me into this?'

'Pure chance. I would have left it with the bag but when I looked into your details there was something about you that suggested you would be interested in something a little more exciting, perhaps more dangerous than some duller than dishwater office job.'

He was right there. 'And you didn't leave the bag to entrap me?'

Barclay smiled. 'No, like I say, it was pure good fortune on my part. I did not deliberately entrap you, Claire. That would have been naughty. I met you. I liked you. I saw opportunities. I sensed a wildness that I could use.'

I smiled. My closeted Bohemian side liked the idea of being regarded as 'wild'.

'Besides,' he continued. 'Even I would not leave such an expensive and dangerous item just lying around for any Thomas, Richard or Harold to pick up, would I?'

I guessed not. Barclay was, for once, being surprisingly honest and open.

'So who's this associate you're off to meet?' I asked.

'Change of plan. I'll skip that. Look, seeing as you're getting cold feet, why don't I show you first hand the kind of individual I'm talking about?'

It was all getting too real, but he was so convincing, so involving, so goddamned logical, I was in deep and thrilled by the danger, the illegality of it all and Barclay's curious take on moral justice.

Tom was wrong. He should go after the real criminals. This

was different. Personal. Besides, it was simply too late for me to step off the Barclay merry-go-round.

Chapter 19

'That's the guy?' I pointed at a short, overweight City-type, smart in his pinstripe suit, pale blue shirt and woven tie. He didn't give an immediate impression of being a likely blackmail victim, but then who did? Even from a distance he didn't look like the kind of guy I'd trust with my money.

'Don't point,' said Barclay. 'It is rude, you know. Did your parents not teach you that? Besides, it may give us away.'

We were sitting outside a Costa in a quieter part of Docklands, away from the upmarket shopping arcade and its lunchtime heaving throngs of already-exhausted office workers. It was mild for January but not mild enough to be comfortably seated outdoors. I was wearing too light a jacket for the time of year that needed an additional layer or two underneath it to stop my teeth chattering.

Barclay had surprised me by lighting a cigarette but had not been smoking it, just letting it rest between his fingers.

'I didn't know you smoked.' I said.

'I don't. But why else would we be sitting outside when there are plenty of empty seats inside?'

'Clever.'

'Thank you.'

'And that's him?'

'Yes. Queues for his sandwich every day at that little Italian place. Every lunchtime the same routine, even the same lunch – chicken escalope and salad in a ciabatta roll. You would have thought he would be a few sizes bigger as a result but he's quite trim, considering.'

'Predictable chap. So what do you know about him? What's he done that is so bad?'

Barclay stirred a sugar into his macchiato. 'His name is Anthony Bartholomew. He's fifty-nine years' old and is a senior director at one of the major trading houses around here. Which particular one is irrelevant to what we are doing, but they're a household name even if he isn't. He would be though, if what I have on him ever became public knowledge.'

'Dirty is he?'

'Unbelievable. He's been creaming off the top, bottom and sides of almost every business relationship he's had for years. No single big take, just a plethora of just-below-visibility dips into the swill. When all added together it runs to millions, tens of millions even. He is one of those I have absolutely no remorse for; he already earns more than he could ever possibly spend in a single lifetime, several in fact, and yet he still has the greed to take more and thinks nothing of the consequences of his actions. He has no scruples over what he dabbles in as long as it lines his pockets. He's traded arms with terrorists, committed financial fraud on a global scale, many of his clients, friends even, have gone to the wall because of his actions, yet there's no regret or remorse on his part. He's very clever, he would be the last any of them would suspect but I got him.'

'How did you find him?'

Barclay hesitated before replying. 'I was put onto him by someone I know. Initially we were looking at someone else but that one turned out to be of no use. Then we saw that Bartholomew was involved in a few of his larger transactions, acting as an 'advisor'. I hacked into his personal laptop and looked a little closer. He's so clever yet so dumb – his password was just 'password1'.'

I laughed, making a mental note to change my laptop's password when I got home, from something that was awfully similar to something that wasn't. Barclay continued:

'And I saw that this advisor role consultancy was off his company's books, very much off-the-record pieces of work. It wasn't the day rate that he was charging that alerted me – that was pretty modest in the banking game – but the travel and expenses he was passing through. Tens of thousands without receipts or an audit trail. So I dug a little deeper and found that it was the tip of the proverbial iceberg. Expenses fraud that would make even an MP blush. By my estimate he draws over three million a year through this additional income.'

'Wow.'

'Oh, that's pretty small in the circles Bartholomew mixes in – you wouldn't believe the bonuses they get just for turning up to an office three or four days a week.' Barclay pushed over his phone to me which displayed a small spreadsheet with some very large numbers on it. 'That's his additional income for last year. He won't be paying tax on it as it's undeclared, its privacy secured by his friendship with clients. He harvests broadly – think of paying a builder cash in hand, we all do it if asked, small amounts, where's the harm? – but if you add it all up it soon takes on a different dimension. That's thousands by the way.'

Oh. My. God. The numbers were dizzying. I sipped my flat white: suddenly Costa coffee didn't seem quite the extravagance I'd previously regarded it as. The money involved was astronomical. I think it was fair to say that I was not feeling any sympathy for this guy.

'And how easy was it to get him?'

'He was easy. He does everything on his laptop and smartphone but never updates the software on it – it's wide open, easy pickings. Spends a fortune on cars but has the cheapest, most vulnerable technology you can imagine. I just phished him, and once he clicked the link I was in and I had everything I needed. He's a dangerous thief, ruins lives. Deserves to be stung.'

'How much for?'

'He's in a different league from the business I usually do. I normally keep it small, a few thousand here, a few there, below the authorities' radar and nothing that's going to bankrupt anyone. No point in being greedy. 100k. Small change to him, but he'll be nervous about the drop. When we ... I made the demand he offered to do a bank transfer – a bloody bank transfer! Does he think I'm stupid? Always cash and always in person.'

'There's no danger of him getting someone else to do the drop, someone we should be scared of?'

'I doubt that very much, he's not going to involve anyone else. We'll have Number Two along just as a precaution. I do undertake a full and extensive background check on targets before I put in the first call – I've never been wrong in the past. Nearest to that was the guy with the dog. I should have seen that he takes the bloody mutt everywhere, can't leave it on its own or it would tear up his furniture. I won't make that mistake again.'

Bartholomew had reached the front of the shuffling queue and had collected his sandwich. He didn't look any different from the dozens of other suited gents quietly milling around the small parade of lunchtime eateries amongst the towering glass edifices of Docklands. Who would have thought, eh?

'So what time tonight?'

'Pick me up at 1am, I'll have Number Two already, and we're not going far from home ground.'

'Good,' I said. 'I'd still like to get more involved if you need me.'

He smiled. 'I'd appreciate that. I think we're a good team, Claire, and I'm glad you are a little more comfortable with what we do. I was cautious about involving another person but this feels good and you're right, I should have told you earlier.'

I smiled back. Now that he'd been open and I knew what was going on in detail I was more at ease and happy. He was a bright man, had thought of every angle, every nuance, every possibility. It seemed so simple.

I couldn't imagine anything going wrong.

As I put my key in the door I heard laughter from within, then two familiar voices loudly entwined. Dawn and …

'Henry?' I gasped.

'Hi there!'

My Ex was sitting there at the kitchen table, a mug of tea, that wretched old mug of his, I noted, steaming in his hands.

'You're back?'

'Yep.'

'Already?'

'Yep.'

'That was…quick,' I observed needlessly.

'Turned out I'm too sensitive a soul for the first-hand experience,' he was beaming, like it had all been a big joke. 'And now I'm back.'

'So I see.' I pulled out the spare chair from around the table and sat with a bump.

'Tea?' asked Dawn. 'The kettle's just boiled.'

'Yes. Thanks.' It was taking a few seconds to get my head

around this. I thought I'd seen the last of him.

'Yes, I was explaining to Dawn who I was and where I've been,' he didn't appear to be capable of stopping the grin and nodded to the younger Barclay who looked to her lap – was it my imagination or was there something between these two? Surely not.

'You never told me much about Henry,' said Dawn.

'I didn't see the need to be honest. I thought he was confined to history,' I said.

'As if,' said Henry. 'You can't keep a good man down.'

'Or a boring one, apparently.' I wasn't buying that 'all friends again' crap.

'It's nice to see you too, Claire. You look well. Dawn was telling me that you've got a new job.'

'I've got new work, I wouldn't call it a job. You couldn't cut it in India then?'

He shrugged. 'Not my thing. I'm more useful here I think.'

'Couldn't stomach the poverty and distress up close? Too painful for you?'

Looking down he shook his head. 'It's difficult. More difficult than I thought I'd find it. I've seen things…'

'You were only there a few weeks.'

'It felt like forever.'

'I'm sure it did. What did you expect?'

'Look, it's easy to sit here and criticise from wintry Deptford but…'

'I don't want to hear it, Henry. I'm not interested.'

'I am,' said Dawn. I wasn't mistaken. She was looking at him with something somewhere between fascination and adoration. What had happened between them this morning? Had I misjudged her? Him? Was this a 'love at first sight' thing going on? In my kitchen? Ridiculous.

He smiled at her – he always lapped up any female attention going and certainly wasn't getting it from me. It was more cloying than touching.

'Nice of you to drop by,' I bit.

'I thought you might be happy to see me. But sadly it appears I was wrong. I'd forgotten to take my favourite mug.' He held it aloft for my benefit.

'You're lucky I didn't bin it.'

'I recall it was you who bought it.'

Not exactly. It was something I'd stolen from the office from the IT guy. 'Have you tried turning it off and on again?' it asked on one side. 'Have you tried fucking off?' it answered on the other.

'Yeah,' I sighed.

He took a final, noisy slurp and rose to leave.

'So I'll pick you up tonight at seven? he asked Dawn.

What?

'Great. See you then,' she said.

Huh?

'Nice to see you again, Claire. I hope the new work goes well.'

I shook my head as if it would get him out of my hair sooner. 'Bye!' I managed.

He was gone. Dawn was grinning. I raised my eyebrows.

'Wow. He's nice,' she swooned. I was beginning to feel nauseous.

'Maybe at first. Seriously? Him? Henry? Where did that come from?' I was shaking my head. 'I should have warned you, should have said something.'

'He turned up whilst you were out. Had a key but still knocked first. Very polite. Quite a gentleman.'

'Him? You'll learn.'

She laughed. 'Well you can't blame me for trying, surely?'

'I don't know why I'm so surprised that I'm surprised. The Barclays are constantly surprising me.'

'It's a family thing, it's what we do. Anyway, Henry's taking me out for a drink tonight.'

'I gathered. Take a good book with you. I give it an hour before you tire of his preaching. Don't bother to set the box to record that film tonight – you'll be home before nine.'

Dawn laughed. 'We'll see,' she said. 'Don't wait up.'

But I knew better.

Chapter 20

I had been wrong. When I pulled away in the Multipla from my building at 1am the next morning there was still no sign of Dawn coming home. I found it oddly unsettling that she seemed genuinely happy with the man I had so easily brushed out of my life just a few weeks earlier. Had I misjudged him or was she not quite the girl I'd thought she was? Maybe she was just too young to know better? Perhaps I should introduce her to TNT. He might be even more her type.

It's not as if my own love life was anything to boast about. My evening reunion with Tom proved a frosty, short lived encounter. Our earlier phone call had clearly unsettled him as much as it had me, and after ordering a couple of bottles of Peroni he was fishing for an excuse to leave early.

'Do you mind if we skip dinner? I've got a lot of work to catch up on. The investigation has been busy and ...'

'Let's not talk about him,' I said.

'Did you talk to him?'

'Let's not talk about him or me.'

'Oh. Okay then.' He couldn't look me in the eye. I couldn't look at him, either. The whole evening had been a mistake, and I'd committed to picking up Barclay and TNT for the Bartholomew job in a few hours.

'I'm not feeling too good,' I lied. 'Can we call it an early night?'

'Sure. Sorry you're not so good.'

God, what a painful mistake the evening had proven. It was supposed to have been a joyous, passionate reunion, but Barclay had come between us and it felt more like a wake for our relationship. The conversation stuttered, stumbled and died, and we left and went our separate ways without even touching once. Broken? It sure felt broken, fragile at best.

But there was little time to dwell on it – time for work. I had to go and collect my colleagues and we were going to get that dirty embezzling fat bastard and extract a ridiculous amount of loose cash from his greedy porky paws.

When I got to Barclay's TNT was already there. At least from a distance I think it was him – it may have been an abandoned overfilled skip.

'Hiya,' I said as Barclay wrestled with the seat belt. 'How are you doing, Number Two?'

Not even a grunt back. I wasn't going to take it personally. He didn't bother with a seatbelt – it's not like he would have bounced around the interior in an accident, jammed in as he was.

I pushed the gear stick into first and we moved off. The traffic was light almost to the point of non-existent and Barclay directed me west into the labyrinth of dual carriageways and roundabouts that form the East India Dock area, brightly lit by the orange streetlights but bereft of any signs of life. So this is what London will look like after the zombie apocalypse.

I was having trouble with the car's gearbox – shifting down to second seemed to be stiffer, jerking and loudly protesting its discomfort when I slowed for corners.

'Wasn't like that the other night,' I said. 'Can't seem to make it any smoother. The clutch feels like it's hardly working.'

'That's not good,' muttered Barclay. He seemed pre-occupied, nervous even.

Nothing from TNT. In the mirror I could see him gazing transfixed at the bright signs atop the Docklands banks and business towers, like a child with the Oxford Street Christmas lights. I half expected him to coo 'Oooh, pretty' but it wasn't happening. At least, it wasn't happening outside his head.

Pity.

'Next left, then a right, then a left,' directed Barclay. 'Right, then left and a sharp left, right and right at the roundabout.'

'Aren't we going to end up back where we started?' I asked, only half joking. This wasn't looking like a straightforward exit route and it was making me nervous. What's more, as we moved from the main thoroughfares into the side streets the lights were further apart and it was getting harder to tell the turnings from the warehouse entrances. I had no idea where we were or how we'd get out in a hurry. It was not feeling good. My stomach was suddenly prickling with nerves.

'Almost there,' said Barclay.

'Did he pick this place or you?' I asked.

'I did, although I have to admit it was easier to navigate on Google Maps than it is in real life at this late hour. Just to the right up here.' He pointed to an entrance to a parking area with a broken barrier. 'Dimly lit' didn't do it justice – there were no streetlights and it was unnaturally dark, countryside blackness in the heart of the new City. The concrete surface was badly pot holed and the Multipla's suspension tackled them with the grace and finesse of a stampeding blind elephant.

'Steady there,' said Barclay.

'Sorry,' I apologised.

I pulled up and dowsed the lights. Not a sign of life. I could just see the dock waters through two dark warehouses, high tide by the look of things, the wind whipping up small, tame crested peaks.

'Okay, Number Two. We're going to wait for him over there

under that light.' It was about fifty yards away and was pretty much the only light in the immediate area, hanging off a broken wooden sign that had promised 'Fresh Fruit and Vegetables' in better, more affluent times.

TNT eased out of the three rear seats, the Multipla's suspension bouncing in joyful relief as his feet hit terra firma.

'Ten minutes. Tops,' said Barclay. It was becoming his catchphrase. It had yet to prove an accurate estimate.

They walked over together to the distant glow, their silhouettes vaguely resembling a diminutive zookeeper taking a giant silverback gorilla for a walk. They reached the spot and Barclay waved. I waved back, involuntarily, forgetting he couldn't see me with the car's lights off.

It was quiet, deadly quiet. We'd driven far enough away from civilisation that there wasn't even any distant traffic to disturb the peace. I wound down my window (electric – the Multipla was an improvement on some of the Uno's more dated 'features') and a cold wind reminded me of the season. Brrrr. Back up it went. Whatever I was about to witness could play out as a silent movie.

This was actually going to be the first time I'd actually seen a pick-up – I'd always been stuck 'round the corner' or 'out the back'. The dream team were quite a distance away and Barclay must have figured it wouldn't be a risk for the car to be in plain sight as it was too dark and distant to make out our getaway car, even one as distinctive as the Multipla.

Lights suddenly appeared around a corner and a second car, a hatchback appeared. It was being driven cautiously, nervously and the driver had just the sidelights on as he approached Barclay and TNT. Barclay raised his gloved hand and waved. All seemed to be going to plan.

Suddenly the car roared and accelerated directly at them, tyres screeching, the headlights blazing on full beam, blinding them with their dazzling brilliance. Instantly the hatchback was on them. Barclay threw himself towards the warehouse with startling agility but TNT was clumsier, slower, too slow, and the speeding car caught him side on. He span, pirouetting with surprising grace as the car swerved, then corrected itself and accelerated away, killing its lights and back into the darkness.

Shit. Fuck shitty fuck.

I needed to stay calm. I turned the ignition, put the lights on and drove rapidly over to Barclay and his fallen comrade.

This wasn't in the script. Someone had torn up Barclay's perfect plan.

Both of them were still lying on the hard, uneven concrete. Barclay was attempting to pick himself up, dazed and hurt, but it looked like he would live.

TNT was motionless, almost as tall horizontal as he had been vertical. His eyes fluttered briefly before closing. There was a dark puddle appeared to be growing under his head. His short legs were lying at odd angles. Not 'funny' odd though, 'badly broken' odd.

'Fuck,' I said, clambering out of the car.

'Fuck,' said Barclay.

That seemed to pretty much sum things up.

I'm no doctor, but I knew who was in more trouble there. I knelt by TNT and could see he needed help, serious help, nothing my fundamental First Responder skills could handle. Even unconscious he was an awesome sight up close, still surprisingly intimidating for one possibly no longer with us.

Barclay stood at my shoulder.

'Fuck,' he said. 'He looks pretty fucked. Let's move him.'

I gave Barclay my most withering look. 'Are you serious? Move him? Us? What's he weigh, thirty, thirty-five stone? Move him?'

'Yeah, maybe. Sorry. I guess I'm not thinking straight. He doesn't look good.'

'No he fucking doesn't. That's blood, isn't it?' In the near darkness the puddle under his head was black and sticky looking, and it was definitely expanding. 'Probably best we don't move him, actually.'

'Yes. Good point. Fuck.' Barclay pulled his phone out. 'I'll call an … shit, no signal. Fuck.'

I got my phone out and found one bar. Sometimes I loved my Nokia more than words could say. I pressed the Emergency fast dial button.

'Hello? Ambulance. Emergency. Hit and run incident,' I sounded remarkably calm, considering. 'Sorry, what?' I looked at Barclay. 'Where exactly are we?'

He gave me the address of the nearest building which I passed on to the operator. 'Ten minutes. Okay. Yes, of course.' I hung up. 'They want us to stay with him.'

'We can't,' said Barclay.

'What? We can't leave him here!'

'How do we explain what we were doing here?'

'We have five minutes to think of a bloody good lie. You can do that Barclay, surely?'

'What good do we do by staying? He's down. Man down. We can't do anything for him. Best leave it to the professionals.'

'What if they miss him, don't find him?'

'Even flat out he's unmissable. They'll find him. Get the torch or warning thing out the back of the car.'

Without thinking I followed his instruction and went to the

Multipla's rear door. In there was a plastic red triangle for use in accidents on motorways and, now, for alerting police after a hit and run on a pick-up. I brought it over to our fallen comrade.

'They won't be able to miss seeing that,' said Barclay. He seemed to be calming whereas I was feeling panic rising. 'We can leave him.'

'I'm…I'm not comfortable with that.'

'Okay. You stay. He's your boyfriend and you got lost walking back from a club. That's easier to explain than if there's three of us.'

'My boyfriend?'

'It'll work. Trust me.'

'But I don't even know his real name!'

'He's just picked you up at the club. You're an easy pull.'

'What?'

'Say anything. It'll work. Trust me.'

'I'm not doing this.'

'Then we go. Your choice.'

My panic levels were rising into the red zone. I looked at TNT. Still no movement. My mind was racing, couldn't think straight.

'Okay. I'll stay. You go,' I said.

'Good girl.'

'Okay. Okay. I'll be okay,' I muttered to myself, not convinced.

Barclay quickly climbed into the Multipla. 'You call me as soon as you can.'

'Yes. Sure.' My voice had shrunk like my confidence. 'I'm doing the right thing, the good thing.' Barclay drove off. Illegally, but that was the least of our concerns right then.

I knelt again by Number Two, bravely brushing his cheek with the back of my fingers. He was still breathing but it was shallow and almost imperceptible.

'Stay still, Number Two,' I whispered. 'Help is on its way. You'll be okay, it's just a little knock. It's all going to be okay.'

But I wasn't convinced, and when the tears came I was crying both for him and me.

Chapter 21

Well, that sure went to hell in a hurry. I wanted out.

I tried calling Barclay when the ambulance had arrived, just minutes after he'd departed the scene. No luck. I was probably too generous in assuming that he was still out of signal. Bastard.

The ambulance crew were fast but there were only two of them and they immediately called for further assistance once they'd assessed the situation. Moving the unmovable was a challenge beyond the two strapping young chaps, I was told. TNT was all muscle, heavy muscle. They'd need a small army to move him.

They asked me to step away and leave them to it, which I willingly did. I thought of mentioning my First Responder course but decided against it – there was nothing I could help with.

The police arrived ten minutes later and I stuck to Barclay's hastily concocted story. I was shaking, partly due to the cold, more likely in shock and the adrenaline. The police and crew were gentle with me, caring even.

'Which club did you say you were at?' asked the policewoman who had introduced herself as Joan.

'I don't know. It's over there somewhere.' I waved vaguely in the direction Barclay had indicated. 'We were lost. I'm not sure.'

'And you don't know his name?'

'He said…' think girl, quick. 'Derek.' Ridiculous. TNT was no more a 'Derek' than I was.

'No surname?'

'I don't recall. Sorry. I'm not thinking straight. I had a few Breezers and it's all muddled.'

'Understandable, Miss. I'll slow down. And you didn't see the other car at all?'

'It was very fast and the headlights were really bright. I don't even know what type it was. I'm not very good with cars. Small. Smaller than…Derek.'

She scrawled something on her notepad, angling it to try to catch enough light from the police car's headlights to write by.

'Is he going to be okay?' I asked.

'Probably too early to say. He's breathing and they've staunched the bleeding from his head. They're trying to figure out how to move him.'

There were now five figures clad in luminous yellow safety coats gathered around TNT discussing the logistics of lifting him.

'I'm not judging you, but he…he is a big fella.' Policewoman Joan was stating the bleeding obvious. She'd made me a cup of instant coffee, primed with about a dozen sugars. It tasted good. Anything would have.

'I like them big,' I lied. 'He makes me feel… safe.' Which was less of a lie. But not safe enough, apparently. Joan nodded.

She took a few more of my details and said I could go. 'Can I have a lift?' I asked.

'Is there no one you can call?'

'I'll try. But it's late. What if he's not answering?'

'Try him first. We'll be here a while and you probably need to get safely home. Bit nippy, isn't it.'

More in hope than in expectation I made one last attempt and called Barclay. He finally answered, but only after it rang for all eternity.

Barclay pulled the Multipla up a good fifty yards from the Police and Ambulance, who had now called for even more reinforcements to try to move 'Derek'. I strode angrily over to the banned driver. He vacated the driver's seat for me. Big of him.

'I take it you don't want to get too close in case they remember you're banned from the wheel?' I bit.

'That's the least of our problems. What did they say? Is he okay?'

'Like you care.' He looked shamefaced and offered no response. I put the car into gear and we pulled away.

'I can't believe you were prepared to leave him there,' I eventually said, almost too angry to speak.

'He knows the risks of this work.' It was lame and indefensible and we both knew it.

'If that had been me, would you have left me?'

'It wasn't you.'

'But if it had been me, would you?'

'Probably not.'

'"Probably"? That's not very reassuring.'

'It's better than 'possibly'.' He attempted a smile.

'This isn't a joke, Barclay. I'm serious. If that had been me knocked down, would you have stayed?'

He hesitated before answering. 'Yes. You're different.'

'In what way?'

'You're my responsibility. I got you into this. It's new for you and that's down to me.'

'What if I want out? I didn't sign up for this.'

He didn't respond and we sat in awkward silence as I drove us cautiously back to Barclay's place, his only words a quiet navigation of 'left heres' and 'next rights'.

'What is his real name? The police asked and I said Derek. I'm betting he's not a Derek.'

'No, not a Derek. He's an Hugues.' Barclay pronounced it 'Oog'. 'He's French, you know? I can't pronounce his surname but he'll have fake ID on him for the hospital.'

French? I'd never heard TNT say anything but he didn't look particularly foreign. Mind you, he looked unlike anyone, any*thing* I had ever seen before.

'You think he'll be okay?' I asked.

'What did they say?'

'They said it was difficult to tell and he'd been hit pretty hard. Any one smaller may have been killed instantly.'

'Then he's lucky. I'm lucky – could easily have been me. He pushed me away at the last moment.'

I had been mistaken – it was TNT's reflex reaction that had saved Barclay, not his. Lucky, lucky Barclay. What had he done to make Number Two so loyal?

'Wow.' Under my breath. 'And you would have left him?'

He didn't hear that, or least pretended not to have. 'Wow indeed. I owe him,' he sighed.

'Let's just pray he's around to know that,' I said.

'Amen.'

The flat was silent when Barclay dropped me off. There was no sign of Dawn or Henry. Good – I don't think I could have coped with the sounds of a noisy first date fumbling from her room.

I stripped and had a shower. I felt dirty and suddenly I was trembling. The shock and emotion quickly returned, bubbled over and I crumpled to my knees, shaking uncontrollably.

Chapter 22

'He's okay,' said Barclay.

'Thank god for that,' I sighed in relief. 'How okay?'

'Well, he's alive but a little bit broken.' Barclay seemed a little broken himself. His usual overpowering self-confidence had seemingly deserted him and I was surprised to still find him shaken by the previous night's events.

'How broken?' I asked, sipping my morning brew. We were always the only customers in Barclay's Docklands café and I was starting to wonder how it kept in business. There was certainly no fear of being overheard there, and the tea was certainly a step up from the sludgy coffee. I still didn't think I'd risk it with the food though.

'Cracked skull, four broken ribs, possibly five, left shoulder and arm, possibly multiple fractures in the left leg but they cannot say for sure until some of the swelling calms down. They said they weren't sure what was swelling and what wasn't.'

'Ouch.'

'Very ouch. It will be a while before they let him out. Hopefully he can get sufficiently well before Interpol catches up with him. That ID he carries won't deceive them for long – the physical description is pretty unmistakable.'

Interpol? I didn't know if that was a joke or not. Neither of us were in a joking mood.

'Were you serious? he asked. 'About wanting out?'

'I was. But I'm not so sure now. It was a heat of the moment thing.'

'I need you with Number Two gone.'

'He's out of action for a while?' I asked.

'He will want to lay low once released, go back to France I expect. He has in the past proved to be a fast healer but I have never seen him taken out like that before before. Months, possibly worse.'

'But they expect him to make a full recovery?' I sounded desperate, desperate for good news, better news at least.

'As far as they can tell. Like I said, they don't know the full extent of his injuries yet.'

'What happened exactly? I couldn't see much from the car – it was too dark and all happened so fast.'

'Someone decided it was a better option to take us out. I told him this was too big, too risky.'

'Told who?'

Barclay didn't answer. There was someone else involved?

'It wasn't Bartholomew driving,' Barclay said. 'Someone else, someone brought in to do the dirty work. Maybe Number Two spooked him. Too big, this was too much.'

I nodded in agreement – TNT had spooked me even when he was lying there unconscious and bleeding.

'Has this happened before? Someone tried to shut you up rather than pay up?'

'No.' Barclay couldn't look at me directly. 'This one was bigger than what I'm normally doing. I told him…'

'Told who? I thought this was just us?'

But he dismissed my questions with a wave.

I tried to lighten the mood; 'I wonder how the other guy is, the hatchback?'

Barclay smiled. 'I'd imagine our friend left quite a dent.'

'I'd be surprised if it was still in one piece.' It hadn't been an entirely one-sided content.

'And how are you?' Barclay suddenly asked. It seemed a genuine question and he made a movement to touch my hand but then withdrew it hastily.

'I'm doing okay.' He wasn't convinced. 'No, really. Bit shaken last night but slept like a log and I'm fine now. All okay.'

'You're a tough one, Claire.'

'I'm going to need to be if there are many more nights like that one.'

'There won't be.'

'Is there anyone else you know who can cover for Number Two until he's mended?' I asked.

'There's no one like Thug Number Two,' he said, stating the obvious.

'Is there a Thug Number Three for emergencies?'

'No.'

'And Number One isn't available?'

'I told you, we don't talk about Thug Number One.' Time to change the record, Claire.

'Dawn went out with Henry last night.' I needed to lighten the mood, get things back to what had been counting as 'normal'.

He raised his eyebrow. 'Henry? Your Ex? He's back from India already?'

'Yes. The wayward worthy one turned up on my doorstep yesterday morning and swept your sister off her size fives. Went off on a date last night when we were out there and hasn't come home yet.'

'The tart,' spat Barclay, without much humour.

'Hey, steady on. That's my new best friend forever you're talking about.'

'And my sister. Well I never. No changing some people.'

'I had no idea she was so … easy, so easily impressed. And still not home yet.'

'Probably eloped. If they come back, charge them both rent and double it.'

'She can handle herself for sure, and Henry is hardly public enemy number one. At worst, he'll bore her to death or worthy her into submission.'

He managed a pained smile.

The conversation slipped away, having pretty much exhausted itself. We still needed recovery time and to reflect on what had happened. Then something bizarre struck me; it appeared that we'd somehow mutated into a conventional couple, comfortable in our shared silences. When did that happen? When had I lost that compelling need to fill every pause and gap in a conversation? It was unnerving to say the least.

'We should go,' suggested Barclay. 'I've got someone to update on last night's episode.'

'Who?'

He shook his head. 'Too big,' he muttered.

Thanks for sharing, Barclay. But I guessed the less I knew, the easier it would be to walk away if I needed to.

By the car he touched my sleeve, a token, uncomfortable attempt at comforting me.

'See you later,' I said, finding it suddenly difficult to look directly into his eyes.

Something may have been happening. I was not sure it was to my liking, not sure it wasn't. I was losing control of my life in so many ways I should have been terrified.

But, somehow, despite everything, I just couldn't let go.

When I returned home I was exhausted, the stress and emotion of the last twelve hours were finally catching up with me and knocking me for six.

And Dawn was back. Finally. Sans Henry, but giddy and giggly like a love-smitten schoolgirl.

'What a night!'

I looked at my watch – it was three in the afternoon. I felt like an over-anxious mother, grateful for her arrival but angry that it had taken so long.

I wasn't sharing her good humour. 'Glad for you. Can we talk about it some other time?'

'What a morning!'

'I'm serious, Dawn. I'm not in the mood.'

'H'okay.' She danced off to the bathroom.

Kids, huh?

Was I angry at her, still confused over Barclay or was it delayed repercussions from the hit and run? Or was there a latent jealous over Henry rising? No, surely not. He was history to me and I'd looked under all the rocks and there was nothing there, not a scrap of emotional residue or longing for the guy. I had wanted a clean break and this one had enjoyed the full power pressure hose treatment. Nothing there. Nothing whatsoever. All gone. Nada.

Honest.

(I was almost convinced.)

'Barclay. It's Claire. I've been thinking.' There was no response from him. 'Barclay? You there?'

'Of course. Please share.'

It sounded like I'd called him in the middle of something – I could hear other voices in the background, street noises too.

'Is it a bad time? Can you talk?'

'I can listen.'

'What are you doing?'

'Selling the Fiat.'

'The Uno? Great!'

'No. The Multipla. I'm trading it back for the Uno.'

'What? You're joking?'

I knew he wasn't. Bloody hell. If this carried on I was going to buy my own bloody getaway car.

'You were thinking?'

'What? Oh, yes. Protection – we need a different type of protection now we're without Thug Number … without Hugues.'

'Please don't tell me you are joining a gym… we don't have the time and you won't have the dedication.'

'What do you mean I won't have…anyway, no, I'm not suggesting a gym. Remember how we first met?'

'Yes. My bag.'

'Exactly. And in the bag, the gun. Do you still have it? Can we get another one? Can you teach me how to use one?'

'No.'

'No to what? No you don't have it, no you can't get another, or no you can't teach me?'

'No, I can't teach you. You may recall I'm not very good with guns.'

'So we'll both learn.'

'Claire…are you sure you want to go down this path?'

'Never been surer.'

He sighed. He sounded disappointed, his apprentice was growing up too fast. I was toughening up. We needed to toughen up. He didn't like it? Tough.

'I can't teach you,' he sighed. 'But I know a man who can teach both of us.'

'Good.'

'One slight concern though…'

'What?'

'He's a little… You may find him quite unbearable.'

It didn't matter to me. I had been proving myself a dab hand in dealing with unusual and difficult men.

Chapter 23

His name was Owen Ward but he said that I could call him 'Wardy'. Apparently that's what everyone did, or that's what he told me. He was around Barclay's age, late twenties, early thirties, not as tall and a little stockier, like he worked out a little but not to the point of obsession. He had dull brown hair with a floppy fringe that was last fashionable in the previous century. It was immediately obvious that he quite fancied himself and thought that women were similarly minded. God's generous gift he was not, but sadly no one had actually told him that to his face.

Or, more likely, he just hadn't been listening.

Barclay had said on the way over to Ward's workshop that they had met at university and had been friends ever since, when it proved mutually beneficial to be so. Ward had stumbled along from one job to another since dropping out of the academic rat race, taking cash in hand whenever it was offered and never staying with anything long enough for it to be classifiable as a career.

After a string of failed business ventures, including one that had burned through his entire, not-inconsiderable family inheritance in a single week of breathtaking commercial incompetence, Ward had hit hard times and was taking whatever was on offer. Currently, he was providing MOT certificates for cars that would fail at legitimate garages, a much needed service in some circles, hence the workshop. I wondered if the Uno had been a recent 'patient' requiring his attention – that would have made so much sense.

Whisper it quietly, but Owen Ward was also building himself quite a reputation in south east London as a guy who could get you what you needed and teach you how to use it, no questions asked, cash not credit if you would be so kind. More importantly, Barclay assured me, he was discreet to the point of appearing disinterested.

Unless you were female.

Which, of course, I am. I thanked Barclay for the warning.

It was after sunset when we got there, a cold, damp and dark late January evening like every other January evening. The workshop was squeezed into a crumbling Southwark railway arch under one of the main rail tracks running from the garden of England into the capital. Either business was particularly bad or Ward had already moved out any cars currently under his dubious inspection. The place had been arranged into a makeshift small firing range with some paper targets pinned onto some loose plaster board on the rear wall some twenty or so feet from where Ward was standing.

'Well, hello there,' he said, smiling and striding towards me, openly leering. He walked passed Barclay, seemingly oblivious to his friend's offered hand of greeting. Ward's attention was already focused.

'Uh, hello,' I said.

'Hi Wardy,' said Barclay, unaccustomed as he was to being completely bypassed. I suspected that the snub was 100% deliberate on Ward's part.

'So you're Claire?'

'Apparently so. Hello, Mr Ward.'

'Wardy.'

'Got it.'

'And you need to learn how to hold and fire my weapon?' He made it sound filthy, pornographic and he hadn't wasted any time getting into a practised routine of less-than-subtle innuendos, that was for sure.

'Both me and Barclay, yes.'

'Well, I'm less interested in Barclay's grip,' he winked. It was like sparring with Graham Norton, but without the laughs. 'He's a lost cause,' said Ward with a smile and slight shake of the head. 'But you I can definitely work with.' I smiled back through clenched teeth. 'Ever worked with guns before?'

'No.'

'Lots to learn then.' He deliberately brushed passed me, too close for comfort. I tried to ensure this didn't become difficult.

'Barclay – are you having a lesson, too?' I asked.

'A refresher may prove useful.'

'Oh, you're staying with us? Pity. From what I recall, you're unteachable,' said Ward.

Barclay looked pained. 'I will accept I can be a challenging student, but nothing a good teacher can't deal with.'

'Touché, brother.' Their banter was neither comfortable nor genuine, and felt as though it was being forced for my benefit. So kind.

Ward went to a drawer and adopted a more professional demeanour. Presumably he assumed I would be back for more personal attention from him later, maybe after Barclay had left.

Sucker. Not a chance in hell.

'I've got Claire the same handgun as you, Barclay.' He put on the dirty worktop a gun identical to the one I had found in Barclay's rucksack.

'It's an a SCCY CPX 9mm, the best-selling handgun in the States, and the Yanks know a fine piece of weaponry when they see one. Every home should have one. Take out those pesky raccoons and immigrants without a second thought.' He formed a childish finger gun with his right hand, actioned as if to fire it like a pre-school cowboy and blew on his 'smoking' forefinger.

Sure, that would impress even me.

'May I hold it?' I asked.

He went wide eyed and smiled, 'With Barclay here?' then feigned disappointment: 'Oh, you mean the gun.'

I rolled my eyes. Barclay was already looking at his phone.

'Hold on, before you touch let me run you through the basics. Gun law I call it. Wardy's Laws. Four golden rules. Barclay! Do pay attention 007.' Barclay couldn't have looked less interested.

'Rule one; always treat the firearm as if it were loaded. Never, ever, even if you are 100% sure it is 100% empty, treat it as if it isn't. Respect the weapon.

Duh.

'Rule two: never fart around with a weapon. Always point it in a safe direction and where it can do no one or nothing no harm. It ain't a toy and accidents easily happen. Think safe.'

I was wondering if he'd mistaken us for a pair of six-year-olds. Barclay was already checking his phone again. I was counting bricks in the ceiling.

Ignoring our wandering attention, Ward continued: 'Rule three. Keep your finger outside the trigger guard until you have made a conscious decision that you are going to shoot. That's why there's a trigger guard. Don't be tempted to rest your itchy forefinger on the trigger.'

Barclay yawned but I resisted the temptation.

'And finally, always look not just at your target but what's beyond it if possible. You don't want to hit a passer-by or shatter a window if you can avoid it, do you? All that nasty paperwork and police time can kill an evening's fun.'

I stifled another yawn and nodded. I could have learned this in five minutes from Google. 100%.

'Got that? Good. Now we can start shooting those bad guys.'

('But aren't we the bad guys?' I asked myself.)

Barclay sighed and took his own pistol from his rucksack, ignoring rules one, two and three immediately by waving it around before pointing it directly at Ward with his finger on the trigger. Ward frowned. 'Barclay...' he said in the weary voice of a teacher who had better things to do with his time.

'Whoops. How careless of me. I really should pay more attention, shouldn't I, Mr Ward? You have me, sir. 100%.'

Ward smiled the tiredest of smiles. Barclay really was the most trying of pupils.

Ward may have been even more condescending than Barclay, but he was thorough, which was welcome if draining. He instructed us how to hold the guns and why a two-handed grip was not just essential for the beginner but also even for an experienced gun hand. It was exactly how you see them do it on the telly, one hand on the gun, the other to steady, the pose familiar from a thousand cop shows. My gun was new, slightly oily, cold and so heavy to my hands. My pose was pure Hollywood, legs slightly apart and arms out rigid. Too rigid for Ward, and I tensed as he moved behind me and made tiny, unnecessary adjustments to my posture just for the thrill of the contact. Creep. 'Relax,' he breathed in my ear. 'Not so tense.' I did the opposite.

But the feel of a real, honest-to-goodness loaded gun in my hands was, I can't pretend otherwise, exhilarating.

'Relax,' he whispered again.

It was a clumsy, unsuccessful seduction, and dangerous for him to persevere with it when I had my hands full of lethal metal.

'Barclay! Stop fucking around!' he barked suddenly, making me jump. Barclay pointed a finger at his chest and pulled his best 'who, me?' look. I'd missed what he'd been doing but I would have put money on it contravening those four rules of gun law again.

Ward turned his attention back to his star pupil. 'Are you ready to fire your first load?' he asked.

It was making me feel nauseous. 'Yep.'

'Right. Aim at that target there and take your time.' I closed my left eye, bit my tongue in concentration and took aim. 'Don't jerk it, take the slack out of the trigger then squeeze, increasing the pressure until …'

Fuck me, that was loud. Echoing around the arched walls of the workshop it deafened us all and had both of them covering their ears but too late to save them. Barclay was shouting something at me but I was momentarily deaf. For seconds I thought I would live forever in a world of silence but slowly my ears adjusted and started to make sense of the world again, sounds edging in around the high pitched whine that would stay with me for the rest of the evening. The recoil and shock from the gun hadn't been as bad as I had expected, but the loud explosion of that first shot was painful.

A greater shock though was when we inspected the target. Wellwadayaknow? Bullseye! Slap bang in the middle of the target, which sadly looked larger close up, deflating my immediate sense of achievement. Ten out of ten. Ward looked genuinely impressed and tried to give me a celebratory hug which I stepped quickly away from.

'Complete fluke,' laughed Barclay.

'Do better,' I challenged.

Ward produced three oversized ear protector muff things from a cupboard. 'I should have got these out earlier.'

That was true. Barclay lifted his gun and took the pose, we covered our ears and he fired, not just once but four times in rapid succession.

The bullseye was untouched. The entire target was untouched. He had missed an A3 sheet of white paper from ten feet. Four times. Unbelievable.

'You've been practising, Barclay,' joked Ward. 'Last time you had trouble hitting the wall!'

I laughed and Barclay fired me his most withering glare. Ouch. How come he never missed with that?

'I'm tired, tired and bored,' Barclay offered as an excuse that no one was buying.

Even with the ear protectors my head was still ringing, my hearing dipping in and out as if there were child playing with the room's volume control.

But I didn't care. It was thrilling and I wanted to do it again. And again. And again. The purest of pleasure, firing a gun, was the biggest kick I could think of, better than sex, hotter than Chris Hemsworth, better and hotter than sex with Chris Hemsworth, this was intense yet intimate and just pure fucking amazing. More. I needed more.

And so we continued into the night. Me, an apparent natural even when we lowered the lights to better simulate the darkness we were accustomed to in our work. Bullseye after bullseye I hit, shredding the centres of the paper targets and hammering the wall behind like a drill.

Who would have thunk it?

And Barclay? Best we don't discuss his shooting prowess, as he was a sensitive soul despite all his front and bullshit and even he should have his pride respected.

But let me just say, he was absolutely fucking shit.

'That was unexpected,' said Barclay.

We were driving back from Owen Ward's after our evening of shooting the shit out of a workshop wall.

'You thought you would be good at it?' I asked, incredulous.

'I had to make you look good,' he lied, purely for his own benefit. He knew that I knew and I felt a warm glow inside at that fact.

We were back in the Uno, negotiating the potholes and puddles of an unadopted backstreet in the small hours. Street lighting was at a premium around here and the local council didn't think it was a worthwhile expense. I was enjoying the driving and manoeuvred the Italian antique with skilled dexterity that was not going to do my campaign to get a better set of wheels any good. I decided there and then that with the next pay day I would buy us a new car. I had seen a rather nifty looking black Alfa Romeo going for £5k on a car lot the day before and would make my move at daylight. That would surprise him. Fiat begone!

'Your shooting was exceptional,' said Barclay, a rare compliment indeed.

'You really thought so?' I mocked.

'Yes, Claire, I really thought so. And you know so. So let's stop pretending. I think by your sixth round we all figured it wasn't a fluke.'

'Maybe I've finally discovered my true vocation in life.' I was only half-joking. It had felt surprisingly... natural. I'd never been good at anything before. This was genuinely a first.

'Our gain is the British Shooting team's loss.'

I loved it.

'Claire,' said Barclay, snapping me from my daydream of Olympic Gold glory. It was never going to be an easy conversation when he used my name. There was something quite parental about that. 'Claire, are you absolutely sure you are comfortable with this?'

'What do you mean?'

'With us … and guns.'

'I'm not that comfortable with you and a gun, that's for sure,' I joked.

'I'm serious, Claire. This is not a path I expected us to go down.'

'But after Thug Number Two?'

'That was a one-off. I'm sure of it. It was careless and I didn't see it coming. I should have thought it through. We shouldn't have gone for someone like that, shouldn't have asked for so much but he… We will be more careful in future and shouldn't need the guns. Keep it small, like that school teacher I told you about.'

I wasn't convinced. 'We're playing a dangerous game here, Barclay, and it's only as a deterrent. If it hadn't been this one it could have been the next or the one after that. You know that. I know that. We've been naive thinking we could just walk away with the bag of cash every time and there was no risk.'

'A one-off.'

'It's not a one-off though, is it? That time without me when you shot the dog…'

'In the general direction of the dog,' he corrected me.

'Having seen you shoot, I think you aimed at the dog and missed from a yard away. Whatever. You carried a gun before and we can do that again. If you're uncomfortable with that I'll carry the gun and do the bloody pickups and drop offs and what not.'

'I'm not that comfortable with us being armed.'

'Well I'm not at all comfortable with us being unarmed. Especially as we're going to be without TNT for a few months.'

'TNT?'

'Thug Number Two. I think of him as TNT.'

'That's good. Hadn't occurred to me.' Barclay smiled, possibly for the first time in hours.

'So how about you trust me with this and I carry the gun then?'

'Like I say, I'm not happy about that.'

'Neither am I particularly, but I will feel safer.'

'We'll see,' he said. 'There may be other options.'

I seriously doubted it. We drove on but there were no more words, I wasn't going to change my mind, come what may.

The following morning I found a tired-looking Dawn sitting alone at the kitchen table.

'No Henry today?' I asked, making myself a quick coffee from the just boiled kettle.

'No. He didn't stay last night. He said something about feeding the homeless but…'

'But you weren't really listening?'

She sighed and smiled a defeated smile. 'You got it. Boy, how does he do it? Get him on a worthy subject and you can feel your will to live ebbing away with each word!'

I laughed. 'That is so true.'

'I know, I mean he is a good man, a kind man, a caring man but bloody hell, it can all be too much, can't it?'

'You've not even had a week of it,' I said.

'I'm not sure I can last that long. Surely it gets easier?'

I shrugged. They were doomed. End of story. Sad but inevitable, sorry to be the bearer of bad news. Pick yourself up and get yourself a gun. You won't believe the buzz, Dawn.

But that was a conversation maybe for another day. Instead I said: 'Barclay's in a funny mood these days.'

'How so?'

'We had a little accident the other evening and his muscle man got hurt. Barclay's taking it badly.'

'Losing his nerve?'

'It looks like it. I'm coming over as the tough one now.'

'And this guy's okay?'

'Should be, but its broken bones and they will take a while.'

'Oh.'

I was talking about TNT but my every thought was about the gun sitting tucked in my parka pocket upstairs. I was having trouble containing it, bursting to tell. I couldn't resist.

'I've got a gun!' I blurted.

'What? No way! Oh wow.' I couldn't tell if she was excited or scared. Probably a little of both.

'Have you shot anyone with it?' she asked.

'No. Don't be stupid – it's just for protection. But I had lessons last night and get this – I'm really, really good with it. I mean, Olympic medal good!'

She grinned, pleased that I was pleased.

'That's so cool.'

'Isn't it? I had no idea. Top marks. And get this – your brother can't hit a target from ten paces! Five paces even!'

We both laughed.

'Doesn't surprise me. That must have been so funny to see,' Dawn said. 'You should have filmed it – that's why God invented

YouTube, you know. I love it when he's embarrassed. Hilarious.'

'It was bloody fantastic,' I said. 'The better I got, the worse he was. Not just laughably bad, hysterically bad. And he couldn't see the funny side of it at all, got more and more sullen. We were killing ourselves!'

'We? Who were you with?'

'An old friend of Barclay's, he was the instructor. Owen Ward.'

Even in through the laughter I could see Dawn shudder at his name.

'Oooh, that creep. I don't like him. Tried to feel me up once. Nasty piece of work. Avoid.'

'I think we agree on that one.' I sipped my coffee. Too cold. 'I'm going to make another – want one?'

'Sure. Thanks.'

And with two mugs of Nestlé's finest, we sat and talked the morning away, setting the world to rights and Best Friends Forever.

My Nokia burst into life just as I was preparing lunch, an unappetising sandwich using ancient dry bread, even older shiny ham and cheese that was putting up a losing battle against the gathering mould.

I saw that it was 'Home' calling. What did Mum want? She only normally called at weekends, we had our routine, Sunday mornings at eleven. Odd.

'Hello?'

'Claire? It's Dad.' I don't think he'd ever called me before. My blood turned cold. He sounded serious.

'Hi Dad. What's up?' I was trying to sound flippant but this felt ominous.

'It's your mother, Claire. She's…she's been taken ill.'

I sat down on the kitchen stool with a bump.

'How ill?' a little voice asked.

'She's had a stroke. She's in hospital.'

Ohmigodohmigodohmigod. I couldn't think, couldn't speak. All noise disappeared from the room except his voice.

'Claire?'

'When?' I murmured, as if knowing details would make a blind bit of difference.

'Yesterday evening. It was very sudden. We've been in A&E all night. She's still there.' He was talking dispassionately, a newsreader on the telly talking about a humanitarian disaster thousands of miles away.

'One minute she was peeling potatoes. The next she was on the floor. Staring. She was just staring.' His recall of the details was un-Dadlike and alarming, as if he'd been taking notes for a memoir.

'I'm coming up,' I said without thinking.

'There's no point Claire. She's being looked after and is comfortable. The doctors sent us away. Paul's at school. I'll go back once I've had a few hours' sleep. Sharon from next door will go with me.'

Sharon may have been Mum's best friend, possibly her only friend outside of family, but Mum needed me.

'I'm still coming.'

'No you're not. She's okay. Not fine, but okay. I know it's hard to hear but there's nothing any of us can do and we just have to give her time to recover.' He was trying to sound as if he had this all under control and was an alpha male assuming his rightful position as head of the clan, but Dad was no alpha male, barely a beta bloke.

'I'm coming.' I was determined.

He sighed, resigned to my resolution and perhaps the recognition that I was heading north not just for Mum but for him, too. And me. This was, of course, mainly about me.

Chapter 24

My hands had been shaking as I typed on my laptop's keyboard, desperately seeking the fastest route. Google suggested that the journey from London to Edinburgh would take four and three quarter hours. Trainline disagreed and promised four hours twenty minutes. I booked on Trainline, but they both lied.

The journey took an eternity.

Dad's call had hurled me back down to Earth with an unfeeling, vicious bump. A crashing descent, from the thrill and highs of the shooting lesson to the harsh reality of ageing parents and fragile health. I felt empty, shaky, it was impossible to think straight, I just couldn't relax.

Dad was right: there was nothing else I could do, but I had to do something. Morbidly, I tried to recall my last words to Mum, something about the Attenborough show that had been on last week. So meaningless. So trivial. Was that it? Her last words? It sounded like she'd had a stroke. Would she be able to talk? Walk? Feed herself? Would I ever hear her voice again?

My mouth was dry no matter how much of the bottle of Volvic I drank. I stared, bleary-eyed, at the bleak, grey landscapes flashing by. Did the train normally take this long? Surely we were at least halfway there by now?

My phone buzzed. Three missed calls from Barclay and a text demanding 'WHERE ARE YOU?'. Sorry sir, not today. I checked the time. Barely an hour gone, not even a quarter of the journey completed. Dad said he'd pick me up from the station but I declined and said I'd get a cab.

I didn't want to put him out. He'd never find anywhere to park, anyway. I just didn't want him to drive.

I had no idea what to expect when I arrived and saw her. Strokes and heart attacks were what happened to other people, not us MacDonalds.

Fuck fuck fuck.

My thoughts blurred with the speeding scenery rushing passed the window. I just couldn't focus on anything for more than a second or two.

The rest of the journey dragged by at a snail's pace and I sat numb and dumb, motionless, emotional, still too stunned to move. The texts from Barclay kept coming. By the time we pulled in to Waverley I was exhausted.

Well, she looked fine. Happy and rested even. She smiled at me from her hospital bed and my heart sang and danced with joy.

But she didn't speak. Just smiled. For that moment, that would be enough. She had a loving smile and I felt as warm and special as I ever had in my life. It was all going to be okay. Panic over.

The nurse, far too young for such responsibility, was talking but I was catching one word in three.

'Minor. A few weeks. Too early to tell.' Words, just words. Meaningless words.

I took Mum's hand, ignoring the tube and savage needle that had punctured her precious, pale skin, and smiled back.

My eyes were brimming, cold tears running unchecked down my face.

'I'm here, Mum. Claire's here.'

She smiled. Just smiled. Her eyes moist but the recognition all there.

Like I said, that was enough.

Dad drove me back to our house, their home.

'She's not spoken since she fell,' he said, suddenly looking like a broken man. 'She looks okay but they don't know what's going on inside there.' He tapped his head with his right hand.

'Oh.' There was nothing that I could add.

'The doctor said her eyes are sharp and she's recognising us, but she's very sleepy and keeps drifting in and out. You were lucky; Sharon sat with her for hours and Mum just slept through it.

'Is that normal?' I asked.

'I don't know. Probably.'

I nodded. Life for Mum was going to be a series of 'probablies' and 'possiblies' from now on, nothing certain, nothing definite.

'She may have to stay in care for a while they said, depending how things go.' His voice was struggling to contain the emotions and dark thoughts that were best left unspoken.

'She'll be fine, Dad,' I touched his hand and he smiled at me.

'God I hope so,' he whispered, then he, too, went silent.

Home was cold. Literally and figuratively. Paul had locked himself away in his room and wasn't interacting with Planet Earth. That was a relief.

I made us our millionth cup of tea and broke open a pack of Digestives for comfort. Mine and his.

'She'll be fine,' I said for the thousandth time.

'I know,' he replied for the thousandth.

We weren't fooling anyone: we knew nothing.

My phone rang. 'Shouldn't you get that?' Dad asked.

'It's only work.'

'You shouldn't ignore it. Is it your boss?'

I nodded, torn between two worlds and lost in both.

Dad took his mug in both hands and looked on the verge of tears. I'd never seen my father cry before. Not out of sadness. Not out of fear.

He took a deep breath to compose himself. 'Claire. If she needs … rehabilitation, professional assistance, would you be able to help me with some money?'

I nodded. 'Of course,' I managed, almost a whisper. He was still in shock, struggling to make sense of it all.

'Thanks.'

We stared at our mugs. So little to say.

Dad had been right. There was little I could do there, nothing I could help with. Sharon was 'popping in' and sorting out the cooking and cleaning, Mum's fall giving her suddenly something to fill her empty hours next door, her husband having walked out several months earlier. Mum had always said she was too good for him.

Mum had always said…

'Dad, I can stay for as long as you need me.'

Pulling his shoulders back he straightened up in the kitchen chair he was sitting on, only to slouch again, just too much effort.

'Thanks but you need to get back to your life. We'll be fine. She'll be fine. Stay the night but I think you should get back down to that new job of yours tomorrow. All okay with that?'

'It's going fine thanks. Busy.' Right on cue Barclay rang again. I cut it off and Dad shook his head.

'Don't do that, Claire. It's too important. Your mother won't want you to lose your job over this … little set back.'

Just don't ask exactly what I'm doing, Dad – we didn't need a heart attack to the add to the stroke.

'And the money's good?'

'Better, and I can spare some so please don't worry about it. I know it isn't easy but I've got plenty. I want to help.'

'It will help,' he said. 'I think I'll need to look at moving your mother into a private home. The hospital says she'll be okay to come home in a few days but it will take time and I'll need help. Professional help. Sharon's been brilliant but your Mum needs more than that and I think the hospital needs the bed back. Bloody cuts.'

'Sure Dad. Whatever it takes.'

'Thank you Claire Bear, you're a godsend.'

'How much exactly will it take?' asked Claire Bear.

'It's expensive.'

I knew it would be. 'How much, Dad, and I can transfer some when I get back?'

He took a sharp intake of breath. 'Ten thousand for a few months' care.'

Christ. My silence spoke volumes I guess, and he quickly followed with: 'Too much?'

'No, that's fine.'

'You sure? I hate to ask but…'

'Don't worry about it Dad. I'll sort it out when I get home.'

'Another reason to leave tomorrow then. And thanks. That's tremendous. One less thing for us to worry about.'

'No worries,' I said, but he could tell that I was lying.

Our conversation stumbled and stuttered on through several more cups of tea and the whole packet of biscuits. What to talk about? We didn't want to talk about Mum or the money and I certainly didn't want to open up about Barclay or Tom Thomas and we had nothing else – any family reminiscences would have been tinged with the uncertainty about the future. After an hour I realised that this is why Dad wanted me not to come and was now pushing me out the door as soon as he could – this was almost as hard for him as the stroke that had silenced Mum, the realisation that he didn't know me at all and I hardly knew him.

My visit was proving a sad and empty gesture, salving only my guilt and comforting no one.

The following morning I sat at the breakfast table, the dry toast in my mouth tumbling like laundry, unswallowable. This was doing no one any good. I said my goodbyes and boarded the 9.30 from Waverley Station and back to Barclay.

At least he'd stop bloody ringing me now.

Chapter 25

It was cold and dark outside, but the atmosphere in the Uno was even colder and darker. I had brought my gun with me and Barclay was not a happy bunny, no sir.

'I thought I told you not to bring that,' he said.

'Not in so many words. You made it clear that you weren't comfortable or happy, but there wasn't a definitive 'no'. Besides, you're not my keeper.'

'I am your employer, your boss.'

'I prefer to think of it as you're the brains of our gang, I'm the more practical one.'

He considered that for a few seconds – I don't think he'd thought of it like that before.

'I do not think you should be armed. It's asking for trouble.'

'And I would be happier with TNT with us. But you can't have everything.'

He said nothing.

We were parked around the back of some abandoned warehouses in the East India docks, the demolition notices suggesting that this was the next target for the insatiable developers' non-stop glass and steel roadshow. We were half an hour early, and Barclay had asked me to park a distance away from the pick-up in case I got ideas with the gun.

As if. Even I would have trouble hitting anything from that distance in the dark.

So we had plenty of time to fill the air with a continuation of the stuttering disagreement about my sudden lust for weaponry.

'It's only the teacher this time. You don't need a gun.' He was sounding like a broken record.

'Ward said I should get comfortable with having it on me at all times.'

'What does he know?'

'He knows enough to be the expert you brought in to teach us,' I snapped.

'But this woman is twenty-five years' old and it's only ten grand. Lunch money to her. She's as timid as they come. She is not going to pose a physical threat whatsoever.'

'If she's in a car she's as dangerous as the guy who hit Number Two.'

'She won't be.'

'Or if she's armed, we should be armed too.'

'Great, the American gun lobby argument. There's the arms race in a nutshell. They may have one so we have to have one.'

Silence. He may have had a point but I wasn't biting.

'I think the guy last time was spooked by Number Two. We won't have that problem again,' Barclay said.

'You're not scary on your own. I'm not exactly terrifying either.'

'You scare me at times, Claire. Not who you are, but what you are becoming.'

So dramatic. I attempted to laugh that off. 'You think I'm out of control? Am I not the monster you were hoping to create, Dr Frankenstein?' I mocked.

He almost smiled. Almost. 'I think your independence and appetite for danger are heading a little out of my comfort zone.'

'Not necessarily a bad thing. Beats complacency hands down.'

'Possibly.'

'Definitely.'

'Probably,' he conceded.

I looked at my watch. Almost time. Just as well, the car was getting colder despite the pathetic efforts of the Fiat's blowers.

'I tell you what, I'll prove you can rely on me to stay calm. I'll do this one.'

'What?'

'Let me do this pick-up. Like you say, what's the harm? She's a young teacher at a posh private school for Christ's sake, where's the risk in that? It's ten grand or her career and reputation and marriage and easy life down the pan. She's the easiest pick-up we've done and I won't exactly terrify her with my size 10 mega frame, will I?'

He raised an eyebrow. He wasn't convinced.

'It will be fine. I will be fine. Ten minutes, tops.' I winked as I released the seat belt and opened my door. He shook his head, but knew he was beaten.

'I'll move the car over under that light so you can see it easily when you get back.'

'Keep the engine running,' I said.

'Of course.' He waved and I turned to go, making my way around a high wire fence to the agreed rendezvous point at an old, disused garage just off the main road. Behind me I heard Barclay rev up the Uno's engine and I turned and saw him move it under the street lamp.

I felt pretty pumped up. It felt good. And, more to the point…

I still had my gun in my pocket if I needed it. My TNT-sized worries were a thing of the past.

The pick-up point was around the corner from where Barclay had maneuvered the car. Fifty yards away stood a desolate, deserted petrol station, a long dormant sign had shouted the Texaco brand in more prosperous times. Now it stood as a sad reminder of how the much-vaunted redevelopment of East London in 2012 had stalled and failed to live up to even its modest promise of regeneration for the area. A streetlight flickered and died, then relit itself only to die again. It just couldn't be bothered and I could understand that; as inspiring landscapes to illuminate, this one left a ridiculous amount to be desired.

Barclay sure could pick 'em.

There was no sign of the teacher. No sign of life at all at first, and then, as if to deliberately prove me wrong, a fox ran up to one of the long-dead pumps. At least, I hoped it was a fox – the rats out this way can grow pretty big I'd been told. I shivered involuntarily. Not a fan of rats. I have a thing about their worm-like tails. Urgggh.

I waited five minutes, hands pressed deep into my coat pockets, seeking warmth but just finding some old crumbs and sweet wrappers. And my gun. My breath formed pale clouds in the cold and I amused myself for what must have been seconds seeing if I could form smoke rings with my mouth.

Don't bother trying it. You can't. It doesn't work. Not for the first time I wondered if I should take up smoking for nights like these.

Suddenly the fox scurried away – something had spooked it. Coming from the opposite direction was a huddled figure, glancing from side to side.

The teacher?

But as she neared I realised that there wasn't just one person but two, the taller one's arm wrapped tightly around the shoulder of the smaller. Shit. There was a bag held in the taller person's left hand. Presumably the money. Definitely the teacher, but who was that she was with?

For the first time that morning I had doubts and I found my hand crawling unbidden to my coat's inner pocket, finding and rubbing the gun's grip for comfort, possibly assurance even.

Not to plan. What would Barclay do? Fuck it up probably, going on his recent efforts. Never mind. I strode purposefully towards them and they didn't back away.

It was the teacher.

I was about twenty feet away from them and could now see a blonde woman, dressed in a thick, dark expensive looking coat with a taller young man, much younger than her that was for sure. Her schoolboy lover? He certainly didn't look like a sixty-year-old City millionaire, that was for sure.

Interesting. I coughed to clear my throat and spoke, my voice startlingly me with its nerveless assurance that broke the night's silence:

'Samantha Fielding?'

She nodded but moved behind the boy for protection. In the darkness he looked mature for his fifteen years, already six-foot-tall but slender as only teenage boys can be, a bulky puffy jacket giving the impression of a greater bulk but it was his spindly legs in slim fit jeans hanging below that gave away the true slightness of his frame. He looked vaguely absurd, all Uniqlo bulk and teenage unmuscled gangly limbs, the torso of a dark Michelin man balanced precariously on a couple of spindly sticks.

I could take him. Easy. Was this really the best protection she could find? She should mix in lower social circles.

'You were supposed to come alone. That was the arrangement,' I said, short and sharp in my disapproval. Although the words came from my mouth I couldn't believe that was me talking. I was so authoritative. I was just so in command. There was no quivering of nerves in my clear, succinct delivery.

Claire my girl, you're a natural.

Samantha shrank further behind the puffer jacket's protection.

'Sorry.' So quiet I barely heard her.

'We have the money,' said the boyfriend.

'So you did understand the instructions,' I said. 'You just chose to be selective about which ones you followed.'

'You can't expect Samantha to come here alone. No woman would feel safe in a place like this.'

I don't know – I didn't feel particularly threatened myself. I was actually enjoying how this was turning out, truth be told.

'Bring the bag here, please.' I said, then silently cursed myself for the sudden politeness of the 'please' – and I had been doing so well with my tough girl impression. Damn. Concentrate.

He edged forward, the quaking teacher moving with him, still hiding behind his back as if she thought it concealed her from my steely judgement.

'How much?' I asked.

'Ten thousand in tens, as you demanded,' he said.

'Doesn't she talk?' I asked, nodding at the figure cowering behind him.

'We decided that I'd be better at the talking.'

'But you're not supposed to be here, are you?'

'No, but I am. Here's the money.' He dropped the bag on the floor, but it was still too far away for me to reach it. I took a step forward and he put a foot on the bag.

'I thought we should talk first though?'

I straightened. 'Talk? You are not really in a position to make demands, are you? Neither of you. You've seen what we have on you two. Think of the consequences for Samantha if we shared that. There is nothing to talk about. You've been playing naughty, illegal games and these are the naughty, illegal consequences.'

'If you take this, how do we know that you won't call again and ask for more?'

'You don't. But we won't. You already live with the guilt of what you have done. At best you have my word that this is it, a one-off transaction. You won't hear from us again.'

He shook his head. 'I'm sorry, but that's not very reassuring. All we know about you is that you're blackmailers who hacked Sam's phone. That doesn't make you super trustworthy in my book.'

'Then like I said, you don't know. And chances are you will continue to jump with every phone ring or rattle of the letterbox, fearing the worst. But you already do that. Paying us … me … is the only way you have to stop this.'

'Or I could stop you…'

Suddenly he reached into his inside pocket and before I could register his movement he had a gun in his hand. Smaller than mine, it could have been a fake or a starter pistol – I just couldn't tell. But it was a gun nevertheless. Pointed straight at me.

Fuck.

I froze. The teacher shrank away from him. 'Anthony, you said you wouldn't…'

Instinctively I put my hands up. 'Hold on there,' it was almost a whisper, my bravado just about holding on. 'Don't do anything hasty here.' I needed to step this down a notch. I had to think quickly. In a flash of inspiration, I surpassed myself. 'This is all being filmed by my colleague.'

That got him. Confused, he looked quickly around the open dark spaces behind me, searching for the fictional cameraman I'd just invented. Nothing. Nowt. Well, what exactly did he expect? He'd already said I was untrustworthy.

When his nervous gaze returned to me I had my own gun in my hands, pointing straight at him. A classic Tarantino Mexican stand-off.

His pistol was wavering but I held mine firmly in both hands, my left supporting the rock steady right. Legs slightly apart. The perfect firing posture feeling suddenly so natural.

My finger was tellingly already on the trigger. Unlike him I knew exactly what I was doing. I had been trained by a professional. One whole lesson. I was ready. Steady Eddie ready.

'Hold on there,' he managed, echoing my sentiment of just a few seconds earlier. 'We can talk…'

But he fired, more pop than bang, a clumsy mess of a shot, whistling off into the night's darkness, all bark and no bite.

I didn't make the same mistake. I shot straight and true.

Chapter 26

I had aimed at his shoulder but it was the side of his head that exploded. So much for shooting to wound rather than kill. Shit. What would Barclay say? All those assurances I'd given him and I fuck it up at the first hurdle.

So I ran. Ran like I'd never run before in my life. Drop the gun? Keep the gun? My fingers felt welded to its grip. I couldn't let go, the warmth of the metal strangely seductive. I loved that gun. We were inseparable.

Run.

Was she chasing me or seeing to what was left of her fallen lover? I wasn't waiting to find out, didn't even turn to see. I just ran. Arms pumping, cheeks puffing, breath already shortening. Run, girl, run.

I turned left, down the dark alleyway that led round the side of the abandoned warehouse. There were no lights, no paving and I stumbled on the uneven surface but I couldn't stop, I ran as fast as I could, my legs, sides, lungs all protesting at this sudden call to action.

There was the wire fencing a few yards ahead. Could I take it in my stride? From behind I could hear her shout for me to stop. At least she'd stopped screaming. I slipped the gun back into my coat pocket and took the shorter route, jumping at the fencing, surprising myself by getting a firm grip with both hands and hauling myself up like I was on an assault course.

'Stop, bitch!'

'Well that's nice,' I thought as I dropped over the other side, my ankle turning slightly on landing but just a tweak. I could understand she was upset, but there was no need to make it personal. I brushed myself down then started to run again, though every muscle was howling for me to slow down. I was just too out of condition for this running lark. If it hadn't been for the adrenaline surge I'd have been finished already.

I could hear the blood hammering in my ears, felt my lungs close to bursting. Any further and I was sure I would collapse. I turned left around another building and then suddenly there was a pool of light ahead, a single streetlamp picking out the familiar Fiat parked at the roadside.

Had he heard my gun shot? Or was Barclay oblivious to the drama I'd suddenly ignited?

'Barclay!' I attempted to shout as I neared the car, so short of breath I thought I would die.

He saw me and wound the window down.

'All go to plan?' he asked.

'No it…no it fucking didn't.' I fell against the passenger side and wrenched the door open, clambering in.

'Where's the money?'

'What?' Barely able to speak.

'The money. Where's the money?'

'He's dead. I shot him. He's dead. Drive!'

'Fuck.'

He turned the key and the engine coughed into life. Slamming it into first and flooring the accelerator, we shot off, as fast as my beloved Fiat Uno could manage.

'Fuck. Fuck. Fuck.' He was scolding himself, not me, and he muttered curses under his breath like a repentant litany.

There was nothing I could say. What had I done? WHAT

HAD I FUCKING DONE?

I think I could safely assume that I was not popular. Barclay's near silence was more menacing and abusive than any emotional volley of derogatory vilification he could have thrown at me. I shrank into the passenger seat, cowering in my shock, cowardice and shame.

He drove surprisingly slowly, but snatched at the gear changes and was late to signal when turning. The roads were surprisingly busy and I was for once grateful for the anonymity of the Uno. His ire was all too apparent. I was furious with myself but I didn't think he'd be sympathetic.

It was all Claire's fault. Muppet.

Before we reached the main road he stopped the car and we swapped seats. There'd been a shooting. The police would be everywhere. No point in taking any stupid risks with him driving us.

Any more stupid risks, I should say.

I turned the Uno's headlights back on and we pulled away, just another couple in a clapped-out car on the streets of South London.

'You said 'he'?' he asked, glaring at me.

'It was not my fault!' I pleaded, knowing that was at best only half true. 'The teacher had come with her boyfriend and he did all the talking. He drew a gun on me and said he was going to silence me.'

'Really?'

'It was all so quick. He may have said 'stop' rather than 'silence', I'm not sure.'

'But he had a gun?

'A pistol. Honest, Barclay, honest.' I touched his sleeve to reassure him but he flinched it away. I still could not make eye contact.

'I heard two shots. The first was more a pop,' he said.

'That was him. Not me, him. It was a small gun.'

'So you shot him?'

'I aimed for his shoulder, Barclay, I didn't try to kill him, just wound.'

'His leg would have been an easier target.'

I didn't think so – I recalled the spindly legs – but decided to keep that to myself. It was not a time for flippancy.

'Maybe,' I mumbled.

'And you killed him stone dead?'

It was all so quick. Was I certain? 'There was a burst of blood and stuff.'

He groaned. 'Shit. Not quite the crack shot you thought you were then?'

'No.'

Suddenly I started shaking uncontrollably as I tried to blink away the tears.

Barclay said nothing. He knew there was no need, that the impact of what I had just done had finally hit me. I shuddered in dry sobs for minutes, uncontrollable, inconsolable. There was nothing he could add.

Chapter 27

I couldn't sleep. I lay wide-eyed on top of my covers, fully dressed, waiting for the police to break down the door, surge in, guns drawn, and drag me away.

But there was nothing.

Every muscle tensed with every dog bark and car passing in the street. My mind just wouldn't rest. I tried in vain to sleep. Toss, turn, toss, turn, flip the pillow, toss, turn.

I'd killed a man. No, not even that. I'd killed a schoolboy.

I put the bedside radio on and listened to the local station's all-night phone-in marathon, straining my ears and holding my breath with every news bulletin.

Nothing.

(Not yet, anyway.)

I replayed those final moments of the boy's life over and over again in my mind, the pop of his pistol diminishing in my mind's echoes, the explosion of my gun amplifying.

In my head I shouted, 'drop the pistol or I will shoot' before I fired. I screamed, 'please put down the fucking gun', but to no avail.

I still shot. He still fell.

I tried to slow the harrowing images down to zoom in to assess the impact of my fateful bullet. But there was only the burst of blood and bone, his collapse, the screams of the teacher.

The teacher. No doubt to be referred to in police reports as 'the witness'.

I sat bolt upright. She would be a witness. She had seen me. She could select me from a line-up. She would point the finger that locked me away for life.

My heart was galloping in my chest, my skin suddenly cold and clammy as the penny dropped. I tried to calm the panic, telling myself that the hoodie and bulk of my scarf had hidden my face sufficiently, but I was convincing no one, least of all me.

But it had been so dark out there, I couldn't see them clearly, surely they couldn't see me? Identify me?

I wasn't buying it.

I was, in a word, fucked.

The 6am news was the first to mention the shooting:

'Reports are coming in of an overnight shooting, believed to be gang-related, in South-East London. Police were called around 2am and a fifteen-year-old youth has been taken to hospital with gunshot wounds. Lewisham hospital described his condition as serious but not life threatening. A number of witnesses are helping police with their enquiries.

'In football, Chelsea lost again...'

I sat upright, suddenly alert. The relief washed over me instantly. He was alive. 'Thank fuck!' I cried out.

He was alive! Every word was precious to me.

What did a 'serious condition' mean? Can't be as bad as 'critical', surely? That was good, wasn't it?

Why did they say it was 'gang-related'? There had been the recent spate of shootings across South London at weekends, maybe they thought this was another?

Why the plural, 'Gunshot wounds'? I had only shot once. For a second I started to wonder if this was a report on a different incident, another fifteen-year-old felled in his prime but I quickly dismissed the idea. This was South East London, not LA. No, I guess they wouldn't know how many times he'd been shot until they cleaned the mess up and got the forensic teams in. I could tell them, but there was no way I was going to help in their investigation on this one.

And what was this all about 'a number of witnesses'? Even Barclay hadn't seen what had happened.

My relief at the schoolboy's survival proved momentary as doubt took hold – what had happened? Had we been truly alone? Had there been another car out there in the darkness? Or maybe some over-attentive fly in the ointment passer-by had heard the guns? That would make some sense, although the boyfriend's pistol had made an almost comical pop, no louder than a Christmas cracker, whereas my gun had detonated with a deafening roar, shaking windows and glass for miles around.

My claim to have fired second was not going to stand up in court.

I spent the next hour waiting for further updates but the morning news was all about plunging stock markets in the Far East and tributes to an actor who had died over the weekend, much to the surprise of most of the world who had thought he'd died decades ago.

The 7am bulletin added nothing. I decided to get up and get over to Barclay's as soon as I could. No point whatsoever in hanging around. I knew far more than the BBC and probably the police, and I wasn't going to share with anyone except Barclay.

I was still fully dressed and didn't bother changing. I needed to move quickly, get over to his place and discuss this.

Dawn was in the hallway.

''Morning. What's going on, fake sister?' she asked innocently.

'I need to see Barclay. Now,' I said, pushing passed her.

'Woah. Hold on there, cowboy. What's up? Why all the noise

and naughty words?'

'I…I…I fucking shot someone, Dawn.'

Open-mouthed, she staggered back. 'What?'

'It all went wrong, too fast. He shot, I shot. I shot a boy.'

'You? Shot? A? Boy?' Repeating each word, hammering home my pain.

'Yes. Yes. YES. I'm going to see Barclay.'

'I'm coming with you. Give me five minutes.'

I tried to explain it to Dawn as we set off for Barclay's, but I was making little sense. She couldn't take it in. Shock was the order of the day. We took the train – the Uno suddenly looked even more risky an option than usual.

'So you were shot?'

'Shot at. But not hit.'

'Did it hurt?'

'I wasn't hit. I told you.'

'But you shot and hit him?'

'Yes. In the head. On the head. The side of his head. Maybe his shoulder. He's not dead. It's only serious. It's not critical.'

'There's a difference?'

'I think so. I hope so. Serious isn't critical.'

'Or fatal?'

'You're not helping, Dawn,' I snapped.

'Sorry. Well, that's good then,' she said.

'It's not good. I don't think I'd call it good.' I was talking too fast.

'It could be worse.'

'I'm not sure how. I'm a wanted woman, Dawn. And not in a good way.'

'Let's see what Barclay thinks.'

I think I already knew what Barclay thought.

When we arrived I felt immediately that something was seriously wrong. Correction, something *else* was seriously wrong. Dawn and I stepped out of the lift into the tasteful luxury of the 12th floor hallway. There were just two penthouse apartments, two doors, and one was ajar: Barclay's. Dawn was distracted by the minimalist elegance of the corridor, the art deco wall lights and spectacular Docklands views through the windows, but I feared the worst and muttered 'no, no, no' under my breath as I approached his apartment and knocked tentatively on the open door.

'Hello? Barclay?' No response. I pushed it wider. 'Hello?'

The last time I had been here it had been a stunning, impeccably decorated pristine Man Cave of technology, a dazzling show home designed to take your breath away. But now…

My hand rose involuntarily to my mouth.

'Shit.'

'Wow,' said Dawn. 'Way to go, bro.'

'Barclay!' I called again, louder. 'Barclay!'

The three shattered over-sized TVs hung from the walls by their cables. There was broken glass everywhere; the beautiful smoked surface of Barclay's desk had been destroyed by what looked like crushing hammer blows, the computer monitors suffering similar devastation. No sign of the laptops or computers, but keyboards had been stamped on and cables ripped from their cubby holes were everywhere. The filing cabinets had been forced open and hundreds of pieces of paper were scattered around the room. The leather of the sofa had been slashed with a knife and ripped open, the filling disgorged over the floor. Adding to the disarray someone had kindly thrown old, discarded takeaway food from the kitchen at the room's white walls, adding a pernicious odour to the brutality of the wreckage in the room.

What had happened here? I strode around the room, too stunned to take it all in.

'Barclay?' There was a slight tremor in my voice. I don't know why I was still calling as it was pretty obvious that he wasn't there. Dawn ran into the kitchen where I had previously been so appalled by the filth and squalor. She ran straight out again, a look of disgust on her face. It wasn't just me then.

Had Barclay run riot in his anger? Unlikely. Very unlikely. Someone else had done this…this…

I ripped open his bedroom door, the overturned bed was littered with his expensive shirts, coats and suits ripped from their hangers in some frantic wardrobe search, overturned drawers and their contents strewn around the room, the full-length mirror smashed into a million pieces. There was a smear of blood on the wall. I touched it. Still wet. Barclay's? His attacker's?

Or had he now abandoned me? Damn you, Barclay, we were a team, weren't we? I needed you as much as you needed me.

Suddenly Dawn cried out. I raced out of the bedroom and almost sent her flying as she fled from the bathroom. She turned back and pointed at the sink, staring wide-eyed, hand over her mouth.

There, by the toothbrush and glass, were four adult fingernails. Not clippings, but whole, bloody fingernails. Male. Manicured. And a blood-soaked pair of heavy duty household pliers.

I screamed, too.

We both ran for the door, then stumbled into the lift and out of the building and back outside as fast as we could.

That had been horrible. Unthinkably horrible.

We just had to run.

We clambered up the stairs at the DLR station and threw ourselves through the closing doors of a departing train, breathless and scared. Scared shitless.

Oh Barclay.

Chapter 28

We had only been gone an hour but that had been sufficient time for some arsehole to break in and ransack my place, too. The busted front door was dangling from a single hinge, precariously suspended from the brute force that had torn it open.

Worse, that nosey cantankerous bitch from the flat above was sitting on her stairs judging us.

'What was all that noise?' she demanded.

'What do you think?' I spat, pushing the door open. 'We organised a wild party before we went out.'

She slammed her door at my sarcasm.

Since Henry's departure the place had never been the tidiest, but our uninvited visitor had elevated it to a new level of chaos. In truth, I had actually seen it messier, but this intrusion into my sanctuary had me reeling.

Dawn ran to her room but quickly returned.

'Fingernails?'

'No. God, no. Just all my stuff everywhere. Like they were looking for something. Nothing missing. A couple of bottles of wine smashed but that's the worst of it. The front room doesn't look that different from how we left it.'

She had a point. It wasn't that bad, more tossed than trashed, as if whoever did it had cared a little more than they had at Barclay's where they'd gone for maximum impact. In fact, if it hadn't been for the broken door and Mrs Nosey-bastard I possibly wouldn't have noticed immediately anything untoward had happened.

But that didn't make it good.

'My laptop's gone, the one Barclay gave me,' I said, spotting the empty space on the dining table where I'd left it earlier, the charger still there like a parentless child.

'Anything else?'

'Nothing I can... shit...' I ran into my bedroom, and, ignoring its upturned drawers and my clothes scattered on the bed and floor, reached up to the top of my wardrobe.

It had gone.

'SHIT!' I shouted.

'What?'

'My gun. They've taken the gun.'

The gun with my fingerprints all over it.

'Got any vodka?' asked Dawn.

I shook my head. Henry had left behind some pretty chamomile tea bags at the back of the cupboard. The packet promised that a 'delicious cup of calming tea would ease away the day's tensions and stresses'. Fat chance, but I was willing to try anything. The packet lied about it being delicious: we each took one sip from our mugs, pulled our best grapefruit faces and poured it down the sink in synchronised disgust.

'Coffee?' I suggested.

'That'll do.' She smiled, but it was forced. It was starting to sink in.

'I'll need to get that door fixed,' I said, attempting everyday conversation as I spooned the coffee into our two mugs and boiled the kettle again.

'Do you think it was the same people who turned over Barclay's?' Dawn asked. We were avoiding talking about her brother's disappearance and the grisly nails. It was just too shocking for us to process I guess.

'Could be. Doesn't seem as violent here though. Not much broken – the telly's fine, the bin's been rifled through but at least they didn't hurl the shit inside all around the place.'

'You've no idea who?'

'Not really.'

'And Barclay?'

I put her coffee down in front of her with a little more force than I'd intended, slopping some over the table.

'I think someone's taken him.'

'What do we do now?'

'I don't…I don't have a clue.'

'We can't call the police, not with the gun and everything.'

'No, no,' panic was rising in me again. 'Definitely no police.'

But I had to call the police. Kind of. I had to call the only person I could think of who knew Barclay, who might be able to help. I called Tom Thomas. He said he'd be right over. My hero. My knight in shining … y'know. Help was on its way. Sanity would return and it couldn't come soon enough.

As we waited an eternity for Tom I broke open a packet of Digestives and I tried to explain the shooting to Dawn. In the cold light of day, after what we'd just found at Barclay's and in our own place, it was starting to feel all too real and less dreamlike.

'It was all quick, really really fast,' I said. 'We'd been expecting just this teacher who'd been having an affair, a classic Barclay set up, seemed fool-proof, low or no risk, the simplest of jobs. After the hit and run we were both a little jumpy and we'd been arguing about the gun but I took it anyway. He wasn't happy but if I hadn't made a move we would have been sitting in that bloody poxy car all night quarrelling.'

'And she wasn't alone?'

'No, she had her underage teenage boyfriend with her, fresh out of nappies and all adolescent macho posturing in pimples, trying to impress her.'

'He's not impressing anyone right now,' she said.

I sighed. 'He wasn't exactly wowing the ladies last night either. He had the money but he had a gun, too. I don't think he had intended to kill me or anything, just wave it around a bit to try and scare me. But he was shaking so much when he drew it I thought it would go off whatever his intentions so when he threatened me I drew mine. He shot first. He definitely shot first.'

'So you shot in self-defence?'

'Pretty much. He missed, I hit. I'd been aiming at his shoulder but think I caught the side of his head. There was blood and skin in a puffy cloud but it was all so fast and I hope it wasn't as bad as it looked. It was dark so I couldn't see clearly. You want to know the funny thing? It felt faster than normal speed, like it was all playing on fast forward rather than the slow motion you see on telly.'

'Maybe you should go and see him in hospital, check he's okay?'

'Should I do that before or after I hand myself in to the police?'

Dawn shrugged. I'd thought overnight of both visiting him and the police and neither had made it onto my To Do list for the day.

'What happened then?'

'I panicked. I don't feel so bad about that now – it was a perfect time to panic. I just ran away. All too fast. I just had to get away from there. No point trying to be cool about it, just needed to escape.'

'And Barclay?'

'He wasn't exactly delighted. I don't think he'll be renewing his membership to my Fan Club.'

'He's probably got other things on his mind now.'

'Yep. Tom should be here in a minute – he only lives in Lee. There's something you should know about him.'

'Is it important?'

'He's a copper.'

The look on her face was priceless and I found myself smiling for the first time in what felt like forever.

'Seriously?'

'Well, not a policeman in the strictest sense, he's a consultant. And he's been investigating Barclay.'

I think she had stopped breathing. I started laughing.

'No way.'

'Yes way.'

'Oh, this just got stupidly interesting. At least he may have an idea who's behind this break-in shit and the nails and everything.'

'And where Barclay's gone?' I added.

'That too. Wow. You're a dark horse, dating the guy investigating you! His name's Tom Thomas?'

'Not his real name, that's my joke name for him. His real name's one of those American Polish names, Pedzinski or something like that.' I helped myself to my fourth Digestive. I needed sugar and then more sugar and bugger the waistline. 'When we last spoke I was a bit short with him.'

'Amazing. Play with fire, girl.'

There was a knock on the barely-vertical door and a familiar face poked around the frame.

'You know that door's not very secure and ... Jeezus. What happened here?'

Nice to see you too, Tom.

'We had a visitor,' I said.

'So I see.'

'And this is Dawn, Barclay's sister and my roomie.'

'Hi Dawn.'

She smiled a stupid, tight-lipped smile, suddenly shy.

He took a chair at the table. 'So it was a bit garbled on the phone but you reckon Barclay's been abducted?' He helped himself to a biscuit – supplies were running dangerously low.

'Looks like it. His flat's been smashed up and there's his stuff everywhere but no sign of him,' I said.

'Bad?' he asked.

'Party of the Century bad.'

'And no trace of him at all?'

'Well, that's not strictly true,' said Dawn. 'There was a sign of him. Four in fact.'

I hadn't been sure how much to share with Tom but there was little point in hiding anything now: 'There were four fingernails, covered in blood, in the bathroom.'

'And some bloody pliers,' added Dawn, helpfully.

It didn't seem to faze Tom. 'I told you he played dangerous games, Claire.'

'Yeah, I know, but…'

'No buts Claire. I wasn't fucking about.'

I stared into my empty mug, unable to look into his eyes.

'Have you got any idea where he may be?' Dawn asked.

'I'll have to go back and check the files again, see if there are any clues there.'

'Those…those files,' I asked nervously. 'Do they mention me at all?'

'What do you think?' he asked, his gaze steely and unblinking.

'Yes?' I suggested, barely audible. He didn't answer and just left it there, cruelly, letting me have my moment of stomach-clamping fear. Then, quietly, he said:

'No. There is no mention of you in the files. There should be, but I couldn't do it.'

I wanted to hug him and kiss him and throw him on my bed and break it with my best 'thankyouthankyouthankyou' sex, but it wasn't the time or the place and I don't think Dawn would have enjoyed the floor show. The weakest of smiles crossed his lips.

'Let me check those files back at the office and see what I can find. We may have to try a few places but I guess you guys have nothing else to do today?'

We both nodded and thanked him.

My hero. My knight in shining…et cetera, et cetera.

Chapter 29

It wasn't until late afternoon before we heard from Tom again. The sun, what little of it we'd seen that week, was long gone and a light, irritating drizzle was confusing indecisive umbrella owners in the streets. My Nokia lit shockingly with its oh-so-last-decade ringtone.

'I think I've an idea where we may find him,' said Tom. 'I'm on my way over. I'll be about thirty minutes – rush hour and all that.'

'Okay. Will you need anything to eat?'

'I can pick up some Indian on the way over if you like.'

My stomach grumbled its agreement before I could answer.

'Indian?' I asked Dawn. She nodded furiously.

'Great,' I said to Tom. 'But don't get too much.'

'There's no such thing as too much Indian,' he joked. 'Besides, could be a long night. Best we fuel up.'

He brought too much. If I'd eaten another mouthful I would have exploded all over our newly re-tidied flat. Temptingly, that last poppadum was calling to me.

Man it was good. I was starting to feel human for the first time in an age.

'Where do you think he is again?' I asked.

'It's this Bartholomew guy I mentioned. He's a City financier, but that's just a cover for all kinds of illegal stuff.'

I wasn't letting on that I'd not only seen the guy but had also been with Barclay when our first attempt to pick up the money had gone so spectacularly tits-up, with poor old TNT paying the price – if Tom's investigation hadn't gleaned that, I was buggered if I was going to offer up the info.

'How illegal?' asked Dawn.

'Front page illegal. Headline News illegal. If exposed this guy would be international news, it's that big 'n' bad. We have our own investigations into some of his enterprising adventures but he has friends in very high places and we've nothing concrete to prosecute with. Barclay decided he would take a more vigilante approach I guess, cut out the middle man and just pump the guy for as much as he can.'

'How did he find out about Bartholomew?' Dawn asked.

'His usual methods, I'd suspect. He'd have hacked a laptop or Wi-Fi network or mobile. He's good with that kind of thing. There aren't many software flaws or bugs that Barclay can't exploit. That's how I first got involved. His activities have been known about for years in both good circles and bad, but it's always been anonymous – believe it or not he doesn't have the rampant 'look at ME!' ego that more often than not exposes the bad boys in the hacking community. He's not been after corporate dollars or making political statements, he's so low key, almost out of sight he's so low, never greedy and so … so good it's impressive. Very impressive.' He shook his head and smiled. 'So impressive.'

'But Bartholomew?' she asked.

'Bartholomew's different from Barclay's usual targets. Far bigger scale, a different league from the small fry our friend normally goes for. This guy's massively wealthy, and smart too. He knows people who know how to deal with irritations like Barclay. That's what I don't get – why go for someone who's just going to be trouble? Claire – you must have seen this?'

I was playing dumb and looked down, embarrassed. 'I just do paperwork and driving and stuff,' I muttered modestly to my lap.

Dawn shot me daggers but, fortunately, Tom missed them.

'Maybe it's not Barclay,' suggested Dawn. 'If it's not his normal type, why has he gone for him? He mentioned someone else was involved with this one.'

Tom looked surprised. 'I ... don't know about that. Normally Barclay goes for people with dirty sex secrets they'd rather weren't made public or smaller financial foul play, never too big, never too greedy with his demands, just little and often. He goes after normal people, every day types, people too scared to call for help, terrified that he'll expose them. The dirty little secrets, the affairs, the wicked lies that probably nobody cares about but are distorted and swollen in their own minds. He seems quite honourable, honour amongst thieves and all that. No doubt he considers himself a bit of a Robin Hood character.'

I had to smile at that; it was so close to the truth.

'And you think with Bartholomew he's bitten off more than he can chew?'

'What do you think? Looks like he has mastication issues to me.'

'If you're so sure Barclay is doing this, why haven't you picked him up before? It sounds like you have all the evidence you need,' asked Dawn.

'But I don't have enough for it to stand up in court. The victims won't come forward, too much to lose if word got out, so they never complain, they don't trust the good guys as much as the bad ones. That's where he's so darned clever – he's modest enough in his ambition to keep it low on the list of our priorities, especially with all the other stuff going on around here.'

He polished off the last, lonely poppadum I'd had my eye on.

'And it's very technical how Barclay does his stuff. The British couldn't get their heads around how his hacking works and, frankly, much of it is beyond me, too. He hacks iPhones. No one hacks iPhones. Even the US Government and the FBI haven't been able to do that. Even Apple can't do that. It's a shame he can't see beyond the easy cash. He's really every bit as good as he thinks he is, and that's saying something. I was hoping that the Bartholomew thing would blow it all wide open for us, two birds with one stone and all that, Barclay and Bartholomew. But it looks like Bartholomew decided that he's had enough of Quentin and has done something about it. Speaking of which,' he looked at his watch, 'we should make a move before it gets too late. If Barclay's where I think he is, it won't be pleasant overnight.'

'Assuming he's still with us,' I added, mournfully.

'Yes, assuming that he's still with us.'

And there was a look of sadness in Tom's eyes, and I realised that Tom, too, had fallen a little under the spell of the man known only as Barclay.

Tom hadn't brought his car – he did like his Oyster Card that man – so we all crammed into the Uno: me and Tom in the front, Dawn squeezed into the back. Tom said that Bartholomew had an old warehouse down in Kent, a few miles outside Rochester. It had been part of one of his businesses that had failed in the nineties but he kept the building for reasons the police just couldn't understand. Several raids on it, looking for dodgy imports or stolen goods had yielded nothing but embarrassed looks on the faces of those raiding. Eventually they'd left it well alone and it had sat there, unloved, seemingly unused for years.

But Tom said that he'd put a 'calling all cars, be on the lookout for…' request out on Bartholomew's car and it had been reported going south on the A2 heading just an hour ago, so that looked like as fair a bet as any. And we had nothing else to go on. Things were desperate. We were desperate.

Typical. There'd been some unspeakable accident on the A2 and we were stuck in the long tail back, stationary for what felt like hours in the long snake of impatient commuters' cars desperate for home and supper. Conversation had pretty much run dry, the radio had given up the ghost and all three of us were starting to regret having a large curry so quickly and then confining ourselves together in a small, metal box. The horror. The smell. All four windows were open but you could still almost taste the after effects.

Just when I'd thought things couldn't get any worse.

We edged forward inches at a time, the only notable movement being the flashing blue of the emergency vehicles, tantalisingly just a few hundred yards ahead.

Tom was starting to doze off, gently snoring in what was normally really irritating but strangely, in these most bizarre of circumstances, was quite endearing.

Very odd.

I looked at Dawn in the rear view mirror. She was smiling. I smiled too. Then we both jumped out of our skins as my phone burst into song.

It was Barclay.

I pressed the buttons so fast I almost cut him off.

'Where the fuck are you?'

'Hello … Claire.' It didn't sound like him. He sounded distant, detached, uncertain, almost unworldly. And breathless, as if calling had been agony.

'We've been to your flat. It's been wrecked! What happened?

Are you okay?'

'I'll ... live.' It wasn't the most convincing answer; he was faint and sounded like he was in pain. A lot of pain. His breathing was audible and laboured, distressing to hear between the few words.

'There were fingernails, Barclay, bloody ones. And pliers! Fucking pliers!'

'Yes.'

'"Yes"?'

'Yes, the nails are ... were mine. They'll grow back ... I hope.'

'Who did this Barclay?'

Dawn was desperate to hear and sat close behind me, trying to force her ear next to the phone.

'That ... that associate I mentioned. He's not happy about the Bartholomew thing...'

'The one we fucked up?' I paused. 'The *first* one we fucked up? He's not worried about the teacher fuck up?'

'He doesn't know anything about the ... teacher thing. That was mine, on my own, not him, not big enough for him. No, he's the ...' he was struggling for breath, 'genius behind the Bartholomew thing.'

'And he's not happy?'

'He wasn't happy, no. It got quite...nasty.'

'We saw.'

'"We"?'

'I told Dawn and she went with me. We've been burgled, too.'

There was silence, then he asked gently: 'Are you okay?'

'Shaken but fine. They took the laptop. And the gun.'

'Oh. With your..?'

'Fingerprints. Yes.'

'Oh.'

'What do they want, Barclay?'

'He wants the money from Bartholomew. He wants a quarter of a million from him. I told him it was too much but he says it has to be the full amount. He was quite … unrelenting on that. He wanted me … us … to collect it tonight. I said no and …'

I couldn't speak.

'Claire. I can't do this. I didn't bargain on this. You need to get away. Dawn too. You need to run Claire. You and Dawn, you both need to run.'

'Run? Where?'

'Anywhere. You can't stay there.'

'But we're not there. I'm with Dawn now in the Uno. We're coming to get you.'

'To the flat?' he asked. 'I'm not there.'

'We're on our way to Bartholomew's warehouse in Kent.'

'Why? I'm not doing that pick-up now. I told him I'd quit. Why are you going there?'

I shook my head. It didn't make sense. 'Barclay, what the fuck's going on,' I asked. Then suddenly it hit me. 'Barclay?'

'Yes?'

'This associate? His name's not Tom…Tom…' Damn it. I still couldn't remember his second name.

'I don't know anyone called 'TomTom'.'

'No. Tom…Thomas…'

'Pedakowski,' said Barclay. 'His name's Thomas Pedakowski.' And the line went suddenly dead.

My blood turned to ice. Pedakowski. Tom Pedakowski. That was it. That was him. And then I felt the cold metal of a gun press against my neck.

'Eyes on the road. Keep driving Claire,' he said calmly. 'The traffic's moving.'

I couldn't swallow. Could barely breathe. Dawn screamed.

Chapter 30

'That was him then,' said Tom.

'Yes,' I whispered. 'That was him.'

'And what did Barclay say?' he asked.

'He said it was … you. All of this was down to you, Bartholomew, the break-ins, the pliers … business. All you. All Tom Thomas.'

'Well, he would say that, wouldn't he?'

'You holding a gun on me isn't exactly persuading me otherwise, Tom.' My voice quivered.

'Good point. But needs must.'

'Are we turning back?' asked Dawn, her voice small and trembling too.

Tom twisted around sharply to face her, but the gun stayed pointed at me.

'No,' he snapped. 'We're going to the pick-up.'

'But we are going to find Barclay?' she said, a question more than a statement.

'No. Barclay's gone.'

'Gone?'

He turned back and stared at the dark road ahead, saying nothing.

'We were never going to look for Barclay, were we?' I said.

'No.'

'This is the Bartholomew pick-up, isn't it? You have no idea where Barclay is.'

No answer.

Dawn started crying, childish but it was understandable. I felt like joining her, but one of us had to stay strong and I was probably our best shot. We were on our own. Tom Thomas, you bastard bastard bastard.

In my head I was screaming but in the car we were silent. The traffic had started to spread out after the accident and we were making fair time towards Rochester, but the minutes felt like hours, there was so much to say but so little said.

Why so far this time? Everything with Barclay had been on our doorstep, but for this one it looked like we were heading a distance out of town. I guess the previous fuck up with Bartholomew had pushed both sides close to the edge.

I glanced at Tom, still pointing the gun at me.

'I thought you were one of the good guys, Tom.'

'And you were one of the bad?'

'I wouldn't go that far. Barclay says I'm an 'accessory' at worst.'

'I doubt a judge would see it like that. Some accessories are essential. Shoes and belts are pretty fundamental.' I was beginning to regret the ridiculous clothing analogy – it wasn't helpful.

'I'm not a bad person,' I muttered.

'Everyone has bad in them.'

'But I only got involved in this because Barclay got suspended from driving.'

'We all know that driving while suspended would prove to be the least of Barclay's crimes.'

'Can't we stop and let Dawn go at least? She's completely innocent in all this.'

'Stop? Where?' He had a point – we were in the middle of nowhere, crossing the Rochester bridge. 'No. She stays. She knows too much.'

'I don't know anything,' she managed to say between the sobs.

'No.' Hard. Final. He wasn't open to negotiation.

'We're doing this pick-up, then? The one Barclay backed out on because he thought it was too dangerous, too big?'

'Barclay's biggest problem,' said Tom, 'is that he lacks courage and ambition. Sure, he lusts for the trappings, the designer clothes and snazzy apartment and fast cars, but he isn't prepared to take the risks to get them. He's brilliant technically but wants always to keep it small and manageable. I brought him … opportunities beyond his limited vision.'

'Barclay doesn't let people get close to him,' I said.

'With me he had no choice. When they asked me to pick up the Barclay investigation I saw he was onto something, his scams so simple yet effective. He just needed some guidance to make some serious money though, he needed encouragement, a brain, a partner.'

'And in return you'd keep the police at arm's length, slow things down, send investigations down dead ends when they got too close?'

'It's not difficult when the troops have been cut to the core by your government. Easy to turn a blind eye when there are so few eyes actually open. Besides, they have all that shit kicking off across South London to keep the boys in blue occupied but I've deflected them when I've needed to. We have a window of opportunity and we're using it. Barclay was perfectly happy with the arrangement. Until Bartholomew.'

'Barclay says it's too big.'

He shrugged. 'Typical. It's ambitious, I'll give him that, but Bartholomew can afford it. Barclay got spooked when his man got hit by that car, but I don't think that was planned or pre-mediated, just blind panic. That muscle Barclay took along was fucking intimidating – have you seen that guy? – and Bartholomew's guy panicked. I would have done the same thing. He won't be doing that again.'

'You sure?'

'You're hardly in the same scary monster league.'

'Me?'

'Sure, you're doing this one.'

'No way,' I said, shaking my head. He poked the gun at me then turned to the back seat and pointed it at Dawn.

'You really think this is the time to start arguing with me?' He wouldn't, surely? Dawn was wide-eyed, staring in disbelief at the gun pointing directly at her.

'Not her, Tom, not Dawn.'

'Pow!' said Tom, laughing. What is it with Americans and waving guns about? Didn't Mom and Pop tell them that was not the way modern societies worked? I tried to get him facing front again.

'Why this one, Tom? Why won't you let Bartholomew go? Barclay said…'

'Barclay's gone.'

'So why me? Why take the risk? I'll fuck it up, you know I will. Why aren't you doing it yourself? You know the guy surely in setting this up.'

'Only by text messages and email. We're hardly dating. I've too much to lose. You have nothing to lose – you're already an accessory, remember? Besides, I'm one of the good guys, huh?' He smiled but it was cold enough to freeze hell over.

'You have a funny way of showing it.'

'Besides, you'll have some good old fashioned British male chauvinism to keep you safe. Bartholomew may be a complete asshole but he's a polite British asshole and he'll be less likely to do anything stupid when he meets you.'

'And afterwards?'

He said nothing and the silence returned to haunt us, the unsaid even more uncomfortable than the spoken.

'The turning's just up here. Next left,' said Tom. I flipped the indicator and changed down to second, the clutch fighting back and the gearbox rattling in protest. That Uno would be the death of us, I thought, silently cursing Barclay's insistence we kept it. Cursing Barclay, not for the first time but possibly the last.

At the junction roundabout Tom directed me left, then right, then left again. A mile down the road was a small cluster of derelict buildings, former factories and warehouses that had been abandoned after a fire had ripped through one and left its roof a jumble of dark timbers jutting up into the moonlit sky. The others, forlorn, forgotten, stood silent in the darkness as if mourning their fallen comrade. There was no Bartholomew warehouse, so no kidnapped Barclay for us to rescue. It was just yet another desolate, dilapidated location for another desolate, dilapidated pick-up, this one by disconsolate, dejected me.

The earlier drizzle had cleared and there was a full moon, the sky clear of cloud for once, possibly the first time that entire winter. Barclay had preferred the dark for our work, but after the recent disasters I was quite grateful that we would have at least a little light this time around.

'Here,' said Tom, pointing to the burned out building. Nothing elsc was said as I pulled up on the concrete road by one of the buildings. There were no other cars. We appeared to be early.

'When you're out there, Claire, no heroics, no fucking around.'

'No fucking around,' I confirmed in a whisper.

He ran through what was involved, how I should identify myself to Bartholomew (not that there was going to be anyone else around to get confused with) and to simply collect the money and return to the car, walking calmly, not running. There was a password I had to give: 'Rosebud'. Someone knew their film classics at least.

It all seemed so simple. It was so simple. So why was I trembling? What did Tom have in mind for later?

'He should be in here in a few minutes,' Tom said, checking his watch for the hundredth time since we'd parked. I turned the engine off – it was getting warm in the car with the three of us – but Tom suggested I leave the lights on.

'He needs to know we're here, waiting,' he said. 'Otherwise he could renege on the deal. It will unnerve him that it's you doing the pick-up.' Not as much as it was unnerving me, I was sure.

I noticed that one of the Uno's headlights was dimmer than the other. That car really was a pile of rusty shit. I longed for the relative comfort of the Noddy Multipla Barclay had sold – anything was better than the Uno. I'd fallen out of love with it again.

Another car turned off the road ahead of us and drove cautiously towards the rendezvous. A monstrous Range Rover. A Sherman tank of a car for those who have the money but lack the class. It looked like it hailed from a different species from our humble wheels. Anything would, truth be told.

The Range Rover stopped thirty yards away. The overweight bulk of Bartholomew emerged, wrapped against the January cold in a large overcoat that almost touched the floor. Fat little man. Big coat. Another of us bad guys. Where were the good guys, the men in white? Did nobody think to invite them along?

Bartholomew waved at the Uno, but there was nothing cheery or welcoming in the greeting.

'Ready Claire?' asked Tom, but I had already forced the door open and was on my way, striding purposefully despite the leaden nervous weight in my legs and stomach.

'Good girl,' I heard him say behind me. Dawn let out a small cry and I heard a smack as he cuffed her. Bastard. What had I seen in that guy? Was I just part of his games with Barclay, just another means to an end? I felt sick, used, abused, and foolish. Don't forget foolish, Claire.

Bartholomew put his clenched fists on his waist, elbows cantilevered outwards like an oversized sports cup.

'Who the fuck are you?' he snarled.

Nice.

'I'm Claire,' I said, and then instantly regretted using my real name. Think sharp, girl. 'Dorothy Claire.' Dorothy? Dotty for short? What was I thinking?

'Well, Dorothy, this sure ain't Kansas. You workin' with those wankers?' His accent was East End barrow boy made good, all the clothes in Jermyn Street couldn't hide the origins of that cruder, coarse accent.

I wasn't going to waste time with small talk. 'Rosebud,' I said.

Bartholomew nodded, stood a second longer then went to the back of his car and opened the boot. With a grunt and a groan and more effort than he was familiar with, he pulled out a limp body, bound and trussed and bruised and…Barclay.

He let him fall to the floor. Barclay barely moved.

'This is yours, I believe,' and he spat at the figure at his feet.

Bartholomew turned his back on me and climbed back into his car. He wound down the window.

'No money. Not now, not ever. We will never talk again.' A man who was used to making statements rather than asking questions. 'Oh, and I don't like loose ends.'

Loose ends? What did that mean?

The window slid smoothly up and his posh beast of a car gave an upmarket, luxury growl and it rumbled off over the potholed concrete.

I ran to Barclay, too heavy to carry but I managed to lift him into a seating position. His eyes were closed and his breathing shallow, rasping, bubbly. His face had been battered and broken, his nose shattered, bloody. It had been brutal and unforgiving. Oh, Barclay.

As the Range Rover disappeared from view I yelled out to the Uno for help.

Suddenly a gunshot rang out and my left leg was on fire. I screamed and my free hand grabbed at my thigh as I fell, dropping Barclay and sprawling onto the cold, hard concrete.

I heard Tom yell 'No!' into the darkness. The pain in my leg was blinding, unbearable, I was blacking out. I saw Tom jump out of the Uno and start towards me

Another shot, catching Tom in the shoulder and turning him round. Another. Tom's head exploded before his body could hit the ground.

Another. This one smacked into Barclay's prostrate body. It shuddered with the impact, then was still again. So still. Too still.

Fuck.

I struggled to heave myself up, the pain exploding and stealing my breath. I had to move. Had to get out of range. I could feel hot blood pulsing out, soaking my jeans as I dragged my throbbing useless leg behind me as I hauled myself toward the Uno. Pain. The pain. I'd never known pain like it.

I left Barclay. Fuck Tom. Fuck Barclay. Fuck this.

Dawn was screaming as I clambered into the driving seat.

'Shut it, Dawn,' I snapped and, much to my surprise, she did. Instantly.

I turned the Uno's key in the ignition. Nothing. The engine ignored my frantic action. I tried again. Nothing. Zilch. Nada. No. NO!

'Why won't she start?' asked Dawn. 'Why won't she fucking start?'

I just shook my head.

'Shit,' I said.

Another shot rang out and a bullet bounced off the Uno's bonnet, shattering the windscreen.

Shit indeed.

Chapter 31

Another shot, another bullet fired from god knows where, ricocheting god knew where off the bonnet.

'Is that…that Barclay?' Dawn pointed at her fallen brother.

'Yes. Bartholomew had him … I don't know why I … I'm not sure he's still alive … he's been shot. He's not moved since I dropped him.'

There was nothing I could say. We both just stared in horror at the two bodies lying motionless.

More bullets from the dark, slamming into the fragile metal around us, peppering it with their deadly intent.

'Well, Butch, what are we going to do now?' Dawn asked as we cowered low in our seats, desperately trying to hide from the unseen sniper. She'd replaced screaming with sarcasm. It wasn't appreciated. We'd watched my favourite movies together but this was neither the time nor place to start with the quoting memorable lines thing.

'Not so sure, Sundance,' I replied. I valued her trying to lighten the tension but we were both in shock and it was no time for levity. Besides, Newman and Redford didn't make it out alive in that movie. Was our very own freeze frame moment just seconds away?

Another shot. I'd stopped flinching – they were becoming the norm.

Instinctively I checked my mobile. No signal. And, even more alarming, the text on the screen jauntily informed me that I'd run out of credit and should buy some more. Dawn checked hers.

'No signal,' she said. 'Not a great surprise given where we are.'

'I've no credit, either,' I said.

'I can't believe you're on Pay As You Go.'

'I can't believe we're hiding from a gunman in the middle of nowhere and we're discussing mobile phone plans. I think I'd like my last words to be a little more profound than 'and how many texts do you get with that?'.'

Dawn laughed. It was false and strained, a familiar sound in an unfamiliar place, an odd little chuckle that seemed to neither rise nor fall. Within seconds we were both chortling away like maniacs. Hysterical. Hysteria. Shock and tension and fear make you do the funniest things. Suddenly Dawn stopped.

'Have you got the gun?' she asked.

I stared at her in disbelief. 'Barclay said no more guns!'

'He, whoever he is out there, doesn't seem to know that.'

'No shit Sherlock.'

'So you don't have the gun?'

'I don't, but Tom had one, didn't he?' She nodded.

Tom, or at least what was left of him, was lying a few yards from the car. The gun was still in his right hand.

'I can't go get it, Dawn, my leg's…'

'I'll get it,' said Dawn. Before I could argue she'd opened the door and had sprinted toward my fallen lover. Two shots in rapid succession rang out and bullets bounced off the concrete, missing her by inches. She wrestled the gun from his lifeless grip and ran back. No more gunfire.

Good girl. Thank fuck she was with me.

'Give it here, Dawn.'

She didn't, instead she pulled out the clip and checked its contents. 'Doesn't feel full.'

'You'd know a full one?'

She shrugged and handed the gun to me.

'Thanks,' I said. 'And why are we whispering?'

'I don't know. It's not like anyone's listening.'

'True.' I stared out into the dark but could see no sign of the gunman. Gunmen? There could be two of them. I had a handful of bullets and an unfamiliar handgun to hit someone out there we couldn't even see.

'He moved!' Dawn shouted suddenly.

'What?'

'Barclay. He just moved. Look – he's lifted his hand!'

I strained my eyes but saw nothing.

'Are you sure?'

'I think so.'

'I'll take the gun and see if I can get to him.'

'I'm not 100%.'

'We can't leave him out there.'

'Aren't we better staying here?' Before I could answer another bullet whistled off the bonnet. We were too easy a target in the car.

It was only about twenty feet I had to cover. I could fire the gun until it ran dry, one last despairing effort. Dawn was horrified:

'You can't just run out there he'll nail you in seconds.'

'We can't stay here. You make your way into this building here – if you stay low he won't hit you.'

She wasn't convinced. Neither was I.

'I don't like the odds on that, either.'

'They're the only odds on offer.'

Yet another bullet flew into the Uno's peppered body.

'If you get out through this side he may not see you.'

It was as near a plan as we had. I quickly unbuckled and slunk out onto the cold road surface, the unfamiliar gun heavy in my hand. My leg shrieked as I hit the ground. Dawn, her tall frame making it more difficult, did likewise. Bullets bounced off the concrete around us like deadly hailstones, a few feet from the car. A few feet from us.

'What if he hits the petrol tank?' she asked.

'I wouldn't worry about it. I forgot to fill up earlier, there's hardly any in the tank as it is.'

More gunfire, but this time I saw the flash that went with it. About forty yards away, behind one of the outlying buildings.

'Over there!' Dawn pointed in the general direction and I nodded.

'Right. Here goes.' I held up the gun in my best Bond-like pose, both hands on the grip. 'Good luck.'

Instinctively she pulled me towards her and gave me a hug.

'Stop that. Go!'

She nodded.

She turned and ran. I painfully lumbered my way towards Barclay, suddenly he seemed so far away.

I heard a shot and fired towards it. The gun barked and jumped in my hand, shooting blind into the pitch black. I heard another shot, and saw a flash with the next. I fired and fired and fired for all I was worth, then slipped on something wet and collapsed on the ground. One more from the dark. So close. I writhed on the floor, clutching my leg in agony. Suddenly there was the sound of a motorcycle starting up, moving off. I looked towards Dawn; she'd been hit and was holding her shoulder. I turned and saw a fleeing bike emerge from the moonlit shadow of one of the buildings and sped off. A lone rider. Our lone gunman.

Just a few more yards.

My leg cried in protest as I collapsed onto Barclay.

My God, he was breathing. Just. But they were fast, deep

breaths and there was a gurgling sound that I will remember to my dying day. His eyes were puffed closed and and a ridiculous amount of blood had soaked through his shirt and that beloved Prada coat of his.

I couldn't move. 'Barclay? Barclay!' I yelled.

And then it all went black.

Chapter 32

The policewoman was the nicest person I had ever met. Ever. Even nicer than policewoman Joan.

She'd wrapped my shivering shoulders in a warm blanket and handed me the sweetest cup of black coffee I had ever tasted.

'You're shaking, you poor thing,' she said, brushing my hair from my eyes.

'It wasn't a great evening,' I half-joked, surprised at my calmness given the circumstances. I was probably going into shock. I could feel dark clouds gathering in the back of my mind. It was only a matter of seconds before I'd be a heaving mess of sobs, tears and shakes.

'At least you two are okay,' she said. 'Those chaps weren't so lucky.'

Another policewoman was talking to Dawn, a silver foil blanket draped around her shivering shoulders. Tom Pedakowski had definitely breathed his last, the top of his head now a macabre bloody jigsaw the sight of which made one of the ambulance crew retch. Dawn had been hit in the shoulder and had, like me, been bleeding profusely. They were trying to bandage her up before whisking her off to hospital. Tom they were still leaning over, crowded around making calm conversation as if there was still a chance to save his life if they could just put all the pieces back together, a modern day Humpty Dumpty.

No way, Jose.

And Barclay?

I looked at the policewoman.

'The guy with the curly hair? Is he…?'

'I've no idea, Miss. You say that you thought he was breathing when you got to him?'

I nodded. After coming to I had managed to stumble away from the scene and had somehow, miraculously, managed to get a single bar of signal, just enough to call the emergency services.

An ambulance man pulled away from the group around Barclay and came towards me, the headlights from the vehicles lighting up the scene but turning him into a silhouette as he approached.

'Are you related to the young man?' he asked.

I shook my head. 'He is…was…my boss,' I managed.

'He still is,' he said, 'but you may want to consider a change of profession if this is a typical bit of overtime for you. He's lost a lot of blood but he'll live. It looks worse than it is. He's taken a few bullets but only in the limbs and shoulder. The girl's going to be okay, too. The other chap though is dead I'm afraid.'

It would have been more of a shock if Tom had been still with us.

'So Barclay's going to be okay?'

'Barclay? That's an odd name. Bit of a character is he?'

'You could say that,' I said, and found myself smiling despite the circumstances.

'He'll probably live,' said the medic.

'Of course,' I said. 'He doesn't do death.'

'And the other one, the deceased?' he asked.

I shook my head. 'He is…was…a man I … knew vaguely,' I said quietly.

'He has a police ID on him.'

'Yes. He told me he worked with the police. One of the good guys. He was a consultant. I only met him a couple of times. Not even dates, really. Well, maybe one. Or two. I … he wasn't the guy

I thought he was and he didn't ... sorry, I'm not making a great deal of sense...'

He nodded. 'Understandable,' he sighed.

My head was throbbing, spinning, and I just wanted to lie down again.

'Careful, you've lost a fair bit of blood.' A tourniquet on my leg was doing its job but I'd lost all sensation in my foot. I felt myself going under again.

It hadn't been a good evening.

And then the shock hit me like a tsunami and I lost all strength, dropping my mug and collapsing, sobbing uncontrollably before finally, mercifully, I closed my eyes and it all went away.

Chapter 33

'Black. Filter, not that Americano rubbish. And two sugars.'

The new young Intern sighs and scribbles my order on her Post-It pad. She's already bored with the day. And it is only 9.30. I know that feeling. Boy, do I know that feeling.

'And get one for yourself,' I say, giving her a tenner. 'And we can share one of those blueberry muffin things. Make sure you get a low fat one though.'

She smiles, surprised at being treated like a member of the human race after all. I'm not going to treat her the way they'd treated me when I was an Intern here, that's for sure. I've learned a lot in the last few months, all of it highly suspect and most simply out and out illegal, but that is no excuse for not being a nicer person when the opportunity arises. Maybe I can be a good girl after all. Maybe, though I doubt it, the angelic lifestyle will win me over and my bad days are behind me.

Like I say though, I doubt it.

I am back working at Marshall's. They had called a few weeks after I was released from hospital. I had still needed crutches but they needed the bed back and I was 'good to go'. My leg still hurts a lot and the throbbing pulses its way through the painkillers with remarkable ease, but I had to get back onto life's treadmill I suppose. Marshall's had a big contract land in their lap ('how big?' I'd asked, 'historically big,' he'd replied) and they needed to staff up really fast and, they said, naturally they'd thought of me.

Sure...

Of course, I was stealing stationery almost from the moment I walked back through their doors. This particular old dog isn't one for that new tricks fandango. Besides, it is good to be back amongst all the bored, scowling faces and those oh-so-critical spreadsheets and emails – it reminds me that it is only going to be a matter of time before I need to escape again. I can only take so much excitement.

And what of Barclay?

Ah yes, Barclay.

He is still in hospital, but is sufficiently recovered to have been charged with a whole list of offences dating back years, even back to his time at university with Wardy. They tell me the charge list is extensive and comprehensive, but, somehow, I suspect it's nowhere near complete. He appears to the casual eye to be a broken man, a battered, bruised stammering wreck, incoherent when answering their questions, almost to the point where they think he may have suffered permanent brain damage.

But I know better. It took a while, weeks rather than days, but that sly wink he gave me when the police weren't looking calmed my concern and warmed my heart. He's playing the long game but it's a game he'll win, I have no doubt of that.

Just how much of the stuff that was recorded in Tom's files will stick I have no idea. I do know that there was no mention of me or my part in Barclay's crimes, nor any of Bartholomew, so for that I guess I should be grateful to Pedakowski. From the polite police questioning I've had so far I'd guess that they actually know so little they'll never be able to piece together what happened that night outside Rochester, or any of it, come to that. Tom covered his tracks and Barclay's pretty much too. Peas in a pod, blood brothers, brothers in arms – pick your own cliché.

Of course, Tom was as corrupt and malleable as you could ever find and if they'd had the resources he would have been under far closer supervision and observation, but then you can't blame austerity and budget cuts for everything, can you? Besides, he wasn't really one of them, one of their own. He was an American, a foreigner, and, his worst crime most likely, a highly-paid consultant. He was an outsider from every angle. They got exactly what they ordered.

But Tom's gone now, and there's no one mourning his demise. Was I just part of his games with Barclay or was he genuinely interested in me? Had I imagined it or was there really a spark between us?

I'll never know.

And, speaking of things I'll never know, who was that fucking gunman? Was he someone hired by Bartholomew to clean up after he left, ensure that no one escaped alive? Get us all together and take us out? Had that been his plan? Lure us with the promise of the money then pick us off, one by one? 'I don't like loose ends,' he'd said, and I guess that was all we were to him that night.

I don't know for certain. I never will. And, frankly, I don't care.

Already it seems so long ago, another lifetime almost. I will always have my limp to remind me of my time as low life, bad girl scum, but it seems a small price to pay.

One of the police said that Barclay would be looking at many years, maybe even decades behind bars or Perspex or whatever they build prison cells out of these days. But I doubt it. They won't make it stick, Tom's evidence will be shaky at best, and Barclay's family will lawyer him up big time.

Tonight I'm seeing Dawn back at home and we'll drink ourselves stupid yet again on Prosecco. Mum reckons I may have a bit of a drink problem developing but I can't shee it myshelf. (Did you see what I did there?) Besides, I can afford it even if most of my salary is still heading north to fund her recovery. I just tear up hearing her voice every time she calls. Her sentences can pause at times, her words lost as she reaches into the darker recesses for that *bon mot*. But I can wait – it's just lovely to hear her, not completely well but improving every day. A reminder of the better things in life.

I am grateful for that.

I had the Uno recovered but it was deader than Tom Thomas, my real fumble with the dark side. I bought another one but it's not the same.

I'm a one car kind of girl I guess, the girl in the Fiat Uno.

And if they finally manage to get Barclay to court I'll be there at his side if he needs me, of course, following his instructions and pleading innocence and shock-induced amnesia as long as my acting skills convince. Tears are good – everyone seems to well up in sympathy when I turn on the waterworks big time.

One thing's for certain though; my bad days are done. Finished. Over. Kaput. That's enough veering off the straight and narrow from me. (For now, at least.) You won't find me playing with fast (ish) cars and guns again, that's for sure. (At least, not for a while.) I'd have to be an absolute bloody idiot to get involved in that kind of malarkey again, and there's one thing this girl isn't, it's an idiot.

Honest.

One year later...

It's gone midnight but my new iPhone is ringing impatiently.

'Hello?'

'Claire?'

'Yes.'

'2am. Pick me up. Number Two will be joining us.'

'Of course.'

And I'm grinning as I leap from my bed, the night barely begun, the dawn still hours away. I dress and grab my keys and dance out to my waiting rust-encrusted chariot, no rest for the wicked and all that.

You can't keep a good girl down. Or a bad one, come to that.

Acknowledgements

My thanks to…

…Barbara Henderson for her support and encouragement on the Random House Creative Writing course and beyond

…Kathleen Gray for her reassurances and guidance with the edit on the final draft

…Graeme Elkington for his friendship and parking the world's most beautiful Karmann Ghia outside my house so the other neighbours think it's mine

…Lesley, Mike, Colin, Neil and Jimmie for their understanding and support last year

…Dan, Tina, Mandy, Maggie, Lenny, Leah and all the other friends who have been so supportive and encouraging…

…but, most of all, my love and eternal gratitude to Jen, Els and the little man, who make me so bloody happy every single day.

Barclay and MacDonald will return. Honest.

When She Was Bad Author Q&A

Karen Myers: What came first, the plot or the characters and why?

Neil: The character of Barclay came first. I was on the Random House Creative Writing course and the opening exercise was to create a character and introduced them through an object. I chose a bag, and that was the start of Barclay. That's still the opening of the first chapter, although I had no idea it would evolve into a novel at that stage. I needed someone to find the bag but had no idea who. I decided it would open more possibilities if it was a woman and so I came up with Claire and it sort of snowballed from there.

It was an interesting way to start a book but I think in future I'll start with the story. I didn't have the details of the plot worked out fully until I finished my second draft – the first draft wandered all over the place as I explored the characters more than the story.

Karen: Did you set out to write something with a twist or did it develop that way?

Neil: It just developed that way. I do like a story with a good twist so I was hoping I could squeeze one in somehow but wasn't going to force it. In earlier drafts the revelation was revealed much earlier but in the later versions I thought it would be fun to save it for the story's climax. Some readers have said they saw it coming, others that they were taken by surprise. The end of the story is told at quite a pace and it just seemed to fit and didn't feel too contrived.

Karen: It's clear that some aspects of the plot come from experience, i.e. there's local colour. But how much research did you have to do for locations, journeys, cars etc?

Neil: 'Don't let your research show,' Barbara Henderson told me and I managed to do that by doing as little research as possible!

I live in Greenwich and also know neighbouring Deptford and the Docklands well, but I wanted to steer clear of the famous landmarks in the area. One issue was ensuring I used locations without CCTV cameras – modern technology can be a nightmare when you're writing a crime thriller – but I found that even in Docklands it was pretty easy to find areas with no cameras and poor lighting at night.

The only car I knew personally was the Karmann Ghia, which is owned by my neighbour, Graeme. I haven't been in an Uno or Multipla for years and sadly you don't actually see many Unos around these days. I embellished Claire's experiences with information from a few Fiat drivers' online communities. I did do all the journeys described, but in my less-interesting VW Golf, and at 3pm rather than 3am!

Karen: You're a 50-something man, the main protagonist is a 20-something woman. You found her voice, so how?

Neil: It actually came quite naturally. I surprised myself to be truthful – I think she's my favourite character in the book and that old cliché about stories writing themselves is certainly true in Claire's case. There were a few times in the editing process when I had to change some of Claire's references as they were not what a 25-year-old would be familiar with, but her actual 'voice' came easily.

Karen: I was left wanting more of some of the characters, and to know more of their back-story. Were you writing them with book two in mind, in terms of who would live or be free to see another day?

Neil: I always wanted to leave things open at the end but resisted the temptation to leave it on a cliffhanger – I had toyed with the idea of Claire finding herself pregnant (by Tom) at the end but decided against it was a bit of a cliché and it would limit any future stories by her having to consider her child's welfare.

I have plenty of character back-story I will use in the second book. There's a lot more to Barclay than discovered by Claire in When She Was Bad and it'll be fun exploring that in the next one (and beyond). TNT's story won't remain untold, and you haven't met The Shoe Woman yet…

Karen: The style is very visual with lots of popular culture and product references. Do those come from your own preferences or did you use them as you thought Claire would see the world?

Neil: I've never owned anything by Prada or Fiat but I do love Apple products even if I do sometimes think life would be simpler with an old Nokia phone that just does calls and texts. I think the dominance of brands and mass culture is just the time we live in and that's how kids in their twenties view things now.

Karen: It's also quite cinematic, given the dialogue, the pace and the way it paints pictures. Do you see yourself as a screenwriter?

Neil: I'm just getting used to describing myself as a 'writer', and I'm happy trying my hand at novels and short stories for now. I suppose that my dialogue and action scenes are quite cinematic but there's no ulterior motive in writing that way except that it's an effective way of making the reader turn the pages faster.

Karen: If so, who would you cast in the film or TV version?

Neil: I wrote Barclay with Benedict Cumberbatch (as Sherlock) in mind. Claire I saw as Claire Foy, but she can be whoever the reader wants her to be and I deliberately didn't describe her appearance. My wife has suggested that Tom is Jude Law and I like that but I had a (young) Tom Hollander in mind as I wrote him. TNT would be the guy who plays The Mountain in HBO's *Game of Thrones*.

Karen: As a first-time author, how did you approach the task of writing? Computer or longhand? Storyboard? Short bursts or long days?

Neil: I'm new at this game so I've been making it up as I go along. This book started with the RH course I mentioned, which resulted in around two dozen short pieces which I then used as the basis for the first part of the initial draft. As the story developed though most were dropped as they didn't fit in the story or its evolving style. A few survive: the prologue, the opening chapters, the visits to both families at Christmas.

I type faster than I can handwrite, so I tend to only pick up the pen when I'm sketching out rough ideas. I review and edit drafts off screen though – an old preference from my days as a sub editor.

I did try using the authoring software Scrivener for the planning, but found it too complicated for what I was attempting to do. In the end I covered my office's wall with hand-written postcard outlines before finalizing them with PowerPoint (a slide per chapter). I wrote it in Microsoft Word – I tried other writing tools but Word is still the best for writing and editing. The print edition was finished using InDesign.

There's no pattern to my writing day and I still find myself keeping 'office hours', starting at around nine in the morning, an hour's break for lunch and winding up around five. Old habits die hard.

Karen: I understand you started your career as a journalist. Do you have non-fiction in you too?

Neil: Possibly, but it's not something I'm interested in at the moment.

Printed in Great Britain
by Amazon